CHRISTOPHER BUSH
THE CASE OF THE CHINESE GONG

CHRISTOPHER BUSH was born Charlie Christmas Bush in Norfolk in 1885. His father was a farm labourer and his mother a milliner. In the early years of his childhood he lived with his aunt and uncle in London before returning to Norfolk aged seven, later winning a scholarship to Thetford Grammar School.

As an adult, Bush worked as a schoolmaster for 27 years, pausing only to fight in World War One, until retiring aged 46 in 1931 to be a full-time novelist. His first novel featuring the eccentric Ludovic Travers was published in 1926, and was followed by 62 additional Travers mysteries. These are all to be republished by Dean Street Press.

Christopher Bush fought again in World War Two, and was elected a member of the prestigious Detection Club. He died in 1973.

By Christopher Bush

CHRISTOPHER BUSH

THE CASE OF THE CHINESE GONG

With an introduction
by Curtis Evans

DEAN STREET PRESS

To
WRAY

WHO HAS PERFORMED UPON THE ACTUAL
STAGE THE THING THAT KILLED
HUBERT GREEVE

INTRODUCTION

THAT ONCE vast and mighty legion of bright young (and youngish) British crime writers who began publishing their ingenious tales of mystery and imagination during what is known as the Golden Age of detective fiction (traditionally dated from 1920 to 1939) had greatly diminished by the iconoclastic decade of the Sixties, many of these writers having become casualties of time. Of the 38 authors who during the Golden Age had belonged to the Detection Club, a London-based group which included within its ranks many of the finest writers of detective fiction then plying the craft in the United Kingdom, just over a third remained among the living by the second half of the 1960s, while merely seven—Agatha Christie, Anthony Gilbert, Gladys Mitchell, Margery Allingham, John Dickson Carr, Nicholas Blake and Christopher Bush—were still penning crime fiction.

In 1966--a year that saw the sad demise, at the too young age of 62, of Margery Allingham--an executive with the English book publishing firm Macdonald reflected on the continued popularity of the author who today is the least well known among this tiny but accomplished crime writing cohort: Christopher Bush (1885-1973), whose first of his three score and three series detective novels, *The Plumley Inheritance*, had appeared fully four decades earlier, in 1926. "He has a considerable public, a 'steady Bush public,' a public that has endured through many years," the executive boasted of Bush. "He never presents any problem to his publisher, who knows exactly how many copies of a title may be safely printed for the loyal Bush fans; the number is a healthy one too." Yet in 1968, just a couple of years after the Macdonald editor's affirmation of Bush's notable popular duration as a crime writer, the author, now in his 83rd year, bade farewell to mystery fiction with a final detective novel, *The Case of the Prodigal Daughter*, in which, like in Agatha Christie's *Third Girl* (1966), copious references are made, none too favorably, to youthful sex, drugs and rock and roll. Afterwards, outside of the reprinting in the UK in the early 1970s of a scattering of classic Bush titles from the Golden Age, Bush's books, in contrast with those of Christie, Carr, Allingham and Blake, disappeared from mass circulation in both the UK and the US, becoming fervently sought (and ever more unobtainable) treasures by collectors and connoisseurs of classic crime fiction. Now, in one of the signal developments in vintage mystery publishing, Dean Street Press is reprinting all 63 of the Christopher Bush detective novels. These will be published over a period of months, beginning with the release of books 1 to 10 in the series.

Few Golden Age British mystery writers had backgrounds as humble yet simultaneously mysterious, dotted with omissions and evasions, as Christopher Bush, who was born Charlie Christmas Bush on the day of the Nativity in 1885 in the Norfolk village of Great Hockham, to Charles Walter Bush and his second wife, Eva Margaret Long. While the father of Christopher Bush's Detection Club colleague and near exact contemporary Henry Wade (the pseudonym of Henry Lancelot Aubrey-Fletcher) was a baronet who lived in an elegant Georgian mansion and claimed extensive ownership of fertile English fields, Christopher's father resided in a cramped cottage and toiled in fields as a farm laborer, a term that in the late Victorian and Edwardian era, his son lamented many years afterward, "had in it something of contempt....There was something almost of serfdom about it."

Charles Walter Bush was a canny though mercurial individual, his only learning, his son recalled, having been "acquired at the Sunday school." A man of parts, Charles was a tenant farmer of three acres, a thatcher, bricklayer and carpenter (fittingly for the father of a detective novelist, coffins were his specialty), a village radical and a most adept poacher. After a flight from Great Hockham, possibly on account of his poaching activities, Charles, a widower with a baby son whom he had left in the care of his mother, resided in London, where he worked for a firm of spice importers. At a dance in the city, Charles met Christopher's mother, Eva Long, a lovely and sweet-natured young milliner and bonnet maker, sweeping her off her feet with a combination of "good looks and a certain plausibility." After their marriage the couple left London to live in a tiny rented cottage in Great Hockham, where Eva over the next eighteen years gave birth to three sons and five daughters and perforce learned the challenging ways of rural domestic economy.

Decades later an octogenarian Christopher Bush, in his memoir *Winter Harvest: A Norfolk Boyhood* (1967), characterized Great Hockham as a rustic rural redoubt where many of the words that fell from the tongues of the native inhabitants "were those of Shakespeare, Milton and the Authorised Version....Still in general use were words that were standard in Chaucer's time, but had since lost a certain respectability." Christopher amusingly recalled as a young boy telling his mother that a respectable neighbor woman had used profanity, explaining that in his hearing she had told her husband, "George, wipe you that shit off that pig's arse, do you'll datty your trousers," to which his mother had responded that although that particular usage of a four-letter word had not really been *swearing*, he was not to give vent to such language himself.

Great Hockham, which in Christopher Bush's youth had a population of about four hundred souls, was composed of a score or so of cottages, three public houses, a post-office, five shops, a couple of forges and a pair of churches, All Saint's and the Primitive Methodist Chapel, where the Bush family rather vocally worshipped. "The village lived by farming, and most of its men were labourers," Christopher recollected. "Most of the children left school as soon as the law permitted: boys to be absorbed somehow into the land and the girls to go into domestic service." There were three large farms and four smaller ones, and, in something of an anomaly, not one but two squires--the original squire, dubbed "Finch" by Christopher, having let the shooting rights at Little Hockham Hall to one "Green," a wealthy international banker, making the latter man a squire by courtesy. Finch owned most of the local houses and farms, in traditional form receiving rents for them personally on Michaelmas; and when Christopher's father fell out with Green, "a red-faced, pompous, blustering man," over a political election, he lost all of the banker's business, much to his mother's distress. Yet against all odds and adversities, Christopher's life greatly diverged from settled norms in Great Hockham, incidentally producing one of the most distinguished detective novelists from the Golden Age of detective fiction.

Although Christopher Bush was born in Great Hockham, he spent his earliest years in London living with his mother's much older sister, Elizabeth, and her husband, a fur dealer by the name of James Streeter, the couple having no children of their own. Almost certainly of illegitimate birth, Eva had been raised by the Long family from her infancy. She once told her youngest daughter how she recalled the Longs being visited, when she was a child, by a "fine lady in a carriage," whom she believed was her birth mother. Or is it possible that the "fine lady in a carriage" was simply an imaginary figment, like the aristocratic fantasies of Philippa Palfrey in P.D. James's *Innocent Blood* (1980), and that Eva's "sister" Elizabeth was in fact her mother?

The Streeters were a comfortably circumstanced couple at the time they took custody of Christopher. Their household included two maids and a governess for the young boy, whose doting but dutiful "Aunt Lizzie" devoted much of her time to the performance of "good works among the East End poor." When Christopher was seven years old, however, drastically straightened financial circumstances compelled the Streeters to leave London for Norfolk, by the way returning the boy to his birth parents in Great Hockham.

Fortunately the cause of the education of Christopher, who was not only a capable village cricketer but a precocious reader and scholar, was taken up both by his determined and devoted mother and an idealistic local elementary school headmaster. In his teens Christopher secured a scholarship to Norfolk's Thetford Grammar School, one of England's oldest educational institutions, where Thomas Paine had studied a century-and-a-half earlier. He left Thetford in 1904 to take a position as a junior schoolmaster, missing a chance to go to Cambridge University on yet another scholarship. (Later he proclaimed himself thankful for this turn of events, sardonically speculating that had he received a Cambridge degree he "might have become an exceedingly minor don or something as staid and static and respectable as a publisher.") Christopher would teach in English schools for the next twenty-seven years, retiring at the age of 46 in 1931, after he had established a successful career as a detective novelist.

Christopher's romantic relationships proved far rockier than his career path, not to mention every bit as murky as his mother's familial antecedents. In 1911, when Christopher was teaching in Wood Green School, a co-educational institution in Oxfordshire, he wed county council schoolteacher Ella Maria Pinner, a daughter of a baker neighbor of the Bushes in Great Hockham. The two appear never actually to have lived together, however, and in 1914, when Christopher at the age of 29 headed to war in the 16th (Public Schools) Battalion of the Middlesex Regiment, he falsely claimed in his attestation papers, under penalty of two years' imprisonment with hard labor, to be unmarried.

After four years of service in the Great War, including a year-long stint in Egypt, Christopher returned in 1919 to his position at Wood Green School, where he became involved in another romantic relationship, from which he soon desired to extricate himself. (A photo of the future author, taken at this time in Egypt, shows a rather dashing, thin-mustached man in uniform and is signed "Chris," suggesting that he had dispensed with "Charlie" and taken in its place a diminutive drawn from his middle name.) The next year Winifred Chart, a mathematics teacher at Wood Green, gave birth to a son, whom she named Geoffrey Bush. Christopher was the father of Geoffrey, who later in life became a noted English composer, though for reasons best known to himself Christopher never acknowledged his son. (A letter Geoffrey once sent him was returned unopened.) Winifred claimed that she and Christopher had married but separated, but she refused to speak of her purported spouse forever after and she destroyed all of his letters and other mementos, with the exception of a book of poetry that he had written for her during what she termed their engagement.

Christopher's true mate in life, though with her he had no children, was Florence Marjorie Barclay, the daughter of a draper from Ballymena, Northern Ireland, and, like Ella Pinner and Winifred Chart, a schoolteacher. Christopher and Marjorie likely had become romantically involved by 1929, when Christopher dedicated to her his second detective novel, *The Perfect Murder Case*; and they lived together as man and wife from the 1930s until her death in 1968 (after which, probably not coincidentally, Christopher stopped publishing novels). Christopher returned with Marjorie to the vicinity of Great Hockham when his writing career took flight, purchasing two adjoining cottages and commissioning his father and a stepbrother to build an extension consisting of a kitchen, two bedrooms and a new staircase. (The now sprawling structure, which Christopher called "Home Cottage," is now a bed and breakfast grandiloquently dubbed "Home Hall.") After a falling-out with his father, presumably over the conduct of Christopher's personal life, he and Marjorie in 1932 moved to Beckley, Sussex, where they purchased Horsepen, a lovely Tudor plaster and timber-framed house. In 1953 the couple settled at their final home, The Great House, a centuries-old structure (now a boutique hotel) in Lavenham, Suffolk.

From these three houses Christopher maintained a lucrative and critically esteemed career as a novelist, publishing both detective novels as Christopher Bush and, commencing in 1933 with the acclaimed book *Return* (in the UK, *God and the Rabbit*, 1934), regional novels purposefully drawing on his own life experience, under the pen name Michael Home. (During the 1940s he also published espionage novels under the Michael Home pseudonym.) Although his first detective novel, *The Plumley Inheritance*, made a limited impact, with his second, *The Perfect Murder Case*, Christopher struck gold. The latter novel, a big seller in both the UK and the US, was published in the former country by the prestigious Heinemann, soon to become the publisher of the detective novels of Margery Allingham and Carter Dickson (John Dickson Carr), and in the latter country by the Crime Club imprint of Doubleday, Doran, one of the most important publishers of mystery fiction in the United States.

Over the decade of the 1930s Christopher Bush published, in both the UK and the US as well as other countries around the world, some of the finest detective fiction of the Golden Age, prompting the brilliant Thirties crime fiction reviewer, author and Oxford University Press editor Charles Williams to avow: "Mr. Bush writes of as thoroughly enjoyable murders as any I know." (More recently, mystery genre authority B.A. Pike dubbed these novels by Bush, whom he praised as "one of the most reliable and resourceful of true detective writers"; "Golden Age baroque, rendered remarkable by some extraordinary flights of fancy.") In 1937 Christopher Bush became, along with Nicholas Blake, E.C.R. Lorac and Newton Gayle (the writing team of Muna Lee and Maurice West Guinness), one of the final authors initiated into the Detection Club before the outbreak of the Second World War and with it the demise of the Golden Age. Afterward he continued publishing a detective novel or more a year, with his final book in 1968 reaching a total of 63, all of them detailing the investigative adventures of lanky and bespectacled gentleman amateur detective Ludovic Travers. Concurring as I do with the encomia of Charles Williams and B.A. Pike, I will end this introduction by thanking Avril MacArthur for providing invaluable biographical information on her great uncle, and simply wishing fans of classic crime fiction good times as they discover (or rediscover), with this latest splendid series of Dean Street Press classic crime fiction reissues, Christopher Bush's Ludovic Travers detective novels. May a new "Bush public" yet arise!

Curtis Evans

The Case of the Chinese Gong (1935)

"We spoke about the age of miracles being over. I very much doubt it."

Tempest smiled. "Talking like [G.K.] Chesterton won't get us very far."

"That's where you may be wrong," Travers told him.

The Case of the Chinese Gong

IN COLIN WATSON'S *Snobbery with Violence: English Crime Stories and Their Audience* (1971), an influential analytical survey of "Golden Age" detective and thriller fiction published between the First and Second World Wars, the English crime writer and critic argued that what he memorably termed the Golden Age's "Mayhem Parva"--the stable and socially stratified rural world of the English village, its placidity disrupted only for the briefest of time by the most tasteful of murders--was emphatically a false creation of British mystery authors, "a sort of museum of nostalgia" for the social and political structure of an Edwardian England that had vanished irrevocably with the advent of the First World War. English author Rupert Croft-Cooke, who wrote Golden Age detective fiction under the pseudonym Leo Bruce, evinced just such nostalgia in his tellingly-titled 1958 memoir, *The Gardens of Camelot*, recalling his adolescent years before the Great War as "a most happy childhood" leisurely spent "in the warmth of Edwardian days." For Croft-Cooke, concessions of the unhappy existence of Edwardian political and social inequities tended to remain vague generalities, compared with such pleasant and substantial memories as "strawberries and cream on the lawn and drinks on the terrace for thirty people." "Where could you find the servants to wash up after them," Croft-Cooke fretted of what he deemed drab Fifties Britain, an era of middle-class domestic dependence upon au pairs and automatic appliances.

One of the reassuringly ritualized aspects of Edwardian England that Croft-Cooke recalled in his memoirs and novels was the sounding of a great metal gong to remind dressing guests that their formal, five-course dinner impended. In British detective fiction, we find perhaps the best known example of this fascinating dinner gong ritual in Agatha Christie's Hercule Poirot detective tale "Dead Man's Mirror." Although the novella, in which a dinner gong serves as a key clue in the brilliant Belgian's investigation of a tricky locked room slaying, first appeared in the collection *Murder in the Mews* in 1937, in its original form, the short story "The Second Gong," the tale was first published in magazines in the UK and US in 1932. This was three years before the publication of Christopher Bush's detective novel *The Case of the Chinese Gong* (1935), an ingenious Golden Age mystery that stages, like Christie's "Dead Man's Mirror," a most excellent "gong show" for mystery readers. The novel is one of Bush's most mechanically sophisticated and mentally challenging tales, of which the *New York Times Book Review* observed: "those who like difficult puzzles will find it wholly satisfactory." In more recent years internet reviewer Richard Liedholm has advised, "this is a puzzle mystery, and if you are the type who likes clues, lots and lots of clues, you will enjoy this novel," while vintage crime fiction blogger Nick Fuller (*The Grandest Game in the World*) has proclaimed *Gong* "extremely ingenious and mystifying."

Both Colin Watson and another prominent British crime writer and critical authority from the Seventies, Julian Symons, author of *Bloody Murder: From the Detective Story to the Crime Novel* (1972), contended that out of deference to the sensitivities of their middle class readership, writers of between-the-wars British mysteries in their books deliberately averted their eyes, if you will, from the unpleasant social realities brought about by the Great Depression (or the "Slump," as it was dubbed in Britain), a man-made disaster that wrought havoc in the lives of millions of unfortunates throughout the world. However, *The Case of the Chinese Gong* is one of the not insignificant number of British detective novels from this era where the claims made by Watson and Symons are something less than accurate. To be sure, *Gong* draws on a familiar trope of Golden Age mystery, that of the plight of impecunious relatives dependent on a provokingly stinting wealthy relation. Yet this stock situation is given unusual piquancy in *Gong* by the author's references to the real world economic crisis and its baneful impact on the lives of the characters--one of whom, when the novel opens, has just attempted to gas himself.

Four men—Tom Bypass, retired army officer; Hugh Bypass, schoolmaster; Martin Greeve, engineer (out-of-work) and Romney Greeve, artist--are present in the immediate vicinity (all but one of them actually within the same four walls) when their querulous, crabbed and egregiously tight-fisted uncle, Hubert Greeve, is fatally shot in the drawing room of his country house, Palings, during a seemingly harmless little parlor game of cribbage. Also present are the old man's lawyer, Charles Mantlin, and his butler, John Service, the latter of whom at the time of death was smiting, as per instruction, the eight o'clock dinner gong. The problem for the local police of the lovely little town of Seaborough--the setting of a previous Bush detective novel, *The Case of the 100% Alibis*—is determining how on earth Hubert Greeve could have been indecorously done to death in his drawing room without anyone having noticed the shooter. "Not one [of the suspects] could conceivably have done it—unless he performed a first-class miracle," pronounces one individual of the crime.

It is a challenging problem indeed, reminiscent of *Seeing Is Believing* (1941), a classic impossible crime novel by Carter Dickson (aka John Dickson Carr, acknowledged master of the locked room mystery). Fortunately for the bamboozled police, Ludovic "Ludo" Travers, author and amateur sleuth extraordinaire, is on hand in Seaborough as a weekend guest of Major Tempest, the chief constable of the county, and his wife. Travers—he of the "patrician air of breeding. . . . air of pervasive sympathy . . . unforced charm of manner and wholly ridiculous generosity"--has become fast friends with the Tempests since he helped the Major out with that 100% alibis affair.

We learn that Travers is writing a new book, this one something in the way of a true crime study, for aficionados of high-

THE CASE OF THE CHINESE GONG

faluting foul play: *Kensington Gore: Murder for High-Brows.* During the investigation of the seemingly impossible murder of Hubert Greeve, Travers has occasion to ruminate about this matter of murders and miracles. "Murder ceased to be killing only when it was a fine art," reflects Ludo. "A perfect murder must escape detection; therefore it must be proofed against human inquiry, and in that manner achieve something of the miraculous." Fortunately for those tasked with solving the seemingly unsolvable puzzle at Palings, Ludovic Travers--like John Dickson Carr's Gideon Fell and Sir Henry Merrivale, Agatha Christie's Hercule Poirot, and G.K. Chesterton's Father Brown --is one of those rare murder investigators who can explain miracles.

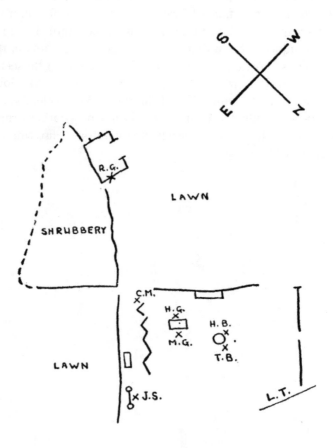

PART I
A MURDER IS PLANNED

CHAPTER I
THE WRONG MAN

Tom Bypass called at the Bond Street shop to see Brenda Greeve, and to make sure that Martin, her husband, would be at home. When the Greeves lost their money in the early days of the slump, through the toy-factory failing, they sold their house and car, dismissed their maids and fended for themselves in a modest flat till Martin should find some sort of a job. A year later the Greeves were pretty desperate and Martin himself almost at the end of his tether, what with living on relatives and spending days answering advertisements in person and nights answering them by post.

Then the Greeves came down to that awful three-roomed flat in Camden Town, though grateful enough to Martin's brother Romney who got it for them from a friend, and with thanks to Tom Bypass, whose money kept them going. Then Brenda found a job in the Bond Street photographic shop, which was run by a friend of her mother. Martin tried canvassing, and threw it up in a month by Tom's orders, or it would have killed him.

Brenda's face lit up when she saw who was waiting in the shop.

"Hallo, Brenda," Tom said. "Just running along to see Martin, so thought I'd pop in here first and get the news."

"Tom," she said, "you're an angel. I've been worried to death about Martin. Do cheer him up—" She broke off, shaking her head. "I shouldn't have said that. You always do cheer him up. He's different for days after you've been to see us."

"Oh, I don't know," said Tom diffidently. "But the poor old chap's a bit down in the mouth, is he?" "Tom, he's worse than he's ever been," Brenda told him earnestly. "That dreadful time he had on that canvassing job pulled him all to pieces. All he does is sit and fret. He won't even walk on the Heath now; he's just lost all heart."

"Bad as that, is it?" He nodded, then his own face lighted up. "I know what'd do him good. I'll take him out this afternoon and buy a jolly little pup—a cocker or a Cairn. That'll make him go out for walks!"

She shook her head quickly. "No, no, Tom; we can't take anything else from you. What with us, and Hugh and Romney, you're spending everything you have." She had been watching him rather puzzledly. "You're looking frightfully peaked yourself, Tom. Anything the matter?"

Tom, at forty, was what was known as a quiet old stick. But for that gas attack in Frame he would still have been in the service, and in spite of his stoop there was still a lot of the soldier about him—his lean six feet, his trim moustache and clean-eyed way of letting his eyes rove round. A good-looking chap, Tom Bypass, and smart; though not so well groomed perhaps since he had thought it his duty to lend a hand to such members of the family as had all at once fallen on hard times.

And he smiled serenely enough at Brenda's alarm. There was nothing new the matter. Everyone knew his lungs had been dicky since that whiff of gas; and a hot August, with stinks and dust and heaven-knew-what, had been giving him rather a thin time.

"I hate to see you looking so ill," Brenda said. "Can't you get away somewhere for a bit? Some quiet little seaside place. It'd do you no end of good, Tom."

"Seaside?" He chuckled quietly. "Aren't we due at Seaborough next Monday—the whole four of us?" Brenda clicked her tongue annoyedly. "That's what's getting on Martin's nerves. He can't stand the thought of it. It's horrible to have to go down there to that wicked old man, just because he happens to be his uncle and it's his birthday and he can order all of you about—that's what it really amounts to. He knows you all hate him and that just gives him the chance to make it worse."

"Well"—he grinned slightly—"so long as he knows it, what's it matter? Besides, you've got to pocket a certain amount of pride. There'll be forty thousand coming to each of us one day—if he doesn't change his mind."

"If he doesn't change his mind!" She sniffed. "It's absolutely fiendish the way he deliberately keeps you on tenter-hooks. And it's our own money really."

Tom shook his head. "You mustn't harp on that, old lady. There's not a penn'orth of proof it's our money."

"Why doesn't he help some of us out now, instead of doing as he does?" She shook her head fiercely. "If I had a hundred or two now, he could keep his wretched money." She remembered something. "Oh, I forgot to ask you about Hugh. How did he get on?"

"Well"—he hesitated—"what you'd expect. He went down to Palings in spite of the old man's letter saying it'd be no good. He wouldn't see him, but Service, the butler, came out with word Hugh was to write down anything new he had to say; then in a minute or two Service brought word back that Mr. Greeve regretted he could do nothing. You've never seen Service, have you?"

The question had turned aside Brenda's indignation, and now he went right on.

"He's an awful good chap. Got Hugh on one side and most respectfully asked if there was anything he could do, he and Alice—that's his wife, the housekeeper, you know." He broke off. "Still, I mustn't stand chattering to you all day. What about your keys in case Martin should happen to be out?"

He took the Tube for Hampstead and walked down the hill towards Camden Town, through mean streets that kept their smells and lost some of their squalor under the August sun. It was not his way to harbour the furtive, and yet in some vague way he was glad things had come to a crisis with Martin—glad because of the astounding thing he himself was about to suggest. And more than ever a fury was filling him against old Hubert Greeve. Brenda had been right. It was damnable that four men should so lose all pride and respect as to go down there and sit with patient eyes and quiet tongues like dogs waiting for a bone. No wonder the old man despised them—as much, perhaps, as they loathed the sight of him.

Then he began thinking of Martin, almost fifty and with never a hope of a job, with the slump still on and the world crowded with bright young engineers, full of the latest notions. And again he had that furtive feeling of satisfaction, for Martin might perhaps find not so fantastic the proposition he himself was about to make.

The flat lay above a greengrocer's shop. It was about a quarter to two, and the shop was closed for the dinner hour, when he let himself in at the side door. As he mounted the stairs the house had that empty silence that told him he was alone. The shaft of sun that came from a roof window made the darknesses of the bare landing more intense, and it was only when he found that the door was bolted as well as locked that he became aware of a paper fastened below the knocker:

Don't come in here. Send for the police.

He stood for a moment with breath held, then lurched his body back and sent it crashing. A hinge weakened, then gave way, and a mad stamping with his heels forced out the other. He wrenched the whole door aside and squeezed his way through.

Martin Greeve was in the kitchen, head in the gas oven. In a flash Tom had him out and the window open and both their heads outside for a gulp of clean air. Then he somehow hoisted Martin's spare body over his shoulders and laid him in the bedroom chair, working at his arms to get the foulness from his lungs. Only then he remembered the gas jets that were still hissing, and when he came to the bedroom again, Martin seemed to be breathing better. But now he was feeling faint himself, and it was a minute or two before he could make his way out for a doctor.

He found one less than two hundred yards away. In two minutes he would be along, he said, and Tom went back ahead. But a policeman was standing at the foot of the stairs and looking up suspiciously, hatless man comes frightenedly from a passage and stares about him and leaves wide open the private door to the street, curious happenings seem not unlikely.

"Extraordinary smell of gas here, sir?"

"Yes," said Tom. "The fact of the matter is, the wind blew a jet out when my cousin was having a nap. I happened to come along and find him." He smiled with what was meant to be a confiding confidence. "The doctor's just coming to have a look at him. I thought it wouldn't do any harm."

And at that very moment the doctor came. The constable gave an official nod or two, cast another suspicious glance round, then moved off.

"Keep this to yourself, doctor," Tom warned him when they got to the landing. "I'll tell you all about it when you've finished with him."

In a quarter of an hour the doctor had gone again. Martin Greeve had had a narrow squeak, having lapsed into unconsciousness at the very moment when his cousin first sent his body crashing at the door. Now he lay half sleeping in the bed, a yellow pallor about his face and a strangeness which a man well might have after a peep over the edge of eternity. Then the doctor's boy came with the powder the patient was to take, and inside five minutes he was sleeping soundly.

That afternoon Tom Bypass repaired the door. He got the last whiff of gas from the house and he bought some flowers to make the living-room more cheerful, and he had the kettle boiling for Brenda's tea, Monday being her early day. Then just before six he stirred Martin gently.

"Time to wake up, old chap." He smiled down at him. "Brenda's coming in a minute."

Martin looked at him puzzled, then remembered—and his face turned away.

"For the love of God, don't let anything out, old chap," Tom told him. "It's all fixed up with the doctor and everything. It was a heart attack. Nothing serious—just the heat. Is that all right?"

At half-past six Tom had to go, and Brenda was following him into the bedroom.

"You let me have a quiet word with him alone," Tom smiled at her. "It'll do him more good than you being there."

Martin's eyes lifted to his. There was almost a reproach in them, and an infinite sadness, and a curious something that was like worship. His voice was a low whisper.

"What'd you bring me back for, Tom?"

Tom shook his head at him, smiling queerly.

"You lie quiet, old chap, and we'll talk about that—some other time." He shook his head again, then all at once stooped till his voice was inaudible save to the sick man's ear. "You'll never try that way out again? You won't, Martin? Promise me you won't!"

The eyes dosed for a moment, opened, and looked away.

"All right, Tom. I'll promise."

He got to his feet, his voice raised for Brenda's benefit.

"Well, look after yourself, old chap. I'll be along first thing Wednesday."

But he paused at the door like a man still in some doubt. Then he opened the door the merest crack and listened, till he heard Brenda and the rattling of washing-up at the kitchen sink. The door was closed gently and he went back to the bed. His head lowered again.

"I'll be in on Wednesday morning, Martin old chap. Perhaps I'll have some good news. And will you do something for me?" He shook his head gently. "No, not work. Something I'd like you to think over in your mind." His eyes rose quickly to the door; he listened for a moment, then whispered again, "Ask yourself this question. Ask it damn seriously, but don't let it worry you. *Don't you think you tried to kill the wrong man?*"

That was on the evening of Monday, the twenty-third of August. On the Tuesday morning Inspector Carry of Seaborough was in the police-station when a message was coming through, and he waited till the station-sergeant had rung off with, "Yes, sir, we'll see to it at once."

A Mr. Hubert Greeve had been ringing up to request police action in the matter of some intruder in the grounds of his house—Palings—the previous night.

"Who is he?" Carry asked.

The constable on duty knew all about him.

"He's a queer old boy, inspector, up at that big house on the London Road; you know—right-hand side as you come in. Palings, the name is. Pots of money, so they say."

Carry nodded. "I know where you mean." Then he grunted. "Might as well run up and see him myself."

So he got out his car, took his sergeant—Polegate by name—with him, and drove off. Palings lay a couple of miles north of the town at the end of a two-hundred-yard drive, with a fine view west along the Downs and south across the Channel. It was a biggish Victorian house, with gardens as chock-full of second-rate rubbish—monkey-puzzle trees, laurel shrubberies, mossy croquet-lawn and miniature temple-cum-pagoda summer-house—as in the year its first owner had had them laid out.

John Service, the butler, warned Mr. Greeve as soon as the two arrived. He was an oldish man of quiet, gentle manner and some natural dignity; tall, rather venerable in appearance, and entirely devoid of pomposity.

"Nice old boy that," Carry whispered to Polegate. "The old man's a queer one by all accounts, so mind your step."

Hubert Greeve came out to the hall at once; a dried-up, suspicious-eyed old man of seventy-four. He supported himself by a stick in his left hand, for rheumatism had somewhat twisted his knee. A general thinness was about him—thin, sallow cheeks, thin, bluish lips, thin neck and spindly shanks; but his manner was alert and even aggressive. Carry asked for information, and at once the old man rounded on his butler.

"Tell them about it!" he glared round at him. "Don't stand there looking like a fool."

"Well, sir, it's the gardener who knows, really—"

"Then fetch him, damn you, fetch him!" the old man roared.

Inside five minutes old Greeve, the gardener and the two detectives were on the steps of the summerhouse that lay not twenty yards from the drawing-room door, that being the handiest spot for the gardener to tell his story. It was there—at about eight-thirty the previous night—the gardener had seen the flash of an electric torch, and his own presence on the premises at that hour was accounted for by some greenhouse lights he had thought best to come and lower. When he made for the spot, he heard someone making off, but it was folly to go in pursuit in the dark with nothing to guide one but rapidly disappearing sounds. Two traces remained of the man's presence: a rose-bed that had been trampled on, and one of those coiled, metal measuring tapes in the usual metal pocket-case. This he produced.

"Whereabouts, exactly, did you find it?" asked Carry.

The gardener showed the spot on the brick surround which made a sort of loggia for the summerhouse.

"And where did the man make to, to the best of your knowledge?"

"Through the shrubbery there," the man told him, pointing to the bushes that lay behind the summer-house and ran as far as the drawing-room doors.

"What's behind the shrubbery?"

"The lawn," the man told him. "The lawn that's both sides of the drive."

Carry turned to old Greeve. "He was taking the shortest way back to the road, sir. And about this case," he said to the gardener. "Anyone opened it?"

"No, sir," the gardener said. "I left it just as I found it. I knew what it was, so there wasn't no real point in opening it."

"Right," said Carry. "Let the sergeant take your finger-prints to make sure, then we'll take it away and try it for prints when it's uncoiled. Then we'll search the shrubbery to see if he's dropped anything else."

He put another question or two to the man, then let him go.

"Now, I'll have a look through this shrubbery, sir," he said to old Greeve, who had been standing there glowering and glaring. But as soon as he set foot between the outermost bushes, the old man let out a roar.

"Damn you! Mind where you set those great feet of yours!"

"Feet, sir?" said Carry, and drew back. Then he became aware of the edging of ragged pinks on which his foot had been neatly planted. "I'm sorry, sir. I thought they were weeds."

"Weeds!" The old man looked murder at him. Then he stamped off a yard or two as if afraid to trust himself in the company of so utter a fool.

Carry blushed up to his ears and stepped gingerly inside the shrubbery again. In a minute the old man was behind him, and watching. Carry puzzled his wits how to make the atmosphere more genial.

"I expect you're fond of gardening, sir?"

"Well, and what if I am?"

"Oh, nothing, sir," Carry said. "Only it seemed to me as if you knew a good bit about it, sir."

The old man seemed slightly mollified; at least, he growled and said nothing.

"You know, sir," said Carry, straightening his back, "I reckon this'd make a rare fine spot for roses—I mean if this old shrubbery was grubbed out and some good soil put in."

The old man stared at him with the black hate of hell, turned in his tracks and hobbled off to the house again.

Carry and Polegate found nothing except some prints on the measuring tape itself, but the usual inquiries were put in hand. Then that same evening, Major Tempest, the Chief Constable, sent for Inspector Carry and told him he had had a complaint. Hubert Greeve had demanded the Chief Constable on the phone, and when at last he got him, said that not only had the police been represented at the Palings inquiry by a fool, but by a grossly impertinent fool as well. Carry's manner, according to old Greeve, had been deliberately insulting.

Carry was so indignant that he could scarcely splutter his defence. Polegate, equally injured, gave corroborative evidence.

"That's all right," Tempest told them, when he had satisfied himself. "Still, the best way when you're doubtful is to keep your mouth shut altogether. But you needn't worry about this. I'll smooth him down."

Carry went out to his own office, and there he let fly to Polegate.

"Well, of all the damned old swine!" There was a good deal more to it than that, and Polegate also respectfully contributed his quota. Then Carry smiled grimly.

"What'd you do with the prints you took off the tape?"

"Got 'em here," the sergeant told him.

"Lose 'em," said Carry laconically. "And put the tape away in the safe. Let the damned old liar do his own detective work." His growlings rumbled to an end with a last dire threat. "If you and me weren't what we are, we'd go up there one dark night and root out every perishin' rose he's got."

CHAPTER II
MURDER IS EASY

Tom Bypass turned up at the Camden Town flat that Wednesday morning a good hour earlier than Martin Greeve expected him. Martin himself was looking older and more drawn, though the last year he had always looked older than his age; but now there was some colour in his cheeks, and bodily he was himself again. But there was something strange and stilted about the meeting of the two men: Tom with a wonder how the other would react to the thing at which he had hinted and was now about to propose, and Martin with a kind of dogged shame for the coward's way out he had almost taken.

"Feeling more yourself?" Tom asked him.

"Yes," said Martin, and avoided his eyes. "I can't say I feel absolutely fit, but I'm not so bad." A bitterness came about his mouth. "Rather a funny thing for me to say to you—considering everything."

"Don't look at it like that," Tom told him. "Tell yourself it never happened—the same as I shall. And cast your eye over this."

He produced a letter from his pocket. It was from Charles Mantlin, old Greeve's lawyer; a Seaborough man who had been at school with Tom and had known the cousins for years.

Most Confidential.

DEAR TOM,

I think I ought to let you know that H.G. had me in yesterday and broke to me the astonishing news that he was proposing to make changes in his will in favour of his sister Ethel. I was unaware that such a person existed, but I gathered that she compromised herself many years ago and was disowned by the family.

I cannot say whether this is some cunning variation on the annual game he plays of cat and mouse to try and provoke you people into an open breach, but he certainly seemed to me to be in earnest, though that may all be part of the game. He did mention that he was of the opinion that restitution ought to be made for what she had undergone, and I gathered that her husband was a worthless individual who might make trouble. I should be glad of any supplementary information you can give me in confidence. Shall be seeing you next Monday in any case. Destroy this when read.

Yours as ever,

C.

Martin's eyes bulged in astonishment. "Aunt Ethel? I thought she was dead years ago."

"So did I," the other told him. "As a matter of fact, though, she never was more than a name as far as I'm concerned. What'd you know about her yourself?"

"Well"—he pursed up his lips in thought—"I never actually saw her, but I remember her name being mentioned, and then being told as a boy that I wasn't to ask questions about her. Later on I wormed the story out of my father, and according to him—as far as I remember—she ran off with a valet or somebody, in Moscow, and the family promptly regarded her as dead. These last years I've always thought of her as dead. I don't know why I should have done, but I have. The husband I've never even thought about."

"The same with me," Tom said. "I don't suppose I've even had her in my mind twice these last ten years. Hugh may know a bit more, being older." He put the letter carefully away again. "I think I'll run down to Bromley and see him to-morrow, and if I learn any more I'll let you know. But the real point's this. As Charles says, is she alive, and does he really want to do anything for her, or is it only one of those damnable yearly stunts of his? Last year, you remember, he said his conscience was troubling him about the unemployed. The year before, it was the hospitals. Anything to humiliate us and try to provoke us into a row."

Martin grunted. "It's about time we forgot the decencies and told him just what we think. Yet, it's hard luck we should be deliberately forced into giving him an excuse to rob us of what belongs to us. That's the damnable part of his policy." He stirred for a moment in his chair, frowning to himself as if hunting for the right words. "There was something you said to me, just before you went out the other night. Would you mind saying it again?"

Tom began slowly filling his pipe, and from the rampart of that small action, spoke his mind.

"I'd rather put it another way. And I'll absolutely open my mind to you, Martin, even if you happen to think I've gone mad. What I said to you was just the wonder whether you'd chosen quite the right way out—whether you'd tried to kill the right man, in fact." He shook his head. "I'll start at the beginning. Do you mind?"

Martin shot a look at him—and waited.

"Now take the slump. It's absolutely uncanny how it's hit you three people so hard. You've been wiped out clean. Romney can't sell a picture and he's dead on the rocks, and just when those two kids of his were due for school. Hugh invested everything he had in that private school, and threw up a good job, and there he is with not enough pupils to keep the place afloat. His boy Jim has had to chuck Oxford and become a kind of usher. The first mortgage on the place has gone, and Hugh doesn't know where to turn. And the damnable thing about it all is, that if this uncle of ours liked, he could set everybody on his feet again till things righted themselves. It'd only cost him a trifle compared with what he has, and after that he could leave his money—"

"Our money."

"Have it either way. He could leave the money where he liked. But you applied to him; so did Romney, and now he's turned Hugh down—and most insultingly. Yet we'll all four of us go down there on Monday and try to act like decent people, according to our agreement, and put up with whatever he likes to hand us out. You know what he'll be like—sneering and gloating and hinting; just because we once took collective action and asked for an inquiry into the 1915 smash."

Martin nodded.

"Now do you see?" Tom went on. "If a man does you an injury or lets you down, do you get your own back by knocking your own head against a wall? You'd come to the end of your tether, so you tried to get out by eliminating yourself." He leaned forward in his chair. "I asked you if you hadn't killed the wrong man. If someone had to be killed, why you? Suppose, for instance, you are now dead. What good has it done a soul—even Brenda? *But suppose you'd killed Hubert Greeve.* Your heir would have been debarred from inheriting, but the rest of us would have seen Brenda was all right. As far as we know this very minute, we four inherit. If you'd taken a dud life instead of a damn good one, then you'd have put everything right; Brenda and Romney and Hugh. That's acting on the assumption that the police would have discovered the murderer, in which case you could always have taken your own way out afterwards. Only you see, *you wouldn't have been found out.*"

"Why not?" Martin fired at him.

Tom smiled dryly. "Not a fortnight ago, in this very room, you and Brenda and myself were arguing about murder. 'Murder is easy,' you said. 'It's child's play to commit murder and get away with it.' You got quite annoyed when we disagreed." He leaned forward again. "You were serious enough, Martin. And if you were so sure, one thing follows. You'd thought it over quite a lot. And there's only one man you'd like to murder—our uncle, Hubert Greeve. Therefore you must have often wondered whether or not it was worth the risk to kill him, and you've got so far as to have found a fool-proof way. Am I right?"

Martin looked away for a moment, then all at once gave him look for look.

"Well, and suppose you are?"

Tom shrugged his shoulders. "Then why say more? Wasn't I also right when I suggested that you'd tried to kill the wrong man?"

"Yes," said Martin slowly. "Perhaps you were." Then he looked up, shaking his head, and in his eyes all sorts of unspoken things. "What's come over you, Tom? I'm different, I know, but it's just like some other man in the room." He shook his head. "We're both of us mad—that's what it is."

"Oh, no, we're not," Tom told him cheerfully. Then once more he leaned forward. "You three have envied me sometimes this last year or so, haven't you? Five hundred a year and nothing to do but live on it?"

Martin shook his head. "Not envied, Tom. We were glad you hadn't got the troubles we had. And five hundred a year's wrong. You've been giving us best part of it. You've been as hard hit as any of us. You gave up that flat of yours in town and—"

"Now, now, Martin; you're getting away from the point." Then he smiled quietly, like the old, sane, steady-going Tom. "But I wasn't serious about your doing in Uncle Hubert, Martin."

"You mean you were just trying to—well, to talk away to keep my mind off things?"

"Not at all," Tom told him cheerfully. "I was merely trying you out."

Martin looked puzzled. "Trying me out?"

"Yes." There was something whimsical about the way he smiled. "You do know a way, though, don't you?"

"Yes," said Martin. "At least I think I do."

"Right," said Tom, and drew his chair in farther. "Now I'll tell you something. I went to a local man about my breathing apparatus a fortnight ago. He sent me to Wintsor, the Harley Street man. He told me if I spent another autumn and winter in England it'd be the end of me. What he advised was a sanatorium in Switzerland at once; failing that, residence in South Africa."

Martin was staring. "My God, no!"

"So you see now what I was driving at. I can't go either place because I've got no money. What's become of it doesn't matter—besides, I've committed myself in writing as a sort of backer for Hugh. All that's left, then, is a choice like your own, my dear Martin. Am I to kill myself or kill old Greeve? I choose the latter. And you're going to hand over to me that fool-proof way of doing it."

"I won't do it!"

"Oh, yes, you will. You wouldn't force me to your own way out?"

Martin's eyes were on the bare fireplace. For a long two minutes his lean fingers curled and uncurled restlessly about his chin; then at last he spoke.

"Well, I might. But I won't promise till next time I see you."

"Take your time," Tom told him. "I know it's none too easy to find the right way. Ever since I stepped out of that Harley Street door I've been worrying my wits to know how to kill a man and get away with it." He shook his head. "It was all providential, really."

"How do you mean?"

"Well, all we've been talking about this morning was what I was coming round to see you about last Monday afternoon."

Martin turned his eyes quickly to the fireplace again. His fingers began that restless curling, then he nodded to himself.

"You still a super-shot with a gun?"

"Not by a long chalk. Still, if you give the word go, I'll soon get some of it back."

Martin grunted, and nodded again as if to himself.

"If I were you I think I would."

Ludovic Travers was putting in a long week-end at Seaborough with the Tempests. Tempest had been overwhelmed by Travers. There had been that murder case with its water-tight alibis—the first Seaborough had ever known—and Travers himself had done some spectacular and eccentric deduction that had fitted in well with the more sober unravellings of Superintendent Wharton, whose shadow he had insinuatingly become.

But Major Tempest was not unique in finding a strange fascination in the personality of Ludovic Travers. For one thing there was about him a perfect disregard of shams and conventions. Afflicted, as he would have put it, with more money than he could spend, his tastes lay in simplicity and middle-class comfort, and outward show was the last thing that concerned him. If he drove a Rolls, it was, as he would have told you, because as an economist he regarded it as a safe investment, particularly in the essential matter of getting with reasonable speed from place to place. If he had a superb flat in St. Martin's Chambers, it was because he had inherited the whole block, and a man must patronize his own property.

His manner was a mixture of diffidence and disarming geniality. He was an elongated lamp-post of a man, with friendly, dark eyes hidden beneath monstrous horn-rims, and when in any mental travail he would take them off and polish their glasses, blinking away like a genial owl. He had a first-class brain, and a queer one, with humanity his study and the world a perpetual theatre. George Wharton, in the nearest he ever got to an epigram, remarked of him that the fact that there were two sides to every question was for him merely an incentive to find a third. And when one adds to those original qualities of the man his patrician air of breeding, his air of pervasive sympathy that could extort a confidence and give it, his unforced charm of manner and wholly ridiculous generosity, then the reason becomes more apparent for that week-end which the Tempests had long been trying to extort from Ludovic Travers.

It was the Saturday evening, and Tempest and his guest had been playing a round on the local links in the comparative cool of after tea. Travers had driven his Rolls, and on the way back the Major had asked for a detour to the police-station. Just a call, he said, in case anything had turned up, and to ensure a night undisturbed by interruptions.

The station-sergeant was talking over the phone as the Major came in. His expression immediately altered.

"Here is the Chief, now, sir. Hold the line a second and I'll see if he'll speak to you."

He whispered with a tremendous caution, "That Mr. Greeve, sir. The one at Palings. Wants to speak to you personal, sir. Wouldn't have anything to do with Inspector Carry."

Tempest nodded knowingly and took over the phone. So clearly did the words come through that Travers could listen unashamedly where he stood.

"The Chief Constable, Seaborough, speaking."

"Ah! thank you. This is Greeve—Mr. Hubert Greeve. You remember?"

"Yes, Mr. Greeve; I remember. But we haven't found out anything more for you about that affair. Our opinion is that it was some chance tramp or unemployed man looking for a night's shelter in the summer-house."

"It's not that. It's not that . . . Are you there?"

"Yes, I'm here."

There was a growling, like a clearing of the throat.

"It's something most confidential." There was a pause as if the speaker had looked round to be sure he was unheard, and then his voice appreciably lowered. "I have an idea I'm likely to be visited shortly by an impostor who wants to blackmail me."

"Blackmail you?" A grunt. "Look here, Mr. Greeve, don't you think it would be better if I ran up and saw you personally? We can be along in five minutes."

A brief hesitation, then, "Yes, perhaps you'd better. I'll wait for you myself."

"Very good. In five minutes."

It was well inside the time when Travers guided the Rolls in at that narrowish gateway to the drive of Palings. The old man came hobbling down from the porch to meet them.

"Here you are then," he said, glaring from under his thick, white eyebrows. "Come this way, will you?" He was off at once without looking to see if the two were following, and he cast the explanations over his shoulder as he hobbled along. "Can't be too careful . . . This way, gentlemen, please . . . Round here . . . That's the summer-house—er—Mr.—?"

"Major Tempest."

The old man gave that curious growling clearance of the throat, as if he resented the information. At any rate he disregarded it, and no word was said till the three were entering the drawing-room by the opened, twin french doors that overlooked lawn and summer-house both. He waved the two men to chairs. Tempest caught Travers's eye and received a scarcely perceptible wink.

In a moment old Greeve was explaining—and, obviously, only too guardedly. There was, too, an air of much mystery about everything, on a par with that circuitous leading round of the two to avoid the front door. His voice was a cracked whisper, and he would lean forward till Travers was fascinated by the tracery of cracks in his thin blue lips and the spittle that lay at the corner of the crafty mouth.

He had a sister, he said, now about sixty or more. He had lost sight of her for many years, but had lately become aware of her whereabouts. She had kept herself apart from the family on account of some scandal, but now as an old man he was minded to let bygones be bygones and do something for her. The trouble was that at that same identical time he had also received a communication from some scoundrel purporting to be her husband, and making threats of what he would do unless his wife were properly treated.

"Might I see the letter?" Tempest asked. "I take it it was a letter?"

"It's not available at the moment," Greeve told him. "Later, perhaps—if the need arises."

"If I might ask a question," said Travers in that pleasant voice of his, "just why do you suspect the man of being an impostor? I mean, mightn't he be her husband?"

"I rather gathered the husband was dead," said Tempest.

"Yes, yes," the old man said quickly. "If he was dead he couldn't be her husband."

"Unless she married again," said Travers casually.

"She hasn't married again." He shook his head. "Oh, no. She hasn't married again."

There was a perfunctory tap at the far door, it opened and Service, the butler, came in. Before he could open his mouth, the old man was getting to his feet and glaring.

"What the devil do you want in here?"

"Sorry, sir," the butler began. "I thought—"

"Damn what you thought!" the old man roared at him. "Get out!"

Service went.

Old Greeve sat down fuming and muttering.

"Just what is it you'd like us to do, Mr. Greeve?" put in Tempest suavely. "Be here when this impostor calls, hear what he has to say, and then, if you wish it, arrest him? That's the usual procedure." "Yes," the old man said. "Yes, that'll be the way." He chuckled to himself, and Travers marked the little sneer that went with it and thought of a thin, leathery spider peering from the web corner at an unsuspecting fly.

"Then you'll ring us up and make the necessary arrangements?" suggested Tempest. "If, of course, the necessity arises."

"Yes, yes," the old man told him fussily, getting to his feet.

Travers, with the natural curiosity of the antique collector, had let his eyes rove the room, and now as he rose and a blank came in the conversation, he had a remark to make.

"What a perfectly charming screen that is, sir."

It was a tall, eight-fold screen of carved, pierced mahogany; each upright fashioned out like the thin branch of a tree with interlaced twigs and perching birds.

The old man glared at him suspiciously. "You can't buy that. It's not for sale."

Travers smiled charmingly. "I never dreamt it would be, sir. I was merely admiring it." His long fingers stroked the polished wood. "Chippendale never made a better."

The old man thawed miraculously. His old parchment face wrinkled with pleasure as he stood there surveying it as if for the first time. It had come from a certain Russian palace, he said, and he had managed to smuggle it to England in 1915. He chuckled wickedly at the memory, then he bustled off along the wall and Travers saw why. He himself had been puzzled at the curious piece of furniture, but now he knew what it was that the old man was so anxious to show. It was a gong. The suspended, brass gong itself was of no consequence; the two carved mahogany supports were the things that mattered, matching as they did the uprights of the screen.

"What do you think of that?" the old man said. His thin mouth widened, and his voice cracked with the excitement of possession.

"Very fine," said Travers. "Very fine indeed." His fingers fumbled at his glasses. "Once upon a time, I should say, a porcelain vase or figure stood where that gong is."

The old man nodded, then gave a chuckle. "It got broken on the journey. I had the gong put in instead."

Five minutes later Travers was steering the car out to the main road again.

"Disagreeable old swine," remarked Tempest. "What'd you think of him?"

Travers smiled. "I had the idea that all that yarn of his was a myth. He was too interested for my liking. Reminded me of an elderly baboon concealing a nut."

"Bit of an old pig, too," said Tempest. "The way he spoke to that butler of his. And a mean old devil. Decanter of sherry on that side table by the screen, right under our noses, and he never even suggested a drink. Not that I wanted his damn sherry, but after going up there specially—"

Travers laughed. "As if I didn't know that, my dear old chap. But what amuses me is having a gong in the drawing-room."

"I thought you said it was a fine piece of furniture?"

"So it is," said Travers. "I'd like to have it myself. But rather funny, don't you think? Fancy being in that room and the butler coming in and giving it the devil of a wallop, and then bowing with very much gravity and remarking that dinner was served." He gave a little chuckle of his own. "As I once said on a certain occasion—truth will out, but there's no need to use a megaphone."

John Tempest smiled, then frowned. "Wonder why he wouldn't let me see that letter he was supposed to have had?"

"Because he obviously had too much to conceal," Travers told him. "Where there's blackmail there's always dirty work on both sides." He smiled. "Wish he'd die and leave me that screen."

"He's the kind that never dies," said Tempest morosely.

"You never know," said Travers amiably. And it was Travers who was to be dumbfoundedly right.

CHAPTER III
MURDER EVE

ON THE MONDAY AFTERNOON the four cousins went down to Seaborough. Romney Greeve had the longest journey, coming from his Essex village to the motor-coach station in town, where he met his brother Martin and Tom Bypass.

Martin and Romney Greeve, sons of old Hubert Greeve's brother George, were unlike as two men might be: Martin, clean-shaven and spare, with hair almost white; Romney plumpish, with black hair that grew along his ears, black moustache, and a tiny black imperial that seemed to buttress his full lower lip. Martin gave the impression of quiet strength—a man to lean on and trust. Romney had a liking for the velvet jacket and flowing neck-tie, but there were few such flamboyances in his manner—save perhaps an occasional volubility—and his quietnesses always seemed like taciturnity.

At Bromley the coach picked up Hugh Bypass, whose private school lay near by. Tom and Hugh Bypass, sons of old Hubert's sister Caroline, had fine dark eyes and sensitive mouths, and there the resemblance ended, for Hugh was as spare as Martin and had the look of a mild parson in mufti. He had, too, all the fidgetiness of a schoolmaster, and a trick of snapping his eyes as if he had continually mislaid his glasses, and maybe that added to his air of unworldliness and made him likeably forlorn. Yet sometimes he could show unexpected obstinacies and touches of temper which no one took too seriously, for they were gone almost before one was aware.

Three days was the usual extent of the stay, and each man's suit-case seemed more than sufficient luggage.

"I've sent some stuff on ahead," Romney said. "Service is seeing to it for me. Just an easel and one or two things."

"You're not going to work?" asked Martin.

"Yes," Romney said casually. "I've always had my eye on that little bit from the summer-house; you now, looking towards the pond."

"Lake, my dear fellow," Hugh reminded him dryly. "It wouldn't do for you to call it a pond. The old gentleman's as proud of it as he is of the garden."

"Gentleman be damned!" said Romney testily. "He can call it what he likes so long as he doesn't object to my painting. There's a fine vista when you look towards the woods from the summer-house in the late evening."

"He won't object," Tom said. "He'll be proud as Punch."

"What's the idea of going in for landscape?" Martin asked. "I thought you always kept to still life."

"Everyone goes in for landscape, as you call it," Romney told him. "And if you're interested, there's something I'd like to put up to you. I've got the idea we ought to regard landscape as a sort of flux. . . ."

He expounded his theories for a good ten minutes. Hugh listened with the courteous interest that was part of him, Tom looked amusedly bored, and Martin was too busy with his own thoughts to follow the intricacies of another man's. Then Romney came to an end of his lecture.

"You think that a perfectly sound argument?" he asked Hugh.

"Well, I'm no expert, but it seems reasonable enough," Hugh told him.

"Good." He took the three into his confidence. "What you've been listening to is a kind of tryout. A man I know suggested an article on those lines, and he can use it for the *Dilettante*, so while I'm down I thought I might write it. I shall use that view from the summer-house as a kind of general illustration."

But from all the topics that helped to pass that hour and a half's journey from Bromley, Palings and its owner were deftly kept apart. There was indeed at times a stiltedness in the conversation through the careful avoidance, and yet somehow in the unreality each man knew what the other thought. Then just about five o'clock the coach flashed past the drive that led to the house. Ten minutes later it drew up in Seaborough itself, and Charles Mantlin was as usual waiting.

There was no mustiness of the law about Charles Mantlin. He was red-faced, fleshy and of immense sturdiness. There was much of the open air about him, and it was that which gave such an incongruity to the curious trick he had of eternally clutching the lapels of his jacket. He was like a man who leans heavily on his own shoulders, and so set was he in the habit, that when one hand was needed for use, the other still maintained its grim hold. As he amusedly admitted, whereas most men had two pairs of breeks to a suit, he always ordered two jackets.

"I expect you're all ready for a cup of tea," he said, when he had shaken hands all round. "I've got a corner reserved for us, so we'll go right in as soon as you're ready. My man will see to the bags."

That preliminary cup of tea in Milani's restaurant was always the curtain-raiser to the Palings trip. It gave a chance to hear the latest news, and was a kind of bracing-up for what had come to be regarded as an ordeal.

"Sorry you couldn't tell us any more about that Aunt Ethel business," he said to Hugh.

"Dash it all, man; you seem to forget it took place forty and more years ago," Hugh told him, and somewhat abruptly. Of the four cousins he alone had never wholly trusted Mantlin, though his views had been kept to himself.

"Be reasonable, Hugh." Tom was throwing oil on the waters. "After all, you might have heard something let fall years ago. Besides, Charles is only trying to help."

"The thing is," put in Martin, "is it genuine or merely one of his craftily thought-out tricks?"

"I think it's real," Mantlin said. "But you never know with him. He's got a twisted mind."

"If he saw her, where did he see her?"

"Ah!" said Mantlin. "That's the point. I had a quiet word with Service—you can trust him, as you know—as to whether there'd been any callers, and all he knew about was two men who came on Saturday night and were closeted with the old boy in the drawing-room. On the other hand he goes out for a drive every day in the hired car, so heaven knows where he goes or whom he sees. He's secretive as blazes. He's as suspicious about me as if I wanted to rob him, and he never tells me a thing till he's absolutely forced. Mind you, we could always find out in confidence from the driver of the car."

"Little bit too much like snooping, don't you think?" said Tom. "It's a good enough idea, Charles, but I think we'd rather leave the dirty work to him. And what about Uncle X-Aunt Ethel's husband? The one who caused the flutter forty years or so ago."

"Don't know a thing," Mantlin said. "I asked if there were a husband when he mentioned the matter. Then you know how he is. He got that crafty look on his face, just as if he was playing a game and he was the only one who knew it. But he distinctly said he was a rascal who had to be watched. That's all he's said, and now you know as much as I do."

Mantlin himself always stayed at Palings those three days, and his man drove the party and the luggage from the town. Hugh, as senior of the four, had one last word to say.

"The usual line of conduct; I think we're all agreed on that? No matter what's said, we behave with utter disinterest. We take him for what he ought to be and not what he is."

Service was waiting in the porch, and everyone had a smile and a handshake for him. It was his thirteenth year at Palings, but the manner of an old servant of the family came natural to him.

"How are you, Mr. Hugh? Very glad to see you again, sir. . . . Mr. Jim is well, sir? . . . Glad to hear it, sir."

And so on with Martin, Romney and Tom. Charles Mantlin received something purely deferential, and once the six were in the hall, Service's manner became wholly that of the servant who must insist on knowing his place.

"The master will be down at the usual hour, gentlemen, and begs to be excused. Mrs. Service will show you your rooms, as there've been some alterations. Thank you, gentlemen."

Alice Service had been waiting in the background, and now she came forward—a white-haired, genteel and rather nervous old lady for whom the four had long felt something of affection. Service watched from below till the pleasant chatter was lost up the stairs.

Hugh stopped on the main landing.

"Not there, sir," the housekeeper told him quickly. "Mr. Romney is having the south-west room this year, sir. He wrote and asked for it specially."

Hugh stared. "Dash it all, Romney, I think you might have said something to me. I've always had that room ever since I've come here."

Romney clapped a placatory hand on his shoulder. "Sorry, old chap, I ought to have done. But you see, I want it on account of that work I'm doing. You get the same view as from the summer-house, or near enough."

A quarter of an hour later the party assembled in the morning-room. The old uneasiness hung heavily about the room, and though there was much talk of the year that had gone, and themselves and an optimistic future, there was always an unreality and an awkwardness that made them choose their words and weigh the unspoken comment. Eyes would rise towards the clock and there was almost a relief when the butler's tap came at the door, and he entered with the usual announcement:

"The master's in the drawing-room, gentlemen."

It was Hubert Greeve's custom on those state occasions to come down to the drawing-room at a quarter-past six precisely. There could thus be a formal reception and an exacting of respect that gave an ironic pleasure to his warped and impish mind.

Then once he had rid his mind of the sneers he had rehearsed or that came readily to his tongue, he would play cribbage with Martin till seven-thirty. Then the gong would go for first warning, a formal glass of sherry would be drunk, and the party would go up to dress. Dinner was always at eight.

He stood leaning on his stick as the five men entered, with Mantlin apart as dissociating himself from the function. Service was at his elbow, and through him the old man would often talk. Hugh, as the eldest, came forward first.

"How d'you do, uncle? Glad to see you looking so well."

The old man kept him waiting for the handshake. His mouth twisted ironically as he surveyed the three.

"Here you are, then; come all this way just to cheer an old man's heart. Thoughtful and unselfish—just as you always are."

His eyes fell on Hugh again, and he held out his hand. It was a limp hand, and Hugh, who had experienced that form of greeting often enough, could still be somehow startled when his own fingers closed about a something warm and yet utterly devoid of life.

"How are you, Hugh?" the old man said. "More like your father every day. You agree?"

He had flashed round on the old butler, who now gave a little bow.

"I'm afraid I never saw Mr. Hugh's father, sir."

The cold eyes ran contemptuously over him, but the butler gave no sign. Martin came up, then Tom, who happened to be nearer, and Romney last of all. The old man turned to his butler again.

"A wonderful gift. Just to dab a little paint—and have the knack."

Service gave that little bow. "Yes, sir." And as the cold eyes again contemptuously surveyed him from crown to toe, he bowed again. "Mr. Romney hopes to do a painting of the garden, sir. I'm sure he'll pardon me mentioning it."

"The garden?" He flashed round on Romney at once. "You're thinking of painting the garden?"

The garden and all its contents, as Inspector Carry well knew, was one of his passions. In less than no time he was hobbling out to inspect the proposed spot, and the whole party, save

Service, went with him through the twin french doors to the left. That drawing-room was thirty feet by twenty, its narrower side heading south-west, and there were twin french doors at each corner which the old man would have open in summer, so that in his chair he had the cool of the room, and air, and the gardens beneath his eye. Now as the party left by the left-hand doors, their way to the summer-house lay along the shrubbery that had caused trouble for Carry. The summer-house itself had its back in the shrubs and was twenty feet or so from the drawing-room doors. It had a brick surround which made a sort of loggia and looked due west across the farther lawns and the tiny lake, which once had been a dew-pond. The woods closed in there with a gap between them, and through it, where the plateau ended, was the bare slope of the Downs and the more distant evening blue.

Romney halted on the summer-house loggia and began to explain. The old man kept nodding away.

"If you'd like it," Romney ended, somewhat taciturnly, "I'd like you to have it. It'd be a kind of present from the four of us."

Again the old man seemed pleased, and then, as if he suspected some ulterior motive, he gave a glare and began hobbling off to the house again. Besides, a quarter of an hour of his cribbage time had gone, and he was anxious to get to his game. Hugh was walking with him. Romney and Charles lagged behind at the summer-house, but Martin and Tom followed in the rear. There was a quick interchange of glances as the two came through the doors again, as if some plan of campaign had been agreed upon and its running looked like being smooth.

Service had the table ready, with the cards and marker. Old Greeve took his seat with a rubbing of bony hands. Martin sat facing the open doors. Hugh shifted the small table to the middle of the room and sat with back to the empty fireplace, and Tom faced him. Romney and Charles still lingered in the garden.

The cribbage game began. The old man hated like sin to lose, though the stakes were no more than sixpence an end. When things went wrong he would grumble and glower, and he would cheat flagrantly with reckoning up his score and furtive additions to the pegging. Then when things went right for him, he would

crow and be offensively genial. Martin would suffer with philo-
sophic indifference and would even make foolish discards to give
the old man an advantage, being of the opinion that sixpence an
end was a small price to pay for peace and general harmony.

A game had been played and the old man had won. Martin
caught Tom Bypass's eye. Tom leaned forward and asked Hugh
a question. Hugh frowned, screwed up his eyes and thought.
Martin nodded and turned again to the game. His opponent was
already shuffling the cards impatiently, and in a minute the two
were at it again.

But before that second game was over, dusk was heavy in the
sky, though the air as yet had no chill. Sweet, dewy scents were
coming through the open doors, and as the old man marked up
his score the quiet voices at the small table suddenly ceased and
Tom got to his feet.

"Hallo! There's somebody in the garden. Looks like a
stranger."

As he craned round the obscuring Hugh to get a better view,
Old Greeve was also turning round, stick in hand, and regarding
him with a strange intentness. Tom's eyes bulged.

"He's gone!" He went forward to those right-hand doors
and had a look. Then he turned back. "Curious thing. I'd have
sworn I saw a man out there—and it wasn't Charles or Romney.
Looked more like a tramp to me."

"Romney's sitting in the summer-house, writing," Martin
said. "I can just see him from here."

"And here's Charles," said Hugh. "I expect your man, if you
saw one, was one of the gardeners."

Old Greeve sat down again. "Your deal!" he snapped at Martin, and glowered round for quiet. But at that moment Service
entered by the far door and made for the gong. Charles Mantlin stood by the screen, fingers, as usual, Balfour-wise round
his lapels, and as he spoke, the butler lifted the gong-stick. *And
though it was not that night that Hubert Greeve was to be
killed, the room was in every essential detail and circumstance
as it would be when he met his death.*

Charles stood then by the door, the screen at his right shoulder, and he was looking down benevolently at the card-players, with, "Well, still at it then?"

Just as he spoke, two things happened. Martin dropped one of his cards and stooped to pick it up. At the gong there was a faint rumble like very distant thunder. The rumble grew louder, became a din that almost deafened, and died away again. The first gong for dinner had gone.

But at the first rumble, Old Greeve had thrown down his cards. The gong had been the miracle that had saved him, for a last marvellous hand had put Martin practically out. And as the last sound of the gong died away, Romney came in.

"Did you see anything of a man in the garden?" Tom asked him.

"A man?" He looked puzzled. "What sort of a man?"

"A tramp-looking fellow. I thought I saw one in the garden."

Romney shook his head. "I was too busy writing."

"Old Greeve turned on Charles Mantlin. Did you see this man of his?"

Charles made a face. "I've been sitting over there"—he jerked his head back—"having a look at the view."

Service came up then with the tray and placed it on the small table.

"Leave it there," the old man snapped at him. "Get hold of Matthews and tell him and the other gardener to look through the grounds." He watched morosely till the butler was at the far door, then called. "They're to patrol the grounds to-night. Do you hear?"

He poured himself a glass of sherry and waved his hand as if people might help themselves and be damned. Hugh waited till the five were ready, then wished him a formal good health. He muttered a something, nodded curtly, then drank.

"I hope this hasn't upset you, uncle," Tom said. "After all, I might have been deceived. It might have been Charles here, coming back to the house."

The old man ignored him, finished his short drink, and with another general nod hobbled off across the room. The far door closed on him.

"Better shut these doors up if we're going upstairs," said Hugh.

"You push off and I'll do it," Charles told him. "I'm a quick dresser."

Hubert Greeve was accustomed to leave the dinner-table for his bed, spinning out the meal till about half-past nine. At ten o'clock the guests were supposed to go up, and at ten-past ten that night, Tom Bypass slipped cautiously into Martin's room. Martin, fully dressed, was sitting on the bed.

"Well, see your way clear?" Tom asked him quietly.

Martin nodded. "Yes—don't you?"

Tom shook his head. "Afraid I'm a bit dense. Anything to do with that question I had to ask Hugh?"

Martin smiled grimly. "Everything to do with it."

"Want to know what he said?"

"No," said Martin. "What he said doesn't matter a hoot." He cocked his ear and listened for a moment, then relaxed. "Let's get the final details worked out." And as he drew up a chair, he chuckled quietly. "It's going to be a darn sight easier than we thought."

PART II
ENTER THE POLICE

CHAPTER IV
CAT IN THE RIDDLE

LUDOVIC WAS STILL in Seaborough on the Tuesday. There was no urgency to call him back to town. Mrs. Tempest was away keeping an ancient engagement, and the Major craved company. The evening found the two on the golf-course; the somewhat later evening found them on the club-house veranda, taking their time over a drink, and it was not till well after half-past seven that they came home, in the deepening dusk. Travers drew the car up at the door and left her there.

"We might want her again later," he said. "If not, Palmer can put her up before we turn in."

He had not wished to encumber the Major's none too roomy house with his man, but it had been at Tempest's own insistence that Palmer had come down. He too had played some part in that affair of the first Seaborough murder. "A darling of an old man," was Mrs. Tempest's somewhat whimsical if not unapt description of the confidential servant who had once been valet to Ludovic Travers's father, and had doubtless seen the infant Ludovic in his pram.

And as the two came into the lounge at about a quarter to eight that Tuesday night, Palmer himself entered by the kitchen door.

"Anything you want now, sir?"

As he spoke the telephone went in the outer hall, and he made an unobtrusive exit. In half a minute he was back, and giving that funny little bow of his to Tempest.

"You're wanted, sir. Very urgent."

The Major scowled and departed. Travers smiled up.

"Well, did you have a good bathe?"

"Not bathe, sir." There was no reprimand, but merely a reminder; the years had inoculated Palmer against all such amiable quips, which were rarely more than an outlet for effervescence. "It was the pictures, sir. A murder film, sir." He shook his head. "Most disappointing, sir. Untrue to life, if I may say so."

Travers smiled once more. In the dozen cases or so that had come with his own experience, there had been never a one so far-fetched and fantastic as those of which he had merely read in the daily press. But while he was hunting for some new quip to cheer the disappointed Palmer, Tempest came in like a whirlwind.

"Come on, quick! That old fellow Greeve's been killed."

"Killed?" said Travers, hoisting his six foot three off the chesterfield. "You mean, murdered?"

"Looks like it," Tempest told him. "Carry's on the way up there already. The doctor'll be waiting for us, he says."

The car soared away up the hill. Shinniford, the police-surgeon, was picked up on the way, and off the Rolls soared again. It nosed its way into the drive of Palings, and as the three got out, Service appeared on the porch steps. He gave Tempest and Travers a quick look, remembering doubtless that conference into which he had come unawares on the Saturday night.

"Are you the police, sir?"

"Yes," said Tempest.

The butler gave him another quick look, and Travers felt all at once a thrill and a premonition. It was the chase itself that was his passion. Murders, inquests, blood and hangings were sickening things.

"This way, sir," the butler said, and turned and made his way across the hall.

All lights were on in the drawing-room, and it seemed to be full of people. Tempest caught sight of one he knew.

"Hallo, Mantlin! What brings you here?"

"Pleasure—and business," Charles said, like a man taken unawares. "I'm his lawyer."

Tempest nodded.

Inspector Carry came forward then from the chesterfield by which he had been standing. Polegate was there too.

"I've just been telling them, sir, they oughtn't to have moved the body."

Travers had caught sight of that body and had moved his eyes quickly away. Then he looked again, for there seemed to be no blood. Just a stain against the white hair, and what looked like a brown spot on the edge of the skull.

Tempest nodded again, cleared his throat and addressed himself to the room.

"I'm Major Tempest, the Chief Constable, gentlemen. What's happened here I don't know, but I take it you're all ready to help. Mr. Greeve, I may say, I know, and have had some recent dealings with, so perhaps while Dr. Shinniford makes his inspection you'll all stand back, and perhaps one of you will give me a rapid account of everything."

Again Travers felt that little thrill. Eyes had narrowed and had sought each other when Tempest had mentioned dealings with the dead man. But Hugh Bypass was stepping forward.

"I'm the eldest of us," he said, casting a mild glance round. "Bypass is my name. Hugh Bypass. I'm Mr. Greeve's nephew, down here with my brother"—he pointed each man out—"and my two cousins for the usual celebration of his birthday, which was—er—to-day."

"Just a moment, Chief," said Shinniford, and Tempest went over. There was some whispering, and no sooner had it ended than the butler was approaching.

"Pardon me, sir, but some more police have arrived."

Sergeant Polegate attended to all that. Tempest faced the group of men again.

"Now, Mr. Bypass, tell us what happened."

Hugh blinked for a moment. "Well, we think he was shot."

"You *think* he was shot! Didn't you hear the sound of the explosion?"

"Well, we did and we didn't."

Tempest nodded patiently. "And why, precisely, was that?"

"It was the gong." His finger went out towards a point beyond the screen. "You see, it made such a noise that we weren't quite sure if there was any other noise—not till my uncle collapsed and fell on the carpet."

"And what time was it?"

"Well," said Hugh mildly, "it was half-past seven—or should have been. I'm afraid I don't carry a watch."

Tempest turned to where Service stood motionless by the far door. At his voice, the butler came forward.

"You sounded the gong?"

"Yes, sir. At seven-thirty, sir."

"And how do you know it was seven-thirty?"

"The master was very particular, sir, about keeping to time. I put my clock right by the wireless, at six o'clock, sir."

"Capital!" said Tempest, and turned to the others. "At seven-thirty precisely the gong went, and then it was thought there was a noise like a pistol going off. Is that right?"

"Yes, that's right," Hugh told him.

Tempest kept his eye on him. "You notice I said *pistol?*" A pause. "You still agree?"

Hugh looked rather sheepish. "Well, I don't know. It was a gun of some sort or he wouldn't have been shot."

"And, of course, there was the bullet."

"Bullet?" He looked surprised.

"Yes," said Tempest. "The bullet. The shot caught him on the right temple and came out above the nose."

Hugh shook his head and gave a look round. "Nobody here knows anything about a bullet. We imagined it was still in the wound."

Tempest nodded. "Good. Then we'll doubtless find it somewhere in the room. And now, who moved the body from where it first fell?"

Hugh looked sheepish again. "Well, I was one. I think most of us helped. Except Mr. Greeve here—Mr. Romney Greeve—and he wasn't in the room. And Mr. Mantlin wasn't here exactly either."

Martin Greeve broke in there. "Pardon my interrupting, sir, but we didn't think about anything like murder. We thought he'd had a fit or something, so we got him on there off the floor."

"I follow," said Tempest. "And did anyone touch his pockets or their contents?"

Hugh shook his head. "We only loosened his collar."

"That's all right then," Tempest told him. "And now, if you'll wait a minute or two, the inspector will make an inventory of what's on him."

The pockets yielded little: some small change, a pocket-knife, a stub of pencil and a handkerchief. Tempest pocketed the keys and then resumed his catechizing.

"Now, Mr. Bypass, do you think you could get everybody to occupy the same positions they were in at the time the gong first sounded?"

There was little for Hugh to do. As soon as Tempest spoke, the group broke up and began rearranging itself. Romney Greeve stood disconsolately apart.

"You weren't in the room, I believe?" Tempest asked him.

"No, I was in the summer-house."

"Well, perhaps you'll be so good as to stand over there with Mr. Travers," Tempest told him. "And you, gentlemen, please sit or whatever it was you were doing at the very moment the gong went." He looked round for the butler, but Service had already taken his stand, the padded gong-stick in hand. "Inspector, you take down the names and note positions." And to Polegate, who had just come in again, "Sergeant, you mark the feet on the floor. First, Mr. Charles Mantlin, by the screen, facing the card-table."

Polegate made chalk-marks for the lawyer's feet. Tempest turned to the table.

"At the table—?"

"Martin Greeve."

"At the table, Mr. Martin Greeve. Your uncle was playing cards with you, Mr. Greeve?"

"That's right," said Martin. "We were playing cribbage."

"Perhaps Dr. Shinniford will act for him," Tempest said. "He's just about his build. You place him just how your uncle was, Mr. Greeve, if you don't mind. I take it the table hasn't been disturbed?"

"Well, it was knocked over when he fell," Martin said. "Then it got moved again when we shifted him, but we put it back again. I don't think it's far out."

Tempest made a grimace. "An inch out might make all the difference. We'll have a look, if you don't mind, and see if we can make out the original marks of the feet."

The table had square, narrow feet and the marks were found.

"Now the other table," Tempest went on. "Nearer the fire-place, Mr. Hugh Bypass. This side of it?"

"Thomas George Bypass."

"That's all then," said Tempest, and then, while Polegate was making marks with the chalk, he had another alarm. "This table wasn't moved by any chance?"

"No," said Tom. "There was room to get him round."

"Right." He gave a last preliminary look. "What's your name?"

"Service, sir. John Service."

"Right," said Tempest again. "Let the sergeant mark where your feet were, and then when I give you the signal, sound the gong just as you did to-night."

The signal was given. The gong rumbled, rumbled more nearly, and clattered and dinned to a raucous boom. It died away again, but the expression of amused exasperation on the Major's face remained.

"That's the very devil of a noise," he said. "And you mean to tell me you kicked up all that hubbub to-night with everybody in the room?"

"Mr. Romney Greeve was out of it," Travers put in quickly.

Service gave him a look rather like gratitude. "Yes, sir, he was. Also the master was very proud of this gong, sir. He admired the tone. He liked it to be struck loudly, sir."

Tempest left it at that. "And at what stage in the uproar was the shot heard?" he asked Hugh Bypass.

"Right in the middle," Hugh said, and immediately qualified it. "Speaking for myself, I didn't know it was a shot. All I heard was what you might call a noise within a noise."

"That's right," said Mantlin. "It was just the same with me, only I remembered afterwards that I sort of felt the whiz of something go by me."

"Anybody else hear anything?"

Tom Bypass said he couldn't be sure. Service was positive he had heard no sound above the din he was making himself, and Martin Greeve said that at the climax of the uproar, he had been retrieving from the floor a card he had let fall.

"Well, we're getting on," Tempest said. "Let's imagine the gong is being sounded and it's at its noisiest moment, and then all at once stops, leaving everyone photographed in the air, as it were. For instance, Mr. Martin Greeve, you be picking up your card. Everyone else do just what he was doing, and look just where he was looking at that very second."

He surveyed the result. Mantlin had his head turned towards Service as if wondering how much longer the clatter would last. The Bypasses faced each other inanely across the more central table. Martin was stooping towards his own right side in search of the dropped card. Service held the gong-stick suspended. Shinniford sat upright at the card-table like a dummy.

"Thank you, gentlemen; thank you," Tempest called. "But remain where you are, please. The most important thing is to come. We've got to know precisely where the head of the head man was. If his head was turned even an inch, it'll change the true direction from which we attempt to trace the bullet. You were facing him, Service. Which way was he looking?"

Service shook his head. "I don't remember, sir. I think he was looking down this way."

"Hm!" went Tempest. "What about you, Mr. Greeve?"

"I couldn't tell," said Martin. "Not with my head almost on the floor."

"Mr. Mantlin?"

"I was looking towards Service, I'm afraid." He thought for a moment and his fingers tightened on his lapels. "I seem to remember now that he turned his head this way. I can't say quite when."

"Mr. Thomas Bypass?"

Tom shook his head. "I was looking nowhere in particular. But I seem to recollect him turning towards the door."

"And you, Mr. Hugh Bypass?"

"I've no idea," said Hugh. "As a matter of fact, I was thinking about something at the time."

"Very well then," said Tempest ruefully, "if nobody's certain, we shall have to assume that he was sitting facing down the room, just as Dr. Shinniford is now. One moment, doctor."

The two moved off down the room for another brief, whispered conference. Then Shinniford spent a minute or so with the corpse, probing the wound and taking measurements.

"Ready now," he said.

"Right," said Tempest. "Resume your original postures, gentlemen, please."

He took the card-table seat himself, Shinniford pressing on his head and adjusting his height above the chair seat to that of the dead man. Then there was some squinting and measuring, and it was five minutes before Shinniford announced himself as satisfied.

"If his head was facing down the room, then the bullet came from somewhere beyond those doors. If he had his head turned that way, then it's a certainty."

Tempest flashed round at once. "Were the doors open or shut at the time?"

"Open," said Hugh. "We shut them later, when we all got back."

"Back from where?"

"Well, some of us were hunting in the garden."

"What for?"

"We thought we heard a noise in the shrubs," said Mantlin.

"Gentlemen, gentlemen!" Tempest lost his patience for the first time. "We'll get nowhere if we carry on like this. I ask for everything to be as it was, and now you tell me the doors were open. I ask what you heard, and now you tell me a noise in the shrubbery." He snapped back at Service. "Get those doors open! And what about those other two there? Were they open?"

Service began opening the twin pairs of doors.

"About the exit line of the bullet?" Tempest said to Shinniford. "Acting on the same assumptions, where would it have ended up?"

Shinniford did some more squinting and measuring, then pointed.

"Somewhere in the neighbourhood of that bookcase, if his head was straight, and half-way between it and the far door if his head was turned. That's not accounting for ricochets."

The bookcase was merely a series of shelves; narrow mahogany boxes, in fact, standing one on the other; unglazed and doorless. Its contents were classics that looked as if they had been undisturbed, save for dusting, for a good many years. But three feet from the ground, at the end of the fourth shelf, was a gap where two books were missing. Tempest stared hard. A line from the left-hand doors, through the wound, would come diagonally across the room to the books at its right-hand wall, and roughly at the height of the gap.

"Know anything about these missing books?" he said to Service.

"No more than that they weren't there this morning, sir."

"Weren't there this morning? When were they there, then?"

"They were there the previous night, sir—the Monday night, sir."

"You sure?"

"Quite sure, sir."

Travers was running an eye over the shelf. "'The Decline and Fall of the Roman Empire,'" he said to Tempest. "Volumes seven and eight missing out of ten in all." He was screwing up his eyes in thought, wondering who on earth should want to read those less voluptuous parts of Gibbon's monumental work, when Tempest found some sort of an answer for him.

"Two books missing from here since this morning," he announced. "Can anyone give me any information? Anyone borrowed them to read upstairs, or anything?"

But nobody knew a thing. In the blank pause, Hugh Bypass coughed gently, then spoke.

"It's no business of mine, sir, but as you seem to have several policemen out there in the garden, mightn't it be as well to search the grounds again? We only had time to do it very hastily."

Tempest kept back most of the irony. His eye fell on the mantelpiece clock.

"If you'd committed a murder here an hour or so ago, Mr. Bypass, I don't imagine you'd still be in the neighbourhood— not that there was any harm in suggesting it. Perhaps you'll all go back to your stations, gentlemen, where you were when the gong sounded."

"Now then," he said, when they were once more in position. "Hands up those who heard a noise from outside?"

Up went the hands of Martin Greeve and Charles Mantlin.

"Sorry to carry on like a schoolmaster," Tempest told them. "You first, Mr. Mantlin. Just what did you hear?"

"A sort of rustling in the bushes behind me."

"Before what you took to be a shot, or after?"

Mantlin smiled dryly. "I shouldn't have heard a thing if that gong hadn't finished. That's when I remember I heard it. It was just as if someone was moving in the bushes. I thought it was Romney coming in, and I remember I looked round, only it wasn't him because he was just coming out of the summer-house."

"And what about you, Mr. Greeve?"

"I don't know that I heard anything at all," Martin said. "I saw the bushes rustle as if the wind had got up quickly. It just struck me as curious—at the time."

"That would be well after the gong had ceased?" suggested Travers.

Martin shot a look at him. For a moment he seemed to be thinking hard, then he smiled.

"Why, yes. I was looking down on the floor for that dropped card till the gong had almost finished, so I couldn't have seen the bushes from there."

Travers nodded charmingly in thanks. Tempest raised his hand.

"One last thing, gentlemen. I take it Mr. Greeve slithered over and fell on the floor. What happened then?"

"I think we all rushed forward to him," Hugh said.

"I did," said Charles. "Then I saw his head and sort of gathered what had happened, and remembered the noise in the bushes, so I hollered out something—I forget what—and rushed into the shrubbery." He shook his head. "It was all sort of confused. No one knew what to do—for a minute."

"I know that's right," Tom said. "I gathered what had happened and rushed out too, only Charles had disappeared. In the shrubbery, of course, but I didn't know that then. I sort of ran across the lawn, and Romney was coming out from the summer-house, and he started asking me what the matter was."

Neither Mantlin nor Tom Bypass had seen or heard a further thing. Romney had been wholly unaware of anything happening, except that the gong was going, which meant he must put away the work he was doing and get to the drawing-room in time for that ceremonial glass of sherry.

"Then those who had been hunting for the supposed murderer gradually drifted back?" said Tempest.

"That's right," Hugh told him.

"And who rang up the police?"

"I suggested it," Mantlin said. "To save time I asked if a doctor could come too. You see, we knew he was dead, so there wasn't so much urgency about that—so to speak."

Tempest stood there for an indecisive minute. A score of things were crying out to be done, but it was the overlapping that worried him, and which must come first. So he gave the company his little homily. Murder was a desperate thing; questions must be asked and no offence taken, for the idea would be not to catch people out or trip them up, but to fit in statement with statement and so arrive at the truth. Everything would be voluntary, but he relied on them as men of goodwill to hand over to the law everything which in their considered opinion as citizens might in any way be of use. Travers said afterwards that he had scarcely refrained from applause.

"Is there the chance of these gentlemen having a meal?" Service was asked.

There was. It had been spoiling for an hour, the butler said, and once the word was given could be on the table at once.

"Then perhaps you'll all adjourn to the dining-room, gentlemen," Tempest said. "By the time the meal is over we shall be ready for further inquiries. In the meanwhile, nobody must attempt to leave the house except by my express permission."

The room slowly cleared. A delicious coolness was coming through those doors that opened on the lawn, and moths were flickering madly about the lights. The silence seemed all at once intense. Tempest stirred himself.

"We'd better find that bullet, don't you think, Carry? Get a couple of your own men in and go through the room, that side first, starting at the far door. Sergeant Polegate, you lend the doctor a hand to move the body. Do all you can here, Shinniford, please; then you can get him away to the mortuary."

He stood with Travers by the gong, watching the new bustle that came about the room. Now and again they spoke quietly, and detachedly, as the thoughts came to them.

"Wish I'd got the nerve. I'd have someone listening in on that dining-room. Hardly worth it though. They're a good type, all of them. Look like it and speak like it."

"A curious uniformity of either neglect of appearance or else respectable poverty," remarked Travers. "That blue suit of the elder Bypass was distinctly shiny. That Bohemian-looking chap, Romney, had the sides of his shoes repaired, which is where most people give them up for good. Then there was the elder Greeve. His coat cuffs had frayed slightly, and he'd pressed his trousers himself."

Tempest recorded the items and made no comment.

"What's the best thing now? Have them in singly or in a lump?"

"Singly, don't you think? And Mantlin first."

"Why?"

Travers smiled diffidently. "Well, better the devil you know, so to speak. Also he may tell us about the will. If people are hard-up—of course I may be wrong about that—then it's just as well to see if there's motive."

"Yes," said Tempest, and rubbed his chin. "Any ideas about who did it?"

"No end," said Travers. "That's the whole trouble. Like yourself, I know the one set of circumstances which the murderer must fit. That's why I don't like all that shrubbery business and the outsider."

Tempest frowned. "I don't follow you."

Travers fumbled at his glasses. "Well, the central point of this murder is the gong, because it had to cover the noise of the shot. Therefore the murderer must have been aware that the gong was rung at a certain time. He knew the row it kicked up, and, above all, he knew to a reasonable certainty where the old man would be sitting. Therefore he must have been someone with a very definite knowledge.

"For instance"—he was now polishing those glasses of his—
"why should the murderer take up a position in the shrubbery
when the old man might have been sitting wholly out of sight?
Loth as I am to say it, it looks even as if it was a cat or a dog that
Mantlin heard. And even more loth though I am to say it, there
have been cases of people fabricating noises heard in shrubberies and places." He hooked the glasses on again. "See under
Clues, false: police, for the use of."

"Other people saw and heard things in the shrubbery," Tempest reminded him. "Besides, what about that nocturnal prowler the old man saw Carry about? Wasn't he in or near the summer-house?—and that's virtually part of the shrubbery."

"Yes," said Travers. "I know there's the prowler. There's also
Aunt Ethel's husband who wrote a blackmail letter we weren't
allowed to see." He smiled. "But my small experience of murders
tells me that they've always got something like the cat in the riddle—the one that had fur, kittens, purred, and laid eggs."

"Laid eggs!"

"Ah!" said Travers. "I hoped you'd ask that. The bit about
eggs was put in to make it harder. Which reminds me. Notice
how upset everyone was? When you mentioned dinner, didn't
everybody remark he didn't feel like eating a bit?"

"Not in my hearing, they didn't," said Tempest grimly.

"Exactly!" He smiled to himself. "Uncle's dead, but why
waste dinner? Which also looks like making things a bit more
difficult."

CHAPTER V
THE AGE OF MIRACLES

HAD TEMPEST'S acquaintance with Ludovic Travers been only
half as long as that of Superintendent Wharton, he would have
paid considerably less attention to those first glimmerings of theories that had come with the effervescing of Travers's vivacious
mind. Given a bare moment to collect his thoughts, Travers—as
someone had once said—would have been delighted to provide

a fool-proof explanation of both the larynx of Balaam's ass and the gullet of the whale that swallowed Jonah.

Yet there was always a definite amount of hard sense in Travers's most airy suggestions. And there was something comforting, as Travers himself perhaps knew, in any manner of speculation. After all, if two men are lost in the darkest of woods, nothing is more dispiriting than silence. Better by far the cheery fellow who remarks, "Hallo! Isn't that a light?" or "We'll be out of here in no time"—even when half the time he happens to be wrong.

The whole of that right-hand side of the room had been gone through with a small-tooth comb, and Carry reported no sign of the bullet. But he had a suggestion to make.

"Given certain conditions, sir, mightn't it have gone through these other doors? The ones this side?"

Shinniford was called over.

"I don't see how it could have happened," he said, "unless he was squinting round clean over his own left shoulder. Even then there isn't a foot for it to have got through."

"Yes," said Tempest, thinking aloud. "Two of them said they *thought* he looked one way. If he'd turned his head at right angles they'd have *known* it." He turned to Carry. "Try the other side of the room and both ends. If nothing happens, search every inch of the grounds as soon as it's light—the same time as you do the shrubbery. Have plenty of men on it."

Ten more minutes and the room showed blank. No plaster was broken or scored on walls or ceiling. And Shinniford was ready to go.

"I'd like an expert, soon as you can get one down," he said. "If we can't find that bullet, we've got to have some idea what it was, and how far it was likely to go, considering the resistance after impact, and so on."

Tempest sent him off with a long-distance message for the Yard, and no sooner had the ambulance gone than Service came in. Dinner was over, he said, and the gentlemen awaited instructions."

"Any other keys but those found on the body?" Tempest asked.

"Of private keys, no, sir."

"Where did he keep his private papers? In a safe?"

"Yes, sir. The safe is in the morning-room."

"Can we get at it without going through the dining-room?"

Service led the way across the outer hall to a door that opened into a smallish room looking southeast. The safe stood plain for all to see, and it was an old-fashioned one. Polegate put on his rubber gloves and drew out the contents for inspection. The sheet of paper was the only thing that mattered.

H. GREEVE, ESQUIRE,

I know your little game, but if you don't do the right thing by my wife, your sister Ethel, your number's up. Write to me.

I. N. ERNEST,
Care of Post Office,
Brighton.

The paper was a blue linen of reasonable quality. The writing was round, large and laborious, like that of a child who makes a careful copy. The fold-mark was there, but the safe produced no envelope.

"Get on to Brighton at once," Tempest told Carry. "Use the hall telephone. Get them to see if a letter's been sent and collected. If one's still there, ask them to keep a watch for whoever calls for it."

"Well, there we are," he said to Travers, when the letter had gone into a police envelope. "But why he wouldn't let us have a look at it on Saturday I still don't know."

Had he ended with, "Do you?" Travers might have found a dozen reasons. As it was, Travers said nothing, even when, back in the drawing-room, Polegate tested the sheet of paper for prints and found two distinct sets, one of which belonged to the dead man. Whose were the other?

"Somebody else had his hands on it as well as Greeve," Tempest said. "Still, put it back in the envelope and ask Mr. Mantlin to step this way. Post a man, Carry, to make sure no witness goes back to the others till we've seen the lot. In the meanwhile, you question the housekeeper and check up on the staff—inside and out."

Charles Mantlin came in with his usual methodical tread, and as if pulling himself forward by the lapels of his coat.

"Sit down, Mantlin, will you?" Tempest said in a friendly way. "How's things with you these days?"

"Can't grumble," Mantlin told him, in the tone of a man who is doing very well.

"So you're Hubert Greeve's lawyer. How long have you acted for him?"

"How long?" He thought. "Personally, since 1919, when I came home after my father died. We acted for him before that."

"That's lucky for us," Tempest said, and his tone became still more genial as he delivered himself of the usual invitation that was to precede each interview.

"You won't mind the sergeant taking your prints? Not for record, of course, only we never know what prints we may find, and we'd like to be able to separate the sheep from the goats. Purely a formality, in fact."

Charles Gordon Mantlin, aged forty-three, of 3 Pier Chambers, Seaborough, had his prints duly taken.

"Cigarette?" said Tempest, and pushed his case across the table.

"Light?" smiled Travers, and snapped his lighter.

"Now, Mr. Mantlin"—the voice was the Chief Constable's—"we'd like you to fill in some gaps in our very inextensive knowledge. Do you know any enemy of the dead man? Anyone who'd be likely to kill him?"

"No," said Mantlin slowly. "Mind, it depends on how you mean it. It's possible to find a motive for all of us who were here to-night—myself included." He caught the quick raising of eyebrows. "After all, I'm due to get ten thousand pounds, which isn't to be sneezed at these days."

Tempest smiled. "Well, I congratulate you. Still, we'll put aside your own ten thousand reasons. Why did you say the other men—the four cousins—might have killed him?"

He thought for a moment. "Well, I've no doubt they'll tell you themselves, if I don't. They hated the old man like sin, and if I'd been in their place I'd have been the same."

Eyebrows were raised again.

"If you want the whole yarn, it's a pretty long one," Mantlin went on. "Easy enough to follow though, once you get the hang of it."

The Greeve history was briefly this. The first Greeve was a Russian engineer and general factor called Gregorivitch. He became naturalized—his wife was English—and changed his name. The four children were Caroline, George, Hubert and—born much later—Ethel. When the old man died there was a London office of which George took charge, while Hubert was in Moscow where the company's works were, with a branch at Riga.

Caroline, who married Frederick Bypass, had some money in the business. She became an invalid on the early death of a daughter, and the death of her husband hastened her end, which was during the war in 1915. The youngest child, Ethel, had involved herself in some scandal by marrying much beneath her, and had been disowned by the family.

Tempest interrupted there. "Anything been heard of her since?"

Mantlin told him all he knew.

"He may have had letters from her," Tempest said, leaning over to Travers. "If so, we shall find them later. Sorry, Mr. Mantlin. Carry on, will you?"

Mantlin carried on at Caroline Bypass. Just when her own affairs were disordered on the death of her husband, the major tragedy occurred. The four cousins were all in the army. Hugh went with an infantry regiment to Mesopotamia; Martin was at Gallipoli and in Egypt, and Tom, who got a permanent commission, was in France and Salonica. In Russia the affairs of Greeve Brothers were in hopeless confusion owing to the war, and

George, the senior partner, travelled to Moscow by the trans-Siberian route to try to straighten things out.

Mantlin spread his hands. "After that, the rest is mystery. George Greeve caught some sort of a fever as soon as he arrived in Moscow and died there. Hubert came home after some months, with the firm, of course, hopelessly ruined. George's widow had a certain amount of money, and Caroline left some to her two boys, but nothing like what they'd all have had under normal conditions, for the firm was a very thriving one.

"Then came what the four cousins have always considered a remarkable thing. On his return to this country, Hubert began an engineering concern on quite a big scale. It was just the beginning of the munitions wave, and he rode on the crest, and made a pretty big fortune. When it was suggested that there was some queer work over the closing down of the Russian business, and people hinted at where Hubert had got his money from, he claimed it was his own personal savings, and so on.

"Then the four cousins were demobilized and came home to hear the whole story. They began an inquiry in which I acted as a kind of intermediary, and there were some pretty high words. They didn't get as far as briefing counsel, because Hubert made a settlement without prejudicing his case. He said, in effect, 'Why all this squabble? The money will come to the four of you on my death, which in the nature of things can't be long. It was a sort of gentleman's agreement therefore. Oh, and I forgot to say that the uncle expressly mentioned that whenever he could lend a helping hand—always without prejudice—he'd be glad to do so. That was easy. Nobody expected the occasion to arise as things then were. Also, as a mark of general amity, the four cousins began this custom of coming down here for the birthday of the head of the family."

"That's clear enough," Tempest said. "But if the hatchet was buried, why the hatred?"

"I'll tell you," said Mantlin. "As I said, the four cousins were doing pretty well. Tom was invalided out of the service, and with some money from an aunt, he was all right for life. Romney began to make quite a name as an artist—he was a camouflage expert in the war, by the way—and Martin, who had been intended for the business, began a toy-making concern. You remember a shop in Regent Street, perhaps? Well, that was his, and he had a factory at Slough. Hugh was a schoolmaster, at Fellborough. What I want to point out is that none of the four had the least need of help. As I know, the uncle was always pretty awkward when they came down, but he was never objectionable. He was vindictive—but he didn't make a parade of what he felt.

"Then the slump came. Martin's toy-factory went out as if it had been stamped on, though in his case things weren't helped by a defaulting partner. Romney had a young family and nobody wanted to buy pictures. Hugh had just left his school and invested all he had in a private school of his own, which looked like doing extraordinarily well. Now it's hanging on by its eyebrows. But the real point is this. In some uncanny way, the uncle seemed to know things were going badly. He was most objectionable when the four came down, the first days of the slump. It was just as if the time he'd been waiting for had come. He began a deliberate policy of provocation. He tried, as I admit, to get the four to quarrel with him, so that he might have an excuse for—well, all sorts of things: telling them what he thought of them, and how he'd have to leave his money elsewhere, and so on. Then the time came when three of them—not Tom—had to bring themselves to apply to him for help, and he turned them down. And as I told you just now, his latest provocation, only this evening just before he was killed, was to tell Hugh and Martin that he would be wanting them to witness a very important document on Thursday morning next before they left. That, as we knew, was the will he was going to make—or was pretending to be going to make—in favour of this sister Ethel of his." He let out a breath. "There, that's the whole story as clear as I can put it in the language of the man of the street."

"It couldn't have been clearer," Tempest told him. "But is it permitted to ask how the will stands at the moment?"

Mantlin shrugged his shoulders. "Why not? There are some bequests to local and other charities; annuities of five hundred a year to butler and housekeeper, and the balance to the four cousins. That might be about thirty thousand each—tax free."

"And the four cousins knew all that?"

Mantlin shook his head. "I can't confess to unprofessional conduct. I must leave you to guess."

"Do I gather that there were two annuities, each of five hundred, to the butler and the housekeeper?" asked Travers.

"That is so," Mantlin told him.

"And if you'll pardon my asking such a delicate question, may we assume that you had rendered special services to the late Mr. Greeve?"

"You mean the ten thousand?" Mantlin asked bluntly.

"Yes—and no," said Travers. "You'll see what I'm getting at in a moment." He turned to Tempest. "Mr. Mantlin ought to know that this talk is most confidential. Nothing he says will be communicated to any other party."

"That's right," said Tempest. "Nobody will ever know the source of any information given."

"Then I'll tell you my private ideas about the bequest of ten thousand pounds to myself," Mantlin said. "He never knew just how much I knew—which happened to be nothing. Undoubtedly my father knew exactly the sources of the money with which Greeve began that ammunitions business over here after he got back from Russia supposedly broke. Nothing of that was ever communicated to me—but Greeve didn't know it."

"To put it bluntly, he was afraid of you," said Tempest. "He left you the legacy so that you should keep your mouth shut—not knowing you had nothing to open it about."

"That's right," said Mantlin. "Mind you, I also did some sound work for him when the business in England was wound up, and I've acted for him since."

"That brings me to the real point," said Travers. "It seems clear that to annoy the four cousins, Greeve hinted at breaking his word and changing his will. But he never actually did so. Yet, if he were actuated by animosity and vindictiveness, why didn't he go the whole hog and change his will? Was it, by any chance, because he was still afraid of you?"

Mantlin smiled dryly. "Yes, I think that is so. I was particularly friendly with Tom Bypass, and I knew the other three well enough. I may say I advised him against even his threats to leave his money away from the family, particularly in view of that gentleman's agreement I mentioned."

"Thank you," said Travers. "That's a very important point. For instance, in this Aunt Ethel business, his words were likely to be little more than a threat?"

"Now you've got me." He shook his head. "I had the feeling with him that you never knew when he was about to go off the rails altogether. Also, you must remember that if he left his money to this sister of his, he could always claim that it was in the family, and he could have put the onus on his sister of leaving the money finally to the four cousins. That would have broken the agreement, I admit, but it would have given a plausible reason."

"And three of those cousins are now definitely very hard-up?"

Mantlin made a face. "Well, yes. They're all proud as blazes—in their own way—and they wouldn't have asked him for help if they hadn't been pretty badly in need of it."

"Thank you," said Travers. "That's all I want to know."

Then Mantlin gave him a sudden look. "You were not, by any chance, insinuating that any of the four would have murdered him?"

Tempest cut in there. "Not at all. We'll put it another way if you like. We want to know who didn't do it—then we may find out who did. For instance, you had this room under your eye. Who do you know definitely *didn't* do it?"

Mantlin frowned. "What you mean is, those whose alibis I'd swear to." He frowned again in thought, and his fingers tightened round his coat lapels. "I could swear to all the three that were in the room. Not one could conceivably have done it—unless he performed a first-class miracle."

Travers smiled. "And the age of miracles—we're told—is over."

"Exactly."

"And Romney Greeve?" asked Tempest.

"He was in the summer-house. As I came across the lawn I saw him sitting there writing. He called out to me and asked if it was time for the gong, and I said it was."

"You'd been in the garden?"

"That's right. There's a really superb view across the Channel, and if it's a fine, warm evening I like sitting at the far end of the garden. I was reading a book some of the time—a book of my own I'd fetched from upstairs—and all at once I looked at my watch and saw it was getting on for half-past seven, so I got up and came indoors, as I said."

"And you stopped just against the end of the screen there and had a look round, just as the gong went."

"Well before it went," Mantlin corrected him. "I stood there just as I showed you, sort of watching the two card-players. Then I said, 'Well, who's winning to-night?' As far as I remember, it was then that the gong first sounded."

"And at the same time you thought you heard the noise of what was afterwards known to be a shot, you heard the whiz of what you afterwards took to be a bullet."

"Not whiz. I'd say the zipp. You know the sound of a bullet that just misses you, Major?"

"Yes," said Tempest, and nodded. "But you still couldn't say if the bullet came from behind you into the room, or from the room and out behind you?"

Mantlin thought hard. "Perhaps I couldn't. All I know is it went by me. All the same, it's a thousand to one it came from outside."

Travers broke in again. "There's still one person left for whose alibi you could vouch—using the word alibi in the sense of utter inability to have committed the murder. What about the butler?"

Then a curious thing happened. "Sorry. I'm saying nothing about Service." He was shaking his head doggedly, and then as quickly his expression changed. "Besides, he was sounding the gong. He's out of it automatically."

Another minute and the interview was over, and Mantlin had gone.

"What the devil did he mean about that butler?" Tempest was saying. "He sort of deliberately shut up."

"He's a curious type altogether," Travers said. "In fact, he's a mixture of types. That trick he has of hanging on to himself makes him look like a stage professor; then there's that free-and-easy manner which is a long way off the usual lawyer type. Also he talked rather overmuch for a lawyer. He seemed to be giving too much away."

"And yet it all amounted to nothing!"

"Exactly," said Travers. "He gave the family history—which made out a perfect set of motives for the four cousins—and then proceeded to say he'd swear none of them did it." His hand went up to his glasses, then fell again. "Would you like to hear what interested me most? There were three things, He said he heard the zipp of a bullet, and yet he'd previously said he hadn't heard the sound of the shot itself—at least, not to be sure it was a shot. Then there was the bit about the four cousins all being in the army."

"Well, they all knew what firearms were." The fingers felt for the glasses and unhooked them. "And in that context, recall something else. We spoke about the age of miracles being over. I very much doubt if it is."

Tempest smiled. "Talking like Chesterton won't get us very far."

"That's where you may be wrong," Travers told him. "Besides, we don't want to go far. The nearer we stay, the better. Take Romney, for instance. He was a camouflage officer. Weren't some of the things those fellows did in the war absolute miracles? And take Martin. He had a toy-factory and made his own stuff. Think of it—toys, mechanical wonders, tricks and puzzles! Couldn't a man like that have performed a miracle?"

"You're too clever for me," Tempest said. "I've got to keep to sheer hard facts." He waved away Travers's protest. "I admit yours may be facts, so I'll say more immediate facts. His prints, for example." He called over to Polegate's table. "Any luck with the prints?"

"No, sir," Polegate said. "They're not the ones on the sheet of paper."

"Right," said Tempest. "And who shall we have in now, Travers?"

There was all at once a noise from outside the still open doors. The noise became a series, then hopelessly confused, with shouts of, "Here he is!" and, "This way!" and the running of feet and a scuffling. Tempest gave a startled look, then made for the lawn, Travers at his heels. Then a small group of four people came into the light that flooded the lawn from the room. The sergeant of the uniformed police and two of his constables were holding a man—and even before Tempest and Travers clapped eyes on him they knew from his protesting voice that the man was Romney Greeve.

CHAPTER VI
SCHOOL FOR LIARS

ROMNEY GREEVE stood in front of the table, looking rather like a schoolboy, hauled in from somewhere out of bounds. The sergeant stood at his elbow.

"I'd like to hear your explanations," Tempest said to him. "You distinctly heard my own orders about leaving the house?"

"I know I did," Romney told him. "I didn't know it applied to the grounds as well. I thought you meant we weren't to go away—you know, return home."

"Next time you have any doubts, come to me and I'll explain." He rumbled on for a moment. "Most reprehensible conduct. And what was it that made you so anxious to go out there?"

Romney explained about his painting and that article he was writing for the *Dilettante*.

"I came away in such a hurry when the gong went," he said, "that I hadn't time to bring my things in. Then with all this business going on and people about everywhere, I thought I'd better go and fetch them."

"The police wouldn't have interfered with your belongings," Tempest said. "However, you have my permission to fetch them—later on. As you're here, you might as well do something for us."

He trotted out the usual recitation, and Romney Greeve, aged forty-two, artist, of Lacy's End, Chelmsford, Essex, duly had his prints taken. Tempest stopped him once more as he turned to go.

"When did you begin your picture, Mr. Greeve?"

"I prepared the canvas this morning," he said. "This afternoon we all went out to the town."

"But this evening you were writing."

Romney looked surprised. "How did you know that?"

Tempest temporized. "I had the idea you told us so yourself, or else someone said he saw you writing."

"As a matter of fact I was," he said. "I had intended to begin painting, but I got interested in my own theories and started writing, and then I didn't feel like stopping."

"So I gathered," Tempest said. "You were still at it when Mantlin came back from the garden. You called out something to him, didn't you?"

"Oh, yes; I asked him what the time was. Then I began putting my things together."

"He didn't show any desire to come in and see what you'd done?" Travers asked. "I mean, he knew you were proposing to paint a picture."

"He knew that all right," Romney said. "But he couldn't very well come in the summer-house because he wasn't that side of the lawn. He looked to me to have come from the pond direction. I thought he was going in at those doors there—not the ones he did go in by."

"And you saw and heard nothing at all?" asked Tempest.

"Well, there I've been thinking. Just about seven o'clock I heard a peculiar sound in the shrubbery and I looked out. Then I thought it was one of the gardeners. The whole thing didn't take a minute—looking out and everything."

"A rustling sound, was it?"

"I don't know, really. It was merely a sound—like someone moving about."

"And what was the light like when you left the summer-house?"

"At half-past seven? Well, I'd say it was full dusk. The sun had gone. There're some pretty big trees out there towards the west."

They were disjointed statements that he seemed to think of as he went along. Tempest had apparently no more questions for the moment, and he half-turned as if to go again. Travers's voice it was that this time halted him.

"I had no idea that you went in for landscape, Mr. Greeve?"

Romney shot a suspicious look at him; the suspicion merely of the expert who resents the meddling and the assumptions of knowledge of the uninformed.

"I don't usually. But everybody does landscape at some time or other. It's the bread that goes to an artist's meal. That was all part of the theories I was expounding in that article of mine."

"Which I'd very much like to read one of these days," Travers told him with his most charming smile. "But you don't remember my name. I bought a small still-life of yours in—let me see—in thirty-one, at the Trentham Galleries, where you had an exhibition."

The other had been staring, and now he too smiled.

"You're not Ludovic Travers? 'The Economics of a Spendthrift' man?"

"The very bloke," said Travers flippantly. "I thought I recognized you this evening, but I wasn't sure. Weren't you full-bearded in those days?"

"Foul-bearded would be nearer the mark." He laughed at his own pleasantry.

Travers held out his hand. "Some time later we may have a little talk about art in general. I'm most interested."

"Take Mr. Greeve along now, sergeant," Tempest said. "Let him get whatever he wants and then escort him round to the front door. You've got a torch?"

The sergeant was already showing it, and off the two went. Travers lighted a cigarette.

"Funny how a change of beard makes all the difference. I knew I'd seen that chap somewhere. Weird bird, don't you think?"

"How do you mean?"

"Oh, I don't know." He smiled to himself. "An artist with the changing earth and the unimagined heavens to paint, and he spends his evening—writing theories! And gets so absorbed that he's still at it at half-past seven when only owls can see." Then he sighed. "It's funny he should think the *Dilettante* is going to pay him for that article. The *Dilettante* pays for nothing unless it commissions something from some big pot. I know. I've done a thing or two for them myself in my time."

Tempest smiled. "As a big pot?" And then becoming aware, apparently, of his own flippancy, "Who shall we have in now?"

There were steps on the crazy-paving strip outside the door, and the sergeant appeared again.

"He took his things, sir."

"What things were they?" Tempest asked him.

"Well, there was some writing paper, sir, and a pen and ink and a paint-box—so he said—and what he called a canvas."

"Ah, that'd be the beginnings of the picture," said Travers.

"Picture? That wasn't a picture, sir. It was a sheet of what he called canvas all daubed over with yellow paint, just as if someone who didn't know anything about it had been white-washing or distempering. You know, sir—all streaks, and just put on anyhow."

Travers laughed. "It was only what he'd call a foundation. You and I are no artists, you know, sergeant."

"No, and I don't want to be, sir, if that's what they call pictures." His tone became more official again. "There was also an easel which he left there, sir. Oh, and it appears, sir, he left the premises by a window. Slipped out of the dining-room where the plain-clothes man was and round the back and so out."

"All right, sergeant. I'll have it inquired into." Tempest nodded him out and then turned to Travers. "Well, there's a pretty brazen-faced liar for you. Says he thought it was in order to go out, so instead of leaving by the front door where he'd have been stopped and brought to me, he sneaks out by a back window. What's the idea?"

"Lord knows!" said Travers, at a loss for once for a theory.

Then Sergeant Polegate all at once looked up from his table and finger-print apparatus in the corner.

"Here's a funny thing, sir."

The two went over.

"What's the gong-stick doing here?" Tempest asked.

"That's just it, sir," Polegate said. "I knew nobody but that butler had handled it, so, thinks I, I'll get his prints and save time. And they're the ones on that letter, sir. The paper's all smothered with 'em!"

Five minutes later, the butler entered the drawing-room, and with his usual deliberate, reverent steps. He listened deferentially to Tempest's palaver, and though Travers thought he saw him shy somewhat at the mention of prints, John Service, aged sixty-seven, butler, had his finger-prints duly taken.

"Sit down, will you?" said Tempest pleasantly. "Will you smoke?"

"Not at the moment, sir," Service told him with a solemn little bow.

"How long have you been here, Service?"

"Thirteen years, sir—come October."

Tempest leaned over sympathetically. "And not always the post you'd have chosen for yourself?"

The old butler's lips tightened. Through his mind was doubtless running that night when he had come into that same room, and the old man had stormed at him as if he were dirt—and the two at the table had heard.

"Well, sir," he said, "Mr. Greeve was hasty-tempered some-times—I admit that. But there were worse masters, sir—so I've been told." He shook his head. "And I'm not so young as I was, sir. I doubt nobody else would have wanted me."

Tempest felt uncomfortable for a moment.

"Then you came here just after the war?" he went on. "Of course you were over age for the war yourself."

"I was not, sir," said Service, and drew himself up. "I joined up the first month of the war, sir. I was wounded in France in fifteen, sir, and then drafted to a Labour Battalion and served in Palestine till well after the armistice, sir."

"Good for you, Service!" said Travers. "What was your regiment?"

"I beg your pardon, sir?" He craned over a bit as if suddenly deaf.

"I asked what your regiment was."

"Oh, yes, sir." He smiled. "The Landshires, sir."

"Splendid!" said Tempest. "I hope your wound doesn't trouble you now."

"No, sir; just the shoulder, sir."

"You're left-handed," said Travers.

"Yes, I am, sir." He looked surprised. "When the right shoulder was hit, sir, I had to learn to use my left hand, and I sort of got used to it, sir."

Travers smiled. "Yes, I noticed you smote that gong left-handed."

He drew back and left Tempest to carry on. The second recitation was begun about sheep and goats and elimination of the guiltless, and ended by wondering if Service, who was looking down the room, would be prepared to swear to the innocence of any parties.

"Mr. Hugh, sir, and Mr. Martin, and Mr. Tom; I could see them all, sir," he said. "But not one of them would have done a thing like that, whatever—" He broke off there, with a clearing of his throat, as if the word were part of the cough.

Tempest leaned across again. "You were going to say, whatever provocation they had; isn't that so?"

The old butler shot a look at him. "Yes, sir. Perhaps I was, sir."

"And Mr. Mantlin. You saw him too?"

There was another hesitation, then he shook his head.

"I wasn't looking at him as I was at the others, sir."

"I see." Tempest left it at that. "And now about this particular birthday and your late master's four nephews coming down. Did you notice any difference this time from any other time?"

He thought again. "No difference, sir—except the bedrooms."

"The bedrooms?" Tempest raised his eyebrows. "What difference was there in the bedrooms?"

Merely an interchange between Mr. Romney and Mr. Hugh, he explained. Mr. Romney had written to Mrs. Service a confidential letter asking for the south-west room, as it overlooked a part of the garden he was going to paint.

"That'll be the room above our heads," said Tempest. "Well, I can quite understand that. And no other change?"

Service could think of none. Tempest nodded, then got ready to spring his mine.

"There's a letter we'd like you to have a look at. You mustn't touch it, but the sergeant there will show it to you. Oh, by the way, you've never heard your late master mention a sister of his, Ethel by name?"

As Travers could see, every fibre of the man's being was suddenly still. Then he shook his head.

"Never, sir."

"Then just read that letter, will you?"

Service read it, producing a pair of glasses from his inner pocket for the purpose. His face was blank when he had finished, and the glasses were calmly replaced in his pocket.

"I'm afraid it conveys nothing to me, sir."

"Then why are your finger-prints on it?"

He stared. "My finger-prints, sir!"

"Yes," said Tempest. "Yours."

He shook his head again, then his face lightened. "But, of course, sir. The master must have left it lying on a table somewhere, sir, and I picked it up and put it elsewhere—for safety, so to speak."

"Probably that was it," said Tempest. "Otherwise you've never seen it or read it?"

Service drew himself up with dignity. "Naturally, sir. I know my place better than that."

Inspector Carry came in just then, caught sight of the butler and gave him a friendly nod. Another minute and the butler had gone. He was bringing sandwiches and drinks at once, for the hour was almost eleven, and the maids were in bed.

"What is he?" asked Tempest. "Just a pious old humbug, or what?"

"I thought he was rather a decent old stick, sir," said Carry. "He did all he could to help me—so did his wife."

"Whatever else he is, he's a thorough-paced old liar," said Travers. "Have a look at these prints again. No. Wait a moment. Got a piece of paper, Polegate? Right. I lay it here. I pick it up and place it out of the way, as Service said he did. Notice I couldn't possibly use more than one hand, and the natural inclination is to pick it up by the bottom corner—the right hand for me, being right-handed, and the left hand for Service. Now look at what I do when I read it. I use both hands, and there's where the proof comes. Look at Service's prints. You can see where he used both hands. Then there's a second, overlapping set. Perhaps he tried to read without his glasses, and the second time he put them on. Perhaps he had two independent goes at it."

"Curiosity, I suppose, sir," Carry said. "As soon as the old man's back was turned, he had to stick his nose into everything."

Tempest shook his head. "A paper as important as that wouldn't have been left lying about." He thought for a moment. "The old man went out for his daily rides. That'd give Service the run of the house."

"You think he had duplicate keys for the safe?" Travers asked.

"There's a possibility," Tempest said. "We might lay a trap for him and have it watched all night." He glanced at the clock again. "Time we finished seeing those people. Mr. Hugh Bypass, I think, Polegate. And how did you get on, Carry?"

Carry reported an excellent series of eliminations. With that special dinner imminent, Mrs. Service had had the two maids under her eye, and the cook was naturally hard at it. The house-keeper herself had been upstairs till the very moment before the gong went, but she came into the kitchen to find everyone there. Of the outdoor staff, the senior gardener was at the pictures, and the junior was lending a hand generally in the kitchen on that special occasion. Carry had, moreover, got people talking, and nobody had the faintest inklings of an idea who could have committed the murder.

Three people came into the room together. Hugh Bypass was first, then Service, carrying a tray, and lastly an elderly woman with a smaller tray.

"Sorry to have kept you waiting so long, sir," the butler said, "but the maids are in bed and we had to cut the sandwiches our-selves."

"That's all right," Tempest told him. "And this is Mrs. Service, is it?"

"Yes, sir," said Mrs. Service herself. Placidity seemed her keynote, and a quiet kind of neatness. But she had been crying, and no art could conceal the fact.

"We're sorry to give you all this trouble, Mrs. Service," Tempest said.

"It's no trouble, sir," she told him gently. "I was going to ask you, sir, if the men would like some tea or anything."

"Very good of you, but they've made their own arrange-ments," he told her, and in a moment she was gone. Tempest turned to Service. "We shan't need anything else to-night. And don't be alarmed if you hear people moving about outside. I shall probably try to have a nap in this room myself some time later, but we shan't disturb the house. About the safe, Mr. Travers. We needn't go into the contents till to-morrow, need we?"

"No need whatever," said Travers, who had been making himself agreeable to Hugh Bypass.

The butler left.

"Quite a genuine old fellow, that," said Tempest reflectively, as the door closed on him.

"He's a very good chap indeed," Hugh said. "I only wish I could employ him myself."

"Wife's a nice woman, too."

"A very nice woman indeed," said Hugh. "Ladylike—and most competent."

Then Hugh Bypass, aged fifty-four, schoolmaster, of Yandell House, Bromley, had his prints taken. After Tempest's second recitation, he said he would swear in any court of law that his brother Tom, Service and Charles Mantlin had nothing to do with it—setting aside the indignations that any of them should be suspected at all. In five minutes he had gone again, and Martin Greeve came in.

Martin Greeve, aged fifty, engineer, of 89A Power Road, Camden Town, went through the formalities. As at the one vital moment he had been picking up a card from the floor, and the card had been hard to seize in the way that cards have, he could swear to nothing, he admitted.

"One thing I'd like to ask you, which has been puzzling me rather," Tempest said. "I gather—in fact I know from my own experiences—that it must have been almost dark in this room when the gong went—"

"Not dark," Martin interrupted him. "Just gloomy."

"Well, whatever it was, your game went on and nobody attempted to turn on the lights."

"Yes," said Martin, in the tone of a man who casually discusses a thing of no earthly importance. "My uncle was far too keen on the game to worry about light. He'd have grubbed along for another ten minutes rather than take his eyes off the table. Besides, you know how it is on a summer evening? You rather shy at turning the light on till you're forced. And, of course, Service wasn't there to do it—not that that made any difference."

Lastly came Tom Bypass, aged forty, army officer retired (disability pension) of 7 Aitkin Gardens, Ilford. Travers took to him from the start, he was so quietly spoken, sensible, even-tempered and generally amenable. Of the four cousins, he alone had the sure, consistent touches of quality, though in himself he looked shockingly tired and ill.

"Hugh, of course, is preposterous," he said. "We sat talking not five feet from each other. Martin too—perfectly absurd to think of him. And Charles Mantlin. I could see him out of the corner of my eye the whole time. He never moved a muscle." He smiled dryly. "He was like the rest of us—cursing that damn gong to blazes and waiting for it to stop."

It was after one in the morning when Tempest proposed that Travers should drive him to headquarters, and then go on himself to bed. The Major had no end of things to do, and preferred to use the station phone. A protracted conference over the belated supper had evolved the following lines of immediate action. Local and London Press must, for publicity's sake, be at once informed of the crime. An appeal was to be issued for Ethel—née Greeve, etc.—to come forward at once. The Private Hire Company—open all night—were to be asked to send Greeve's usual chauffeur round in the early morning. Finally, at Travers's suggestion and principal insistence, the necessary local police authorities were to be informed, and asked for confidential information about each of the four cousins.

"About that watch on the safe," Tempest asked Carry as he rose to go. "Got a good man in mind?"

"Would you mind if I did it?" Travers asked, and most earnestly. "Never in my life have I had the chance of anything so thrilling."

"Thrilling, sir!" said Carry, and grunted. "Not much thrill sitting in an empty room, waiting for somebody who, it's a hundred to one against, mayn't turn up."

But Travers had a dozen reasons to confound the opposition. It would be light in an hour or two, when the search of the grounds would begin, and there was always the day to sleep in. Tempest himself could drive the car down, and in a way it would be a blind.

"I don't like it, all the same," Tempest had to add, when he had given in.

Travers clapped him reassuringly on the back and saw him as far as the car.

"There's still a light in the servants' quarters, sir," the officer on patrol duty reported. "I thought I'd better mention it, sir, as it's so late."

"There you are!" said Travers, as a final vindication. "Didn't I tell you that few people in this house would get much sleep?" Then his voice lowered. "And what's Service still up for, if it isn't to take a last peep inside that safe?"

CHAPTER VII
STIRRING TIMES

THERE WAS A curtained recess in the morning-room, and Travers chose it in preference to the window. After all, as he argued it, if Service entered the room at all, his first anxiety would be to make sure the window curtains were drawn and himself unobserved. So Travers moved a chair to the empty recess, sat sideways with ample space, and prepared to await something which in his heart of hearts he knew would never happen.

But Travers was never less disposed for sleep. He was always a night-bird and his brain, he would always assure himself, was never more apt for effort than in the midnight hours. And in any case, that night he had an infallible cure for sleepiness—nothing less than a review of what appeared to himself the salient points that had emerged from the five-hour inquiry. That he would keep the results of his ruminations in his mind for subsequent use and recording, he had no doubt. Without being too aware of it, he had a prodigious memory; one of those photographic minds that can take mental snapshots and develop them at leisure.

And with two hours of darkness before him, Ludovic Travers was in no immediate hurry. A pleasing urge indeed was on him to survey the problem in a leisurely way. The world, Palmer included, was unaware of the momentous fact, but he was engaged on a new book, and in a new line. It had been thrust upon him somehow by his own experiences, and was to have the quaint and wholly Traversian title, "Kensington Gore," with the subti-tle: "Murder for High-Brows."

So that night Travers approached even his own ruminations in a spacious frame of mind. Murder, he felt, should have a slo-gan, and for the life of him he could not find the all-embracing one. And then, before he knew where he was, he was thinking of the murder about which he was immediately concerned, for it had seemed to him that the only murders worth while were those with a claim to the unique. Murder ceased to be killing only when it was a fine art. A perfect murder must escape detec-tion; therefore it must be proofed against human inquiry, and in that manner achieve something of the miraculous.

The miraculous. What, precisely, was a miracle? Something purely relative, he decided, and found the decision obvious. To an aboriginal, a match might be a miracle. Anything that de-ceived was a miracle in its potentialities. Take that fellow Mar-tin, for instance. Mightn't he, in the eyes of small boys and cred-ulous parents, have achieved the miraculous occasionally with the amazing mechanical devices that were needed to titillate the modern young idea? And what miracle or device might Martin Greeve have discovered to kill with impunity? It would have been well worth his while. No weeks of publicity and overhead charges for such a discovery, but immediate and colossal profits. Thirty thousand pounds for an idea!

But try as he might, Travers could compass nothing of his own devising that might even have served the turn of a murder-er in the matter of the killing of Hubert Greeve. Nor could he find one in the case of that other worker of war-time mystery—Romney Greeve, the camouflage expert. And as Travers assured himself, he was taking the two Greeves out of order. The thing to do was to review the evening from its beginning and let each of six men drop snugly into his own natural groove.

There was John Service, the butler; pious humbug or con-scientious servant—which? There had been the queer look he had given at the sight of himself and Tempest. Above all, there had been the flagrant lie he had told about the threatening let-ter. And there had been that strange way in which Mantlin had refused to vouch for him as one impossible to have committed the murder. And could he have done it? Could he have shot with his right hand while his left smote the gong? Could he handle a gun at all? The army mightn't have taught him that, though his hand was steady enough and he had cause enough to exchange old Hubert Greeve for an annuity of five hundred a year. And why had Greeve left him that annuity? Was Greeve a much-slandered man, whose bark had never been meant for bite? And, sole test in the long run, could Hubert Greeve's head have been so twisted to his *left* that a shot would have hit him coming from the place where Service undoubtedly stood?

Travers gave it all up. But there was Mantlin. A queer bird who by no conceivable-circumstances could have fired the shot. But he might have been a confederate—and Travers smiled to himself in the dusky dark of the room when he thought of it—for confederates can make any man a miracle-worker. It might be as well, then, to inquire if ten thousand pounds was desperately needed by Mantlin. And why had he given so much away about the four cousins, and on the mere plea that if he didn't speak, the law would find out?

And those four cousins. Somehow Travers liked them all, and not only because he was always for the under-dog and the man down on his luck. Hugh could have done nothing. His brother Tom could have done nothing, though—and Travers smiled to himself again—by his own theories that made both men the first suspects. And there was that tired-looking, decent soul, Martin. Nothing suspicious about him, unless it were that dropping of a card. After all, if a man dropped a card so that his eyes had perforce to be on the floor, how could he be accused of seeing the things he had no intention of seeing?

Lastly there was Romney Greeve, the man who made some early reputation as a painter of still life, and stood up so valiantly for landscape. The man who was suddenly so keen on writing theories that he forgot to paint. The only one who could have fired that shot from outside the room, but the man whom three people would swear was in the summerhouse from which the shot could hardly have come! And why the careful ensuring that he should have, for this ominous occasion, a special bedroom? If it were wet he could still paint the picture from the summer-house, or write his article with the view beneath his eye. Why, then, the special bedroom?

And then Travers suddenly realized that he had wholly neglected the factor of the unknown man. Had that unknown fired the shot from the shrubbery, so that its zipp had been heard by Mantlin? Was that unknown the husband who had written the threatening letter? And yet about all that side to the inquiry, Travers felt a strange weakening of enthusiasm. Wait, he told himself, till the Brighton police had caught Mr. In-Ernest. Wait till Ethel herself had come forward. And at the same time, in that same heart of hearts, Travers was wishing no such things would happen. In them there would be no mystery and no miracle.

So he began thinking of his own book again, head comfortably in the corner of the recess, and heels hooked round the rail of the tilted chair. In two minutes there came a pleasant drowsiness. Then for maybe a long half-hour Ludovic Travers slept. Then he stirred in his sleep, his chin drooped, rose again, drooped again and then drooped too far. With a crash that must have been heard a room or two away, he pitched forward chair and all.

Not before half a minute did he know where he was. Then he smiled sheepishly to himself, only for the smile to go as soon as it came. How much noise he had made he had no idea, though it had seemed to himself in the split second of first consciousness like the crash of earth's foundations; so in the musty dark he set the chair back and took his seat again, and it was as he drew the curtain across more closely with one hand, and with the other felt with a quick alarm for smashed glasses, that he heard the low voices and the turning of the doorknob.

The light was clicked on and he held his breath. A silence, and Service's voice came.

"There doesn't seem to be anyone in here."

His feet were heard across the carpet, and as Travers felt a new tremendous alarm and his brain hunted feverishly for some excuse that should explain his own ludicrous presence, the window curtains were moved back—then re-drawn.

"The window's all right. Must have been somewhere else."

His feet shuffled across the carpet again. The voice came from near the door.

"I think perhaps I ought to find someone—someone responsible—and say we heard the noise."

"Don't do anything of the kind." It was his wife's voice, and yet the fierce insistence as much unlike her placid self as if she had been some strange, younger woman. "You'd only have to tell more lies." The door was closing again. Travers, peering furtively out, saw the hand that turned down the switch, and heard the last words before the door itself closed.

"Lies? Haven't we *got* to tell lies?"

The faint sounds receded in the dark silence. For a long minute Travers stood listening by the closed door. He opened it, and still his ear caught no movement or voice. Then he moved his chair cautiously to its place again and made his way across the dark hall to the drawing-room door. There, on a sudden impulse, he stayed; felt for the light switch and looked at his watch. Three o'clock, and the first dawn would soon be breaking.

With the light full on he stood there thinking. Then he began a noisy clearing of his throat. At once the door from the kitchen passage opened, and Service, fully dressed, appeared. He blinked for a moment.

"You startled me, sir. Anything you want, sir?"

"Not specially," Travers told him. "But I suppose you didn't happen to hear a noise here just now?"

"A noise, sir?" He shook his head. "Where did you think it came from?"

Travers vaguely suggested the direction of the morning-room. The butler shook his head again.

"You're still up?" Travers said.

"I didn't feel like sleep, sir." His face brightened. "Might I make you a cup of tea, sir? I was just about to make one for—myself."

"Thank you," said Travers. "I'd like one very much."

The lights were still on in the drawing-room as he had left them. Outside, in the now approaching dawn, no sound was heard, till through the closed and curtained doors there came the tread of a constable on his round. Travers, in the brief time before Service should appear, sat with his forehead wrinkled up in thought.

Making a cup of tea for *himself*, was he? And then he had hesitated. *Ourselves* was what had been on the tip of his tongue, and yet why should Service conceal the fact that his wife was still up? But that other matter was more serious. Lies had to be told. What lies? For Service himself, or to shield someone else? And his tone had been a mixture of reprimand and resolve, and reminding. And how was one to know in future what were lies and what were truths?

The door opened and the butler came in with the tray. Travers was sitting there with glasses in hand.

"You and I happen both to be what's commonly called bat-eyed," he told Service jocularly.

"Well, my own sight is very good except for reading," the butler said. "I can't read a thing, sir, without my glasses, but I can see things quite a distance away."

Travers's eyes happened to be on the card-table, and his finger went out to it.

"I'll wager you didn't see the actual card Mr. Greeve was picking up off the floor to-night?"

There was hesitation but no uncertainty. "No, sir, I own I didn't—not to-night, sir." He smiled. "But I did the night before, sir. Mr. Martin dropped a card then too, sir, and I distinctly saw it as he picked it up."

Travers was startled. His fingers went to his glasses, then fell again. He smiled.

"Dropped a card two nights running, did he? That's that gong of yours, Service. Enough to scare anybody into dropping anything."

"It does make a noise, sir," he admitted. "Still, the master liked to hear it, and it was his business, sir—not mine."

Travers nodded. His face took on a considerable concern.

"I wonder what will be the outcome of all this? If only we could rely on everybody telling the truth, and the whole truth, everything might be cleared up in less than no time." His face took on a whimsicality as he smiled, and the light twinkled on the glasses of the monstrous horn-rims. "Why do people tell lies, Service? You and I wouldn't tell lies?"

The butler stood motionless, his eyes set and unheeding. Then he shook his head.

"I don't know about you, sir, but I'm only human." He nodded to himself. "Suppose my own brother was responsible for—for what's happened, sir, and suppose I thought he was justified, then I wouldn't stop short of a lie—not if I didn't get anyone else into trouble."

"Maybe you're right," said Travers solemnly. He got to his feet and his hand fell on the old man's shoulder. "Still, that's merely supposition. You haven't a brother, and he didn't do it. And you'd make a pretty poor liar; don't you think so?" And as the old man moistened his lips and shook his head, "Still, I mustn't keep you here any longer talking nonsense. And I'm very grateful for the tea. Don't bother to come for the tray, because I may be asleep."

But though he was to lie back with eyes closed, there was no more sleep for Travers. Dawn broke and Tempest came with it. Travers drew him aside as soon as Carry had marshalled his men for the search.

"Been up all night, have they?" he said, when Travers had told his tale. "And Service is counting on telling lies. What shall we do? Confront him and admit we overheard?"

"He'd deny it," Travers said. "But if you don't think I'm butting too far in, I have an idea. I expect Mantlin will be leaving after breakfast if you let him, so there'll definitely be a free bedroom. Why not plead that you must have somebody on the spot, and install me here—with Palmer?"

It was at about five o'clock that the grand discovery was made, when a hail from Carry brought Tempest and Travers into the shrubbery, halfway between the summer-house and the drawing-room french doors. A slender tree rose above the outer laurels and looked as if it might be a scarlet may.

"Have a look here, gentlemen," Carry said portentously.

Three feet from the ground, a six-inch nail had been driven into the trunk. Two feet above that was an ordinary staple, and six inches above that a smaller, three-inch nail, from which hung a few inches of stout string, through the staple, and with end snapped off. Tempest frowned.

"You know what it is, sir?" Carry asked.

"I know what I think it is," Tempest told him. "I think it's a rudimentary, but possibly efficient device for filing a gun at a fixed target without being oneself on the actual spot."

"Exactly, sir!" He beamed. "You'll notice the large nail would support the gun, and just in front here, sir, is a handy gap in the laurels with a stout fork the other end can rest on." He had evidently been making experiments, and now he produced a straight stick. "We'll take this for the gun. Now you squint along the barrel, sir."

Tempest squinted and Travers squinted. Then Tempest became quite excited.

"Carry, you go and sit in the very place the old man sat in last night, while we see where the gun points."

Off Carry went.

Travers's eyes left the upper nail which had so interested him.

"I don't quite see how the contraption was going to work," he said, "unless someone was up the tree, and that's manifestly ridiculous, with the string round the trigger and the swivel to give a kind of pulley effect."

"What's it matter?" Tempest told him gaily. "We can always work that out later. You do own that it *is* a contraption for firing a gun?"

"Yes," said Travers. "Perhaps I do. That gap in the laurels, for instance, wasn't made by nature. You can still see where a bushy branch was neatly cut out."

There was a call from Carry, and Tempest squinted again along the supposed gun. Then Travers squinted. The line led clean through Carry's neck—*which would be the head of the dead man.*

Carry came back, settling his foot with heavy satisfaction clean on a clump of pinks.

"What about footmarks round here?" Tempest asked him.

The inspector snorted, and with good reason. "Our men have been through here on hands and knees, sir, and what traces can you see? And if they didn't leave any when they didn't care whether they did or not, what about the one who did this little job, and took darn good pains to leave nothing?"

Tempest nodded. "But if a gun was used, where is it?"

"Where, sir?" He smiled. "I'll tell you what I think, sir. After it was done, the man would bolt that way, farthest from the house, and out into those woods. Therefore, whichever side he took, he'd go by that pond. That's where the gun is, sir—though I may be wrong."

"Personally, I think you're right," Tempest said.

"You'll drag the pond?" broke in Travers.

Tempest pursed his lips. "I don't think so. How deep is it, Carry?"

"Deep, sir? About ten feet in the middle. It's only an old dew-pond."

"Then why not have it drained?" Tempest said. "The bullet may be in it for all we know, and we can't drag or dredge that out. An engine can come up near enough by the drive way, and we can use the Corporation plant."

"Fine!" said Travers, who foresaw a morning of delicious excitement.

"I'll see to it then, sir." He turned away, then stopped. His voice lowered and his eye rose to the windows of that south-west bedroom. With a fearful grimace he motioned the two to follow him, and it was not till they were behind the rhododendrons that backed the pond that he explained.

"Did you realize what all this amounts to, sir? According to those notes you gave me, there's only one man who could have had a hand in this—the one whose window we were talking under!"

Tempest thought furiously. "Yes, you're right. That was why he got out of that back window and came out here in defiance of orders. He came for the gun he'd dropped."

"Or else to make such a mess of the contraption that we'd never quite know what it was," said Travers. "That's why the string was broken."

Tempest nodded, then he frowned again. "Yet at least three people would swear that he was in the summer-house when the shot was fired."

"Exactly, sir!" said Carry. "He was in the summer-house, *holding one end of that string.*"

"Maybe," said Tempest. "But I don't like it somehow. It's all too easy."

Travers's face suddenly beamed. "I'll tell you something that wouldn't be too easy. People may swear he was in the summer-house. They may have seen him come out and heard him speak. Yet all the time he might have been manipulating the string from that bedroom he was so anxious to acquire for this particular visit."

Tempest smiled tolerantly. "That wouldn't be what you called easy. It'd be a super-miracle."

"Precisely!" said Travers, face still beaming. "Remember my first theory? Besides, miracles *are* easy. The whole thing's relative. Once the quickness of the hand has ceased to deceive the eye—"

Tempest smiled and clutched him by the arm. "You can tell me all that when I've got a couple of hours to spare. Now we'll see about having the contraption photographed—what's left of it—and we might have a man inconspicuously handy, to see it isn't monkeyed with further."

It was not till soon after eight that morning that things began to happen. Plant, the chauffeur from the Hire Company, turned up for interview. He had always driven Mr. Greeve, he said, ever since he took his present job, which was two years ago.

"You found him a good client?" asked Tempest, trying to be genial.

"I didn't particularly," Plant said. "Two hours and often three I drove him, and he always give me the same tip—sixpence!"

Tempest smiled. "And where'd you usually go?"

"All sorts of places," Plant said. "Round the villages, away out on the Downs, as far afield as Eastbourne and once to Brighton. Gardens he was particularly fond of, and he'd always be stopping the car and looking over people's gates and hedges."

"And where'd you go the last few times?" Tempest asked him.

"Can't say off-hand, sir." He thought for a bit. "Eastbourne once. That'd be last Friday, sir. Saturday we went round Tonbridge and home by Battle."

"Stop anywhere for long?"

"Not Saturday we didn't. Friday we did. We always stopped when he went to Eastbourne, sir. I had to park the car, and out he'd get and go off on his own, and I had a certain time to be ready for him again."

Tempest nodded. "I see. And how often within the last six months have you gone to Eastbourne?"

"Eastbourne?" He thought. "Twice, sir—no, three times. That's right, sir-three times. Once Good Friday, once in June, and last Friday. Three times altogether."

"Nothing much to be gathered from that," Tempest said when he'd gone. "Greeve evidently didn't go to see this sister of his, therefore they must have corresponded. It wouldn't be a bad idea to go through that safe again."

But the safe and a search of every available drawer produced nothing, and then shortly after nine o'clock a message came through from Brighton. No letter was waiting in the post office for a Mr. I. N. Ernest, and none had ever been received there.

Tempest was puzzled. "Why on earth didn't Greeve ever answer the letter? If he didn't make an appointment with the man to come here and meet him, how could he expect to be in a position to get us to come here and listen to the talk?"

"He was a mean old devil by every account," Travers said. "He'd tell himself that the man knew his address in any case, and if he was coming, he'd come—so he saved himself a stamp."

Tempest and Polegate began a fresh hunting through of every paper and document they could lay hands on, with the hope of running across Ethel Greeve's original letter. Then, shortly after ten o'clock, the phone went.

"I'm Mr. J. T. Bendline, of J. T. Bendline *Sc* Co., solicitors, of Eastbourne," the voice said to Tempest. "They've put me through to you from the police-station. What I want to know is if I can see you this morning at any time convenient to yourself. We're the solicitors of the late Mr. Greeve."

"His solicitors!" Tempest was knocked all of a heap. "You mean you have a will of his?"

The voice now expressed surprise. Certainly the firm had a will of his. The date was June of that same year.

"How on earth did you know he was dead?" Tempest asked.

But he had reckoned without the enterprise of the modern Press. Even the Seaborough *Beacon* was rushing out an early edition, and it was in the Stop Press of a late edition of a London daily that Mr. Bendline had seen the news of his client's hasty death.

"Get here as soon as you can," Tempest told him, and, as an afterthought, "Can you give me a rough idea of the contents of the will? Strictly in confidence, of course."

Ludovic Travers came in while he listened. Then Tempest hung up.

"How long do you reckon it'll take an elderly solicitor to get from Eastbourne to here?" he asked Travers, with a certain complacency.

"If he's a centenarian, and walks it—three weeks," said Travers. "If he comes by car, round about half an hour."

"Right," said Tempest. "Then in half an hour the dog-fight's due to begin."

CHAPTER VIII
CALIGULA'S GALLEYS

ON THE EDGE of the pond, where the rhododendrons ended, Ludovic Travers stood watching the pumping plant at work. His expectations quivered with the quivering of the great hose that led away the water to the hill-side, and leapt as the water leapt on its downhill rush to the valley below. Mantlin, by Tempest's permission, had gone, but the four cousins were watching too, and Travers wondered with what feeling they must be regarding the lessening water and anticipating the ultimate mud.

It was as he shifted ground so as not to miss the sight of the arrival of Bendline's car that the two Bypasses came up. Tom nodded and smiled.

"A perfect morning for the operations."

"Yes," said Travers. "A man might make money by betting there's fish on the menu to-night."

Hugh took quite a time to make sure that Travers was not serious. Tom laughed.

"I'll eat every fish they get out of here. That doesn't include eels, though." A small bout of coughing came on him and he turned away for a moment. "Sorry. This air's a bit keen for me."

Hugh cut in with, "My cousin tells me you're the famous author, Mr. Travers."

Travers hunted for apologies. Tom got there first.

"How'd you come to be mixed up with the police?"

"Ah?" said Travers, "that's a very long story."

"Sorry," said Tom again. "But why are you people draining the lake?"

Travers saw no harm in telling. Someone had committed a murder, he said, and that someone might have thrown away the gun. There was also the mystery of a missing bullet.

"Most interesting," said Hugh, and took another look at the water, as if it might suddenly have sunk a foot or two.

His brother gave a nod that had in it no particular interest. Then a different expression came over his face.

"By the way, we were all rather in a hurry last night." He turned to his brother. "Don't you think I ought to tell Mr. Travers about the man I thought I saw?"

A minute later Travers was moving off to the house with the news, and Carry drew nearer to keep an eye on the watching three. Romney Greeve, indifferent now, apparently, about that subtle evening effect he had harped so much on, was setting out his easel on the summer-house steps.

Tempest looked none too pleased about the news. It did rather cut across that highly promising clue of the tree contraption. Still, there was Tom Bypass's own doubts with which to console himself.

"It was probably Mantlin he saw. He did come that way round, if you remember." He frowned. "For all that, I don't see how the disappearing part was done, unless, of course, Bypass took his eyes off him for a moment, and in the meanwhile Mantlin had moved out of the line of the doors."

A car was heard, and the ringing of the bell. In a minute Service was ushering Jackson Bendline into the morning-room. He was a white-haired, still active man, somewhere in the late sixties.

"All this is naturally highly confidential," Tempest assured him when the preliminaries were over. "But we'd like to know just how you first came in contact with Mr. Hubert Greeve."

"He rang me up," said Bendline. "Got my name from the telephone book, he said, and he liked the sound of my voice. Then he arranged for an appointment—the first week in June, that was, and gave me preliminary instructions over the phone for drawing a will. Then he amplified his instructions in a letter, and when he came over one afternoon, we completed the whole thing. A very brief document, really."

"Anything peculiar about his manner?"

"I don't think so." He smiled. "He was a very queer type of man, of course. Very suspicious—and secretive. His first question was whether his dealings with us would be confidential. I assured, him they undoubtedly would be."

"You were surprised when he saw you last Friday?"

The solicitor himself looked surprised at the question.

"I was," he said. "I was even more surprised when he'd gone." He smiled to himself again. Old Greeve had evidently been in his eyes something of a character. "He said he was in the town so he dropped in to pay his respects I rather pulled his leg, and asked if he'd come to ask us about a new will. Then he laughed. Funny way he had of laughing, just as if he'd something up his sleeve. What he said might interest you: that the will we'd drawn for him would cause enough bother without any other."

Tempest smiled grimly. "He wasn't far out. Still, that's no business of mine. But I suppose you don't know what he did with himself the rest of his time in the town that afternoon?"

"But I do," said Bendline. "My clerk, who also regarded him as a queer sort of man, said he saw him having his tea in a nearby restaurant a few minutes later. He was enjoying himself apparently, and listening to the band."

"That's very useful information," said Tempest. "And I suppose he never mentioned to you, over the phone or otherwise, a certain sister of his, named Ethel?"

Bendline shook his head. "Never. I wasn't aware that he had a sister living."

"We rather think he may have," Tempest told him. "And now the main provisions of the will. Would you mind repeating, so that I can make a private note?"

The solicitor gave them. Ten thousand pounds to each of the four nephews, with special bequest of house and contents to Martin ("He used to play cribbage with him," interrupted Tempest); an annuity of five hundred to the housekeeper, of two-fifty to the butler, and remainder to a short list of charities.

Tempest made a note of them, then exploded his shell.

"You know a Seaborough firm of solicitors, Mantlin & Co.?"

Bendline's face showed a flicker of interest, and even distaste.

"I've heard the name."

"I'll give you the address," Tempest said, "because I think you should see Mr. Charles Mantlin at once. He's acted as Hubert Greeve's legal adviser for years, and he holds a will prior to your own; though yours, of course, takes effect." He seemed surprised. "The news doesn't astonish you?"

Bendline smiled dryly. "Didn't I tell you he was a queer character? Still"—he rubbed his chin "I dare say the matter can be easily adjusted, or explained, as between Mr. Mantlin and myself. He isn't likely to hold a still later will?"

"His dates from at least ten years ago," Tempest told him.

Bendline departed, and Tempest called up Mantlin's office, to give warning of his coming. Mantlin himself answered. Tempest gave Travers a meaning look before he spoke. Travers, straining his ears, could hear no faintest sound across the wire.

The last words were being spoken, and now Travers could gather from Tempest's face what was happening at the other end.

"Well, I'm afraid I received the information in confidence, but I ought to warn you to be prepared for such an eventuality. . . . That's right. . . . Mr. Bendline himself is ringing us up as to what happens with you. . . . Thank you. Good-bye."

"How'd he take it?" Travers asked at once.

"It's hard to judge," Tempest said. "He sounded to me like a man who'd been blown sky-high. He hadn't hit the ground again when I hung up."

"Ten thousand's a pretty good sum to lose." Then he laughed. "He's the one man in this case who's proved himself to be honest. He told us in so many words he could do with the ten thousand; he said Greeve was only leaving it to him because he was afraid of him, and he said he distrusted Greeve, who was likely to do a dirty trick at any moment. Everything Mantlin has even hinted at has turned out right."

Tempest nodded.

"There's only one thing I can't understand," Travers went on. "I won't say there's only one thing I disagree with, because it may be that we aren't holding all the strings just yet. It's this. Mantlin's our chief evidence for the shot coming from the shrubbery and for hearing a noise there. Now the gun that fired the shot couldn't have been left in the contraption or Mantlin himself would have seen it when he searched, even if it was pretty gloomy inside those bushes. Therefore, if we carry on with Romney Greeve as a suspect, we're all wrong. Nothing's more certain than that he couldn't have flicked that gun away after he fired it. He couldn't have dragged it by means of the string to where he was sitting in the summer-house, because the bushes must have held it up. And yet, if Mantlin's right, somebody did fire the shot from the contraption."

"The man who wrote the threatening letter," suggested Tempest.

"Even more impossible," said Travers. "What evidence have we that he had a thorough knowledge of the internal arrangements of the house—and above all, the striking of the gong? Every bit of evidence we have about him is fishy, to say the least of it. Faked hand, faked name, and when there was no earthly reason for him to conceal his name from Greeve, who certainly must have known it. And he's never been to Brighton post office to find out if there was a letter for him. Think back to that interview we had with Greeve last Saturday evening. Why, even Greeve didn't take him seriously. If anything he seemed to be somewhat amused—which appears to have been a way with him when he was up to some particularly dirty trick himself. I shouldn't be surprised if Greeve himself wrote the threatening letter."

"Maybe," said Tempest. "We'll find some specimens of his writing and send it along to the experts."

Travers drove Tempest to the police-station and left him there. That arms and ammunition expert was due at any time, but Travers himself was infinitely more interested in the draining of the pond than in the sawing open of skulls. So he collected Palmer and the baggage, had a hasty meal in town, and hurried to Palings again.

There was no solidity, so to speak, about that triangle about to be composed of Palmer, his employer, and the two Services. Everything was vague and deliberately haphazard. Palmer himself would have resented being a police spy. What he was doing was, as he conveniently saw it, something for Travers; and even then there would be no peeping or prying or putting of leading questions. Travers himself had confidence in his man. Only if he fitted naturally into the butler's parlour would information unsought and naturally come his way.

Palmer then, was a detached, unprejudiced observer, and no man was better fitted for the post. In some ways he resembled Service himself, but whereas the Greeve butler had about him a kindliness, an adequacy and a deference, Palmer had that sureness of bearing, that suave competence, that aristocratic dignity of silver hair and episcopal profile that would place him above all trumpery suspicion. He had a stock of reminiscence that would admit him to the confidences of John Service, and an old-world charm of manner that must fascinate his wife. Above all, Palmer was adaptable, handy in the house, and a master of a good few jobs.

The early afternoon found Ludovic Travers watching again those drainage operations, at his ease on one of the half-dozen seats that Greeve had had placed between the rhododendrons. There was something soothing that scorching afternoon in the gurgle of the water and its splash as the hose discharged it down the hill-side. Travers, in fact, was having in a concentrated hour or two the weeks of thrills that had doubtless come to many a modern Roman who had watched the slow uncovering of Caligula's galleys. And already the water had sunk so low that a branch or two could be seen, and an ancient pail, thrown in by some lazy gardener, was appearing above the surface.

At two o'clock Romney Greeve was seen coming round the far corner from the front lawn, and carrying the unfinished picture. In a minute or two he was at work again on the loggia, untroubled by the incongruous engine and suction plant that hampered the ordinary view. Of the other cousins there was no sign, and as Travers wondered what they might be doing, his thoughts shifted again to the case and was at once busy with speculation.

To be or not to be; that—in the matter of clues—was indeed the question. When was a clue not a clue? The inquiring and eager mind, thought Travers, seized on everything and distorted it, so that a humble sneeze acquired the importance and malevolence of a cyclone. Mantlin, for instance. Bendline had made a faint motion of disapproval at the mention of his name. Or had he not? Or had it been disapproval at something quite different from Mantlin? Or take again Martin Greeve, and the fact that he had dropped a playing-card two evenings running at the same corresponding moment. There might be nothing in it. All life was coincidence, Travers told himself, and nothing more easy than to give a significance to a trivial thing. Why, for example, should Romney Greeve be painting in the afternoon something which he had begun in the morning in light which now made the whole thing quite different? Might it not be—to the distorted, over-eager mind—that he wished to have the progress of the draining beneath his eye, and yet not appear too curious?

But the water in the pond was sinking. Its basin began with steep sides and once the inward bend was reached, the hose gained rapidly. And with the carcass about to appear, the eagles gathered together. The engineer made an inspection and mentioned an hour for the completion of the job. Tempest came back, and Polegate and Carry drew out of their watchful retirement. Romney Greeve put away his canvas and came across to the bank, and soon the other three cousins put in an appearance too.

Carry had drawn in close to where Travers and the Major were standing, and it was he who saw the first object. Polegate was dispatched for the apparatus—a long-handled net and a species of rake-cum-fork—and by the time he was back, the excitement had grown. Two books could now be plainly seen, and the string that tied them together.

"Those two missing volumes for a fiver!" said Tempest. "Hook 'em out, Carry."

But a set of steps had to be brought first, and when Carry got down, the books offered a queer resistance. A stone was tied for weight to the string end, and the fork gadget was brought into play.

"My God! don't touch them," Tempest said when they lay at last on the bank. "Get your gloves on, Polegate, and we'll watch."

So Polegate cut the string and opened the volumes out. The red colouring from the covers had made more mess than the water, but the titles could be plainly enough seen. The missing volumes they certainly were, though the back of one had been cut somehow through its title. But it was not a cut. Something had shorn a clear way diagonally through the back of the book, and had partially penetrated the side of the other. And though that something was not yet to be seen, it was almost certainly a bullet!

But with so great a cloud of witnesses at hand, nothing was said, and Polegate put the find in the folio envelopes. And in the same minute, the next object appeared—the stock of a gun. Carry had a grip on it in less than no time and hauled it out. It was a small rifle, of the kind that will kill a rabbit at twenty-five yards—a .202, in fact.

Tempest addressed himself to the onlookers who were crowding in too closely.

"Sorry, gentlemen, but I must ask you to retire to the other side of the pond. It's highly irregular your being here at all."

"Could a bullet from that thing have killed him?" he asked Travers, when the bank was clear again. "I very much doubt myself if it would have gone right through a man's skull."

Travers for once admitted complete ignorance. All he did know was that a .202 bullet, as far as he remembered it, would have made the hole that was so cleanly cut on the back of the second book.

But the water was now nearing the bottom. Another holler from Carry and a shifting of the steps, and he was fishing out a new object. This time it was a small revolver, the sort that might go into a lady's hand-bag; a neat, compact, white-handled toy of a thing as deadly in its way as a stick of dynamite or a length of coloured snake.

In a quarter of an hour the hoses had gurgled their last and the bottom of the pond was bare. It was not muddy, but the wet clay would send a man slipping as if he walked on sloping butter.

"I don't know how you're going to do it," Tempest told Carry, "but use a draw-hoe or something and take off the whole top and examine it. That bullet's got to be found. If you want more help, arrange for it. And don't allow any unauthorized person to come anywhere near."

He moved off to the house with Travers and Polegate.

"One minute," Travers said suddenly. "I have an idea that the frayed string we found on that nail in the shrubbery is the same kind as what was tied round the books."

"I've got both pieces, sir," Polegate said.

But though the pieces were of the same, whitish, cord-like quality, and a layman would have sworn they came from the same ball, string varies so little within a certain range that the evidence was far from conclusive. What mattered was the gun and the revolver, and Polegate was sent off with both to Shinniford and the London man.

"Hope to heaven he hasn't gone back to town," Tempest said. "But he can't have done, or Shinniford would have rung us up and reported."

A rug had been laid on the table and those two volumes of Gibbon were on it. Both men stood for a minute looking down at them, then Tempest shook his head.

"It's got me beat. Service swears they were never in the case after the last thing on the Monday night—and yet there's the bullet mark through 'em!"

"Lies," said Travers reminiscently. "'You've *got* to tell lies.'"

"I know," said Tempest. "Service may have been lying, but nobody contradicted him about those books. After all, anybody's eye might have caught the gap. It was the only one in the whole set of shelves." He clicked his tongue. "Besides, unless a man had the whole room to himself, he must have been noticed taking out the two books—"

"And abstracting the bullet."

"Yes, and abstracting the bullet, and then walking off with them. They aren't books you could slip in your pocket."

"All the same," said Travers, "we have got the consolation of being pretty nearly sure that the bullet came from the shrubbery—so that Mantlin was right again. I wonder—" He broke off. "What about ringing up Shinniford and asking them to find out any marks of binding on the stock or barrel of that gun? That'd make sure it really had been used in the contraption."

Tempest dashed off at once. When he came back, Travers had another idea.

"That little French revolver looked as if it might be the same bore as the rifle. Wonder if they could fire the same shell?"

"I'll ring 'em up and ask in a minute."

"Personally I don't think it's feasible," Travers went on. "But it certainly looked from their condition as if they were thrown into the water at the same time, and that's only a few hours ago."

Tempest clicked his tongue again. "But why two guns?"

"Lord knows," said Travers cheerfully. Then his fingers all at once began fumbling at his glasses. "Two guns, and only one needed. Remember the cat in the riddle? I wonder if one was put in to make the other more difficult?"

"Damn your philosophies," Tempest told him, half-amused, half-annoyed. "I'll go and ring them up about putting that gun under the glass for marks. You see if Palmer can scrounge a pot of tea."

At about five o'clock the two strolled out to the pond where Carry was hard at it. Before dusk, he said, every inch would have been gone through, but up to the moment there had been no sign of a bullet. A few minutes' watching and the two went back to the house again. The plain-clothes man in charge of the telephone was just coming to look for the Chief.

Travers remained in the drawing-room, eyes on the scene that still remained in its overnight staging. Then he went to the bookcase gap and squinted from there through where old Greeve's head had been, and marked with satisfaction that the line ended at the may tree which stood plain above the laurels. And as an idea came to him, Tempest scurried in.

"You know that rifle," Travers said to him, "and how you wondered if a .202 bullet would have gone right through even a corner of the old man's skull? Well, even if it did, how could it have had the additional force—after emerging—to have gone clean through one book diagonally and part of the way into another?"

Tempest smiled ironically. "Why worry about the rifle? Or the revolver? Neither of them had anything to do with killing him. A much heavier bullet did it!"

Travers's eyes bulged. "What—a third gun!"

"That's right," said Tempest. "A heavy Colt probably. A third gun. One we haven't found—and a hundred to one we never will find."

CHAPTER IX
MORE ABOUT MIRACLES

THE SCOTLAND YARD expert came to Palings personally, and when he departed he left behind him even more mystery for Tempest to make what he might of. Not only was he sure Greeve had been killed by a bullet from a heavy Colt, but he was further of the opinion, after careful examination of the wound, that the bullet had emerged from the wound, and little more. The chances were, in fact, that it had been picked up by an occupant of the room.

As for that small sporting rifle, it had been fired, and almost as certainly its bullet had been the one that had penetrated the books. But it and the vicious little French revolver could never have fired the same size of shell. The revolver, indeed, had not been fired at all. It was scrupulously clean—consistent with its brief stay in the water—and was fully loaded. Neither weapon bore finger-prints, but the fullest details of each had been taken so that the Yard might try to trace.

But the rifle, the expert pointed out, was easy enough to transport. A simple unscrewing—and stock, action and barrel were apart, with the barrel going down a trouser leg and the rest in a full-sized pocket. As for marks where it might have been fastened to the contraption, there was never a one, though a powerful glass had been turned on it.

And finally, after inspection of the contraption itself, its position and the deliberate making of the aperture through the laurels, the expert was of the opinion that a heavy Colt could only have killed Greeve from there if it had been fired by a master hand, for from that distance the sighting would have been a problem. For the contraption, in its then dismantled form, he could find no use, and as for the summer-house as the place from which the Colt shot was fired, he dismissed it at once as wholly out of the question. One gathered, in fact, that without wishing to be dogmatic, he was gently hinting that the firing of the heavy Colt in the room itself would have ideally fitted his own ideas. As to what had happened to the two bullets—the fatal one and the one that had pierced the books—he agreed with Tempest. Each had been probably thrown the farthest possible distance away, and at the quickest moment after they had been picked up.

"And now where the devil are we?" asked Tempest plaintively, when he'd gone.

"Up a gum-tree," said Travers. "Three guns and never a bullet. Everybody vouched for by everybody else, except Ethel's husband—and he probably doesn't exist."

Tempest lowered his voice. "Wonder how that rifle got here? Inside somebody's suit-case?"

"It'd go into any suit-case if stripped and laid diagonally," Travers said, and broke off as Service came in.

"Your pardon, sir," the butler said to Tempest, "but Mr. Hugh wishes to know if you can see him a moment. The gentlemen are anxious about getting home, sir, and they'd like to arrange accordingly."

"Certainly I'll see him," Tempest said. "But just a moment, Service. What's worrying them, I gather, is clothes and things. I take it they didn't bring down much luggage?"

A small suit-case each, Service said. Mr. Romney, of course, had sent his painting things beforehand. Questioned tactfully by Travers, he said it was quite a bulky parcel, sent down by rail.

"One other trifling matter while you're here," Tempest said. "We've been given a very clear picture of what happened last night just as the gong was sounded. What we haven't got so clearly is a picture of what happened when you laid down that gong-stick there, *after* Mr. Greeve was shot. Just try to think back, will you, and tell us what you remember? I take it you stayed in the room?"

"Yes, sir; I stayed in the room—till I accompanied Mr. Mantlin to the phone to inform the police."

Then Service began to think and little details emerged, if not in chronological order. Mr. Mantlin shouted that he'd heard something outside, and out he bolted. Then Mr. Tom mentioned the man he'd seen the previous night, and out he bolted too. Mr. Romney had come into the room and he followed the others out. Service himself remained with the body and Mr. Hugh with him, for Mr. Martin had looked out to see what was happening to the others and then had gone out too. He came back with Mr. Tom after perhaps ten minutes. Mr. Romney came in next, and lastly Mr. Charles Mantlin. At once Mr. Mantlin said the police must be warned.

And as Service said that, a peculiar expression came over his face, so that Tempest said, "Yes, Service? What is it?"

"Nothing, sir," the butler said, and shook his head.

"There was something," Tempest told him sternly. "Come on now. What was it?"

"Well"—his feet shifted uncomfortably—"it wasn't anything really, sir—only when Mr. Mantlin mentioned the police, Mr. Hugh"—his voice somehow instinctively lowered—"sort of left the room rather hurriedly, sir, and went upstairs."

"How do you know he went upstairs?"

"Well, sir, because when I went to the hall with Mr. Mantlin, as I said, Mr. Hugh was already coming down again." He craned forward anxiously. "You won't mention my name in the matter, sir, if you should think it anything? I wouldn't like anyone to think I'd told tales, sir. I hadn't meant to mention it, really."

"That's all right," Tempest told him kindly enough. "No one shall ever hear a word. But those things you've told us were definitely all you noticed? If so, you may tell Mr. Hugh Bypass I'll see him at once."

The door closed on the butler. Tempest let out a deep breath, then buried his head in his hands.

"Lord! What next? Soon I'll be afraid to ask a question for fear what someone'll answer. And what the devil did *he* bolt for, of all people? A quiet, inoffensive little man—"

There was a tap at the far door, and Tempest shot up in his seat as Hugh Bypass came in. It was the funeral about which he was particularly anxious. The relatives would naturally stay, but arrangements must be made. The Friday, Tempest suggested, and left Hugh himself to complete details. As for the inquest, it would be on the Thursday morning, and a pure formality with Mr. Charles Mantlin giving evidence of identification. Hugh seemed most grateful, and even became the least bit talkative after Travers had passed his cigarette-case.

"Service tells me there was a broadcast appeal this evening for this aunt of ours to come forward. He heard it on his set."

"Yes," said Tempest. "But I don't know that we anticipate any results. I believe there was a distinct impression among you people that the late Mr. Greeve might be imagining the whole business for the sake of—well, annoyance, shall we say."

Hugh smiled with a certain bitterness. "Yes, that may have been so. He was a peculiar man—a man with a warped mind."

"Then it may have been imagination. Still, it's as well to be on the safe side, so we'd rather hoped you might have given some help in that matter of your aunt. As the eldest son, we thought perhaps you could recall some mention of her. The name of her husband, for instance."

Hugh screwed up his eyes in thought, and with the effort his face took on a harassed benevolence. Then his eyes opened again and he shook his head. A look of strange discovery came suddenly.

"It's funny you should ask me that. My brother was asking me the same thing last night, just at the very moment—it happened."

Travers leaned forward quickly. "You were sitting talking with your brother, weren't you, on Monday night at the same time? Mr. Romney Greeve was in the summer-house, and the card-players were hard at it." He smiled charmingly. "The same seats, of course."

"Oh, yes," said Hugh. "They've always occupied the same seats ever since I remember them playing."

"And Mr. Mantlin came in," Travers said reflectively. "I suppose he had a look at the game? On the Monday, I mean."

Hugh smiled. "Oh, yes. You see, there used to be curious happenings at times." He shook his head. "But Martin was always very patient."

"Mr. Mantlin dropped in to see who was winning?"

"Well, I believe he actually asked how they were getting along."

"It's not a game I care for a lot myself," said Travers, ignorant of its first principles, but easing the conversation gracefully off. Then he drew back with another delightful smile and Tempest carried on.

"One little thing you might help us with," he said, "and that is what happened after Mr. Mantlin left the room to warn the police. Now you were here all the time."

"Er—yes." He hesitated. Then his face coloured. "I mean, I wasn't really. I had to go upstairs. Merely a personal matter."

"Quite," said Tempest lingeringly. "But you can't be any help to us then." He got to his feet. "You'll pardon my saying so, but I thought your brother looked none too fit."

Hugh told him about Tom, face all concern.

"Frightfully sorry to hear that," Tempest said, then smiled. "Still, a little bird has told me he's going to have some good news shortly. Not nearly so good as he might have wished—but good enough. What was his regiment, by the way? I wondered if I might have run across him."

The two were strolling towards the far door, and Travers, heavy in thought, heard the drone of their genial voices. But Tempest's face had lost its geniality when he came back.

"There's a queer mixture," he said. "A perfectly delightful man in some ways, and yet why did he get all hot and bothered when I mentioned his going upstairs?"

"Lord knows," said Travers, impatient to spring his own mine. "But did you notice the amazing thing he admitted, incident by incident? Do you realize that as far as our information goes, this room, at seven-thirty on Monday evening, was precisely the same as it was the following night?"

"Yes," said Tempest, like a man who ponders the implications, "I wondered why you were getting all that out of him."

Travers began polishing his glasses. "I've got an idea, I may say I've got a staggering idea, and yet it's a feasible one." His hand fell on the other's arm. "Give me just one night's thought and I'll have it licked into shape. But all I'll say now is this. I know we've got to beware of coincidence, and keep a sense of proportion in the matter of clues, but hasn't there been *too much doubling?*" His voice was a tense whisper. "Martin drops a card at the same second and the same spot each night. Each night two identical sets of circumstance, for Tom asks a question and Hugh tries to find the answer; Romney is in the summer-house and Mantlin pauses over there to watch the game and speak to the players. And take the weapons. Three of them altogether—presumably used by three different people, and either for business or to throw us off the scent. And when the murder's committed and Mantlin mentions the police, Hugh Bypass—the now head of the family, and always the spokesman, shall I say, of the four cousins—bolts upstairs!"

Tempest looked away thoughtfully. "You mean, collusion between the whole five of them?"

"Let's be modest," Travers told him gently. "Let's be content for the moment to think of conspiracy—between the four." Then he suddenly whipped round. "Why were you questioning Hugh about his brother?"

"I'll tell you. Tom Bypass was a soldier and likely to be a good shot with a revolver. So I had an urgent message sent through to try and find out if whoever it is at his rooms could be induced to let fall whether he had a gun or not. I'm expecting something through at any time. Also I thought it might be a sound idea to know his regiment, and find out if they knew anything of him as a shot." He broke off. "Hallo! Here's Palmer bringing you some food. And Service too. Looks as if it's going to be a banquet."

He whispered in Travers's ear. "Back in an hour or so. Then a quick conference." And as he passed Service, "You didn't sound the gong to-night."

The old butler shook his head. "No, sir. As long as I live I'll never sound the gong again."

Tempest's head turned, and his eyes met those of Travers. Perhaps both had the same thought. Not a conspiracy of four, or even five—but six! Service himself might have been fully in the swim.

At nine o'clock in the drawing-room, behind closed doors, the short conference began. Carry was there, and Polegate with him. The reports on the four cousins had come in, and Tempest laid them before the meeting, keeping the best wine till almost the last.

> HUGH BYPASS: had an old country house which he had converted into a private school. Began with one assistant master and about twenty boys. The master left at the end of the spring term, since when the school had been carried on by owner and his son, a young man of eighteen. The property had been unsuccessfully offered for sale. Number of pupils at end of summer term believed to be nine. Gardener and caretaker once kept; now only occasional odd man.

"Not too much motive there," said Tempest, "but it goes on to say that the son should have gone to Oxford. A man might do a good many things to get money to further his son's career, and we must remember that he'd applied to his uncle for help—in accordance with that uncle's explicit promise—and had been turned down."

> TOM BYPASS: According to landlady's information, she had gathered that when he came to her rooms a year ago, it was from a high-class service flat in town.

"I mention that particularly," Tempest said, "because it bears out Mantlin's evidence. He had, apparently, a very high sense of duty and began to give help to his brother and cousins. We shall hear something more of that later. Those rooms he took in Ilford are particularly cheap and dingy—compared with what he must have given up, I mean. The move to Ilford shows he had spent most of his money and wanted to economize for the sake of the others. A very fine set of principles, I think you'll agree. But—as Mr. Travers might point out—the same extremely high sense of duty might have induced him to go even further to help his brother and cousins."

"I had my eye on him more than once this afternoon, sir," Polegate said. "He's got a nasty little cough, sir. Between ourselves, he's the kind that don't last long."

"Just what I thought myself," said Carry. "And if he happened to know his number was up, sir, then he wouldn't mind what he did." He took the room into his private confidence. "If I knew I was for the high-jump to-morrow, do you mean to tell me it wouldn't occur to me I might as well pay off a few old scores before I hopped it?"

Tempest smiled dryly. "Well, I won't go so far as that, but I'll admit it wouldn't be a deterrent. But it's funny you should have mentioned it, Carry, for just listen to this report on Martin Greeve. It's rather long, so I'll give you the gist of it."

The gist was the report of a certain constable, forwarded ultimately to Divisional Headquarters, and there filed as for no action to be taken. That constable had seen a man emerge in a state of perturbation from a side entry to a flat, found to be in the occupation of Martin Greeve, he being alone there at the time. The constable noticed a strong smell of gas, and the man—a relation of Martin Greeve and now known from his description to be Tom Bypass—had given a plausible explanation when he came back from fetching a doctor. Later on, the constable had questioned the doctor's boy who brought some medicine, and had learned that the door to the flat had been smashed in. That same afternoon, the relation visited an ironmonger's shop and purchased things for the repairing of the door.

"There's a whole lot more to it than that," Tempest said, "and a lot of it we know already. But what I put to you is this. Martin was alone in this flat of his. Tom came to see him and let himself in with a key of his own. But the top door was bolted, and maybe he already smelt gas. In any case he broke in the door, turned off the gas, got his cousin's head *out of the gas-oven*—and the rest we know." He paused. "You see all the implications?"

"Yes, sir," said Carry bluntly. "If he'd got himself into the state where he'd as good as done himself in, then he wouldn't be likely to make any scruples about getting out of his troubles another way—bumping his uncle off."

"Or you can put it this way, sir," said Polegate. "If Tom Bypass knew his cousin was up against it like that, and he couldn't help him himself, he might have done the old man in and helped his cousin and himself at the same time."

"I quite agree." Then he gave that same dry smile. "The trouble, as far as we're concerned, is that three people would swear that Martin couldn't conceivably have done it—and the same with Tom. How much more forward are we?"

"In the matter of that theory of mine, I think we *are* a little further forward," said Travers, and gave the two a quick idea of what was in his mind. "If there are two people on such close terms of—well, we'll say hostility to someone else—as Martin Greeve and Tom Bypass, they might easily have formed a partnership. Each could have brought in his own brother, and there we are."

"And just how do you reckon they did it, sir?" asked Carry.

Travers had to smile. "What do you take me for, Carry? A magician?" He shook his head. "One thing I will promise you. Let me put in a good night's hard thinking, and I'll either wash it right out or find something we can all get our teeth into."

"Well, we'll leave it for a bit," Tempest said, "and have a look at the last of the four—Romney Greeve. His report says that eighteen months ago he gave up the house and studio he rented near Chelmsford and moved into a small bungalow. He has two children—a boy of ten and a girl of eight—and there was some bother with the local people about their education. He refused to send them to the local school, and won his case for their mother to proceed with their education herself. Their affairs with the local tradesmen are in what I might call a pretty considerable muddle. He also applied to his uncle for help and was turned down. There again then, I take it we have motive."

The plain-clothes man in charge of the telephone came in then. Tempest had a man there day and night, and had rather wondered if it might not be a saving of time to run an extension through. Now he was wanted himself, it appeared, and as soon as he'd gone, Carry was away on an old grievance.

"If I could only get those four by myself for just a quiet little half-hour each, sir," he told Travers, "like we could do when I first got in this game, I'd soon have their jaws prised open."

Travers, with an eye on the inspector's fifteen stone and square chin, remarked that he didn't doubt it.

Then Tempest came back in the middle of Carry's tirade against modern obtaining of evidence. The Chief Constable was streaking across the room like a man with big news.

"What d'you think? That white-handled gun. It was known to be in Tom Bypass's possession less than a week ago!"

His landlady had let fall the information, and, according to her, the gun had been in a drawer ever since Tom Bypass had taken the rooms. She had mentioned the matter to him and said she was nervous of guns. He had laughed and said it was unloaded.

Carry grinned in anticipation. "Have him in, sir. Four or no four, we've got one where we want him."

"No hurry," Tempest said. "Get a man suspicious and you've got him prepared. He'll be here if we want him. Also, the gun you got from the pond wasn't fired."

Carry snorted. "How long would it take to clean it and reload it? After the murder he was out in the dark long enough to do that twice over, sir."

"But he couldn't have done the murder," persisted Tempest. "Every bit of evidence we have goes to show the shot came from outside. If he fired it, then his uncle must have twisted his head clean round over the left shoulder-blade! Somebody must have noticed a movement as distorted as that."

But he had Tom Bypass in, sending Polegate for him. Carry prepared to take notes, and the conference, even to the eyes of Tom Bypass, had the look of a court of law. But he came in quite stolidly, with never the flicker of an uneasy eyelid.

"You wanted me, Major?"

"Yes, Mr. Bypass. Take a seat there, will you? To be perfectly candid, we'd like a short statement from you."

There was a nod, as if he found the request an eminently reasonable one.

"You mean what you'd call an official statement?"

"That's right."

"Fire ahead then," Bypass said, and settled himself more comfortably in his chair.

"It concerns one of the guns found in the pond," began Tempest. "One was a small revolver of French make, with a white composition or ivorine handle. We have information that such a gun was in your possession last week."

For all the perturbation he caused, he might as well have remarked that he had information that Tom Bypass shaved daily.

"Yes," he said slowly, and it even seemed amusedly. "That's right. I did have a gun like that. I've had it for years. It is a Frenchman—at least, a Frenchman gave it to me just after the war."

"And may I ask where it is now?"

"Well"—he grinned sheepishly—"that's rather awkward. Of course, if you insist—"

"I certainly do insist," Tempest told him.

"Well, that's different then," said Bypass amiably. "The fact of the matter is, I got rid of it just before I came down here." He cocked a meditative eye towards the ceiling. "The Friday, it was."

Tempest smiled grimly. "Got rid of it, did you? And how can you prove it?"

He gave another sheepish smile. "Well, you're rather going to let me down if you make me tell you. Really, I'd rather you didn't."

"I must be judge of that," Tempest told him. "And I ask you to tell us here and now just how you got rid of it."

"Have it your own way." He shook his head. "You see, I knew a man who was coming down here who hadn't enough money to do things properly, and I was just a bit short myself, so I raised the wind."

"You sold it?"

"No—pawned it."

Tempest's eyes narrowed. "Got any proof?"

The other raised his eyebrows. "Proof among friends?"

"We'll leave the friendship out of it," Tempest told him wryly. "Give us the proof."

"Have it your own way." He brought out some papers from his breast pocket, chose one and handed it over. It was a pawn-ticket, dated the previous Friday.

A minute later he had gone again and Tempest was raising his hands to heaven.

"Can you beat it? Talk about coincidence!"

"It may not have been the same gun," suggested Carry. "He may have pawned another one."

Ludovic Travers was hooking off his glasses. "I'm open to bet a hundred to one in shillings that it was the same gun. The gun the landlady saw was duly pawned, and we've just seen the ticket."

"The first step we take, and my God! what a damp squib." That was Tempest wailing again.

"On the contrary," Travers told him. "It couldn't have happened better. Tell me if this isn't right. He was confident from the very start. His every act was that of a man who knows himself safe. To put it crudely, Major, he was pulling your leg all the time."

Tempest nodded darkly.

"And why?" went on Travers. "Because he knew he was safe. And why was he safe? Because he'd invented some perfectly fool-proof method of committing a murder and getting away with it. And if he didn't do it himself, then he was in collusion with a party or parties who did."

"You're right, sir," said Carry, and smote his knee.

"Right or not," said Travers, "I'm trying a new tack. Those that like common sense can have it. I'm going back to the age of miracles."

CHAPTER X
PORTRAIT OF A MAN

LUDOVIC TRAVERS went up early to his bed that night, though with no thoughts of sleep. With windows open and in the scented dark he proposed to relax in his bed; the body a thing apart, and the mind focused on two men—the two who in that modern, sceptical world might yet be living in the age of miracles. It was with Romney Greeve that he began, and a review of the art and mystery of war-time camouflage; Martin, the designer of toys and maker of gadgets, could be dealt with later.

But before Travers had been settled comfortably for more than five minutes, there was a tap at the door, and he stirred and opened his eyes. A miracle had indeed happened, for the room was in broad daylight. He gasped—and then knew. The previous night there had been no sleep at all, and the day had been spent in new and bracing air, so as soon as his head was on the pillow he had slept, and there was Palmer coming in with the early morning tea.

"A beautiful morning, sir," Palmer observed. "It seems to me, sir—if I may say so—that we're in for a very warm day."

"Capital," said Travers, reaching for his glasses. A shame was already filling him for the confession he must soon make to Tempest, who would be all impatience to know how the inquiry into miracles had fared.

"The grey suit, sir?" said Palmer.

"Any old suit," said Travers, with an unwonted irritation. And then, ashamed of himself again, "Perhaps it had better be the grey."

"The grey, sir? Very good, sir." He began brushing it and laying it out.

Travers took a gulp at the tea. "And how've you been getting on?"

"Very well indeed, sir," said Palmer. "A very pleasant couple, sir—Mrs. Service especially. Kind-hearted, sir, and very genteel." He gave a queer little clearing of his throat. "But there's something, sir, I think I ought to report. I don't understand it myself, sir, but I have no doubt, sir, that you will—"

"Exactly!" He smiled at the old fellow's windy periods. "What is it, Palmer?"

"It arose out of a question of eyesight, sir. A private conversation between Mrs. Service and myself, by which I mean, sir, that Service wasn't there at the time. She happened to remark, sir, that she had always prided herself on having really good eyesight, but lately she had begun to have doubts, sir—if I may put it that way."

"You may," said Travers facetiously, between the sips at the hot tea.

"There was one particular thing she mentioned that occurred on the Tuesday evening, sir. Mrs. Service was making a quick visit to the bedrooms before dinner, sir, to make sure the staff had left everything in order, and some very little time before the gong went, she was in the last bedroom, sir, which was that one above the drawing-room."

Travers was suddenly all excitement. "Mr. Romney Greeve's room?"

"I believe it was, sir. But what Mrs. Service remarked, sir, was that her eyes began playing her queer tricks. She was looking out at the summerhouse, sir, and it appears she caught sight of that Mr. Greeve, the painter, sir. Then, from how I understood her, she saw him doing all sorts of things, sir. She didn't see him really; it was her eyes playing tricks—if you know what I mean, sir?"

"I know," Travers told him impatiently.

"Well, sir, first she saw this Mr. Romney sitting writing and then, before you could say Jack Robinson, he wasn't writing at all—he was standing up. Then there he was again, sitting writing. Then he disappeared again!"

Travers frowned. "Well, what's wrong with that? How long were the intervals between the movements?"

"That's the very point, sir," said Palmer mysteriously. "According to her, sir, they happened at once! One flash of an eye and he was sitting writing. But he wasn't—if you understand me, sir. He was standing!"

"I see," said Travers, polishing his glasses on his pyjama jacket.

"She asked me not to say anything about it to Service," Palmer went on. "It seems that Service has been insisting for some time that she should wear glasses, sir, and she doesn't wish to." He smiled tolerantly. "Something to do with spoiling her looks, sir, though I must say she's a good-looking woman; handsome, I might say." He picked up the shoes and made for the door, and there stopped. "I should have added, sir, that while Mrs. Service was watching those—er—occurrences, sir, the gong began to sound, and she told me she hurried downstairs at once, because of the dinner, sir."

Travers thought, till the thoughts were a whirlpool. He was still at it when Palmer came back with the shoes. Breakfast found him still at it, and when the meal was over, with a thought of seeing Tempest maybe in his mind, he strolled along the drive to the main road, and smoked his first pipe at the gate. It was there that he had all at once an idea.

That summer-house must be inspected at once—and yet he must not be seen. So he avoided the house and made for the long shrubbery, with the notion of slipping round that far pointed end and so into the summer-house at the side hidden from view—the circuitous way round, in fact, that old Greeve had taken himself and Tempest on the Saturday night.

But as he drew near, voices were heard in the direction of the pond. They came closer, and he knew one voice for Hugh's.

"Breakfast is ready. What about it?"

"Just coming." That was Martin Greeve answering, and with it was Tom Bypass's barking cough. Travers, ducking by the laurels behind the summerhouse, knew what was happening. Martin and Tom had taken a stroll round the garden before the meal, and Hugh had just come from the house to fetch them. Now they were coming back. They had met. They were almost level with himself on the other side of the shrubbery. Then he heard his own name:

MARTIN. Tell him about T.T., Tom.
HUGH. T.T.?
MARTIN. Tom's name for him. Travers the Tec.
HUGH. Tec? . . . Oh, I see. Detective!
MARTIN. That's right. You tell him, Tom.

They had been moving slowly towards the house, and Travers had tiptoed in their wake. Now they halted.

TOM. It was like this. I happened to take a peep out of my door this morning, thinking I heard someone go by, and there was that man of his that T.T. planted in the house. So I shut the door again just as he went into T.T.'s room, and just as I was shutting it, who should come pussy-footing behind but old Service. I had my door shut like a flash, and when I took another decko, what do you think? Service had his ear screwed to the keyhole of T.T.'s door. Back to me, of course, but I could see he was listening like hell.

HUGH. Good heavens!
MARTIN. Extraordinary, wasn't it?

The three moved on again, and Travers with them. The shrubbery now widened and made its own automatic distance, with the voices harder to hear or even distinguish.

". . . had the door shut . . . T.T.'s man came out . . . really amazing . . . Service a canny old . . ."

The voices died away as the three entered the drawing-room. Travers stood for a moment like a man who has had a mortal blow. Service had listened at the key-hole; therefore he knew what the three had guessed—that Palmer had been planted in the house. And why had Service taken the risk of listening at a keyhole? Service—who had told his wife that lies were necessary; Service—for whom Mantlin had not been prepared to

vouch. And what had he heard? Something innocuous enough.
Yet there Travers had a new panic. Innocuous enough, on one
condition. "Something, sir, I ought to report." Those were Palmer's words; the dangerous words, and they had been spoken
long after Palmer had entered the room, when Service's ear was
well in place.

Then Travers smiled, and not only at the remembering of
himself as Travers the Tec. Palmer might be a tale-bearer, but
yet he carried about with him such an impressiveness and vir-
tue that a man who heard the tales themselves could scarcely
believe the evidence of his own ears. No word of warning then
to Palmer. Let him carry on normally, and the virtuous rigidity
and patriarchal benevolence be his own safeguard.

But Mantlin might be spoken to about Service, and as
Travers thought that, he found his feet had brought him to the
pointed end of the shrubbery. A moment and he was in the summer-house for the first time. It was a stone and stucco building,
fifteen feet by ten; with slate roof to match that of the house, a
wide doorway facing the garden, and a narrower one facing the
drawing-room. In the other wall was a window, and supporting
the extended roof in front and at the sides were imitation Gre-
cian pillars.

From the narrower door facing the drawing-room, Travers
glanced up for a quick moment at the windows of the bedroom
from which Mrs. Service's eyes had looked when they played her
what Palmer called strange tricks. The french doors of the drawing-room were open, and though the staged scene had been
shifted, with chalk marks to show where things had stood, he
could still see the end of the screen in its accustomed place.

He turned to the summer-house itself, and its cold stone
floor. A good place to write on a hot day, and a good place to
work. There stood Romney's easel, but no sign of picture, paint-
box or writing materials. Writing—and Travers frowned. Romney had sat in that narrower doorway—or just behind it—facing
the drawing-room. But at approaching dusk the light would be
bad. Back to the main doorway would have been better, where
the full evening light lingered and came from behind his shoul-

der. Therefore, in choosing the other spot for his writing, Romney Greeve had not had that writing in mind. He had planted himself there so that he might be visible to those in the drawing-room, or so that he might have them beneath his own eye.

A brief look round and Travers made his way openly to the house again by the front lawn. The sound of an engine was heard and Polegate came in sight in the office car.

"Where's everybody?" Travers asked him.

"The Chief's seeing about the inquest," Polegate said. "Inspector Carry's doing a job or two, sir, then he's appearing at the inquest too."

But the sight of the sergeant had given Travers yet another idea, and one that queerly fitted in.

"You remember that night trespasser in the grounds here, whom old Greeve had you people in about? The only clue was a steel measuring tape he left behind. No prints were found on it?"

"No, sir." But there had been a quick look, and somehow a suspicious one. And it was followed by the quickest and most complacent of smiles.

Travers smiled too, and knowingly. Never had he looked more cajoling.

"You're sure?"

Polegate hesitated. He had a tremendous admiration for Travers—his shrewdness, his absence of show and his genial courtesy. Moreover, there was about him at the moment something that invited confidences.

"Well, between you and me, sir—"

"Exactly!" said Travers. "Between you and me."

Polegate grinned, and let the whole cat out of the bag.

"Right," said Travers. "Tell you what—I'll drive you down now in my car because I want a word with Mantlin—which is also between you and me. Then I'll come to your office and hear if you've discovered anything. On the way down we'll think of an excuse in case you're found out."

Charles Mantlin was in his office and Travers was shown in. When Mantlin rose to shake hands, one set of fingers still grasped the lapel of his coat, which gave him an air of a man of serious affairs and some concentration.

"Sorry to bother you," Travers began, "but I was just wondering if you would care to give me—confidentially, if you like—a little information." His voice took on a sudden condolence. "Awfully upset, by the way, to hear of the dirty trick old Greeve played you in the matter of that other will."

Mantlin gave a shrug of the shoulders. "I wasn't surprised. I told you the kind of man he was."

"All the same, ten thousand's a bit of a loss—when you've as good as got it in your pocket." An idea came. "I suppose, then, you don't feel sufficiently aggrieved to open your mouth and let out a few secrets about the old boy?"

Mantlin shook his head. He was being far too gloomy about it all, Travers thought. Philosophical but glum, and no rising to the bait of humour.

"What I told you and the Chief Constable was correct," he said. "My father undoubtedly knew a good bit that might have landed the old man in queer street, but he didn't hand it on to me—and there weren't any documents that I've been able to find." He peered up. "Was that what you came to find out?"

"Oh, Lord, no!" said Travers. "All that's your own private affair, my dear fellow. I'm interested in Service." He hesitated artistically. "Certain things have come to my notice—highly incriminatory things—which I can't tell you at the moment; but the moment has come, it seems to me, for you to amplify the reasons you gave—or didn't give—why Service was the only man in the room that night whom you wouldn't speak for."

"Yes," said Mantlin, and screwed up his eyes in thought, while his fingers so tightened on the lapels that Travers wondered if the coat collar would stand the strain. "Yes—in very strict confidence. Even then, mind you, it's only a ridiculous suspicion, as I've since thought. Also my eyes might have been deceived. Still, here's how things seemed to me. Service was doing something curious with his right hand that night, while he was clouting that gong with the left." He waved a hand to forestall Travers's question. "I can't say what it was he did. All I'm doing is thinking back as I did that night; and I say I distinctly have the impression that he was doing something queer with his right hand. If you understand me, what I mean is that he was doing two things at the same time."

"No flash of a gun?"

"Heavens, no! Who could have missed that?"

"Quite," said Travers lamely. "And nothing else suspicious against him—before and after?"

"I think not," said Mantlin slowly. "Motive, of course. He knew he was in for an annuity because the old man had sneered at him about it and sort of held it over his head." He sneered himself. "Just something for the old man to kick round—that's all Service was."

And that, thought Travers, as he drove back to the police-station again, was hardly just. Service might have allowed himself to become a chopping-block for old Greeve's tongue, but he was an efficient servant, and one with obvious responsibilities. Yet it was queer about Service and Mantlin—and himself. Mantlin he distrusted though his every move had been above-board; Service he furtively liked though the butler's actions had been consistently suspicious.

Polegate peeped out from the office door when footsteps were heard, and seemed relieved to find they were those of Ludovic Travers.

"It's all right, sir. Nobody's been in. And here's those prints you wanted."

Travers looked down at them, and nodded.

"Where are those you took at Palings?"

Polegate had them out of his file at once.

"Splendid," said Travers. "Now, compare them with those of—well, try all four cousins."

In a minute Polegate was looking up, mouth agape. "How the devil did you know, sir? They're Romney Greeve's—the painter's!"

"A shot in the dark," Travers told him soberly. "But keep this under your hat till I give the word go." He frowned to himself, then all at once his face lighted up. "I'll do it!"

"Do what, sir?"

"Listen," said Travers, "and I'll tell you." He frowned again. "I don't know. I don't like your running risks. And it'd be the devil of a risk."

Polegate looked disappointed. Travers's face cleared and his own cleared too.

"I'll put it up to you," Travers said. "I want you to steal something—remove it, if you like. You'll certainly stand the faint chance of being blamed for it, and if so you'll have to lie like blazes. I shan't be here to back you up, and if things go wrong and I don't find what I ought to, then I shall be for the high jump too. Now what about it?"

"What about a few details, sir?" Polegate told him. Travers thought for a moment. "Right! Take your own car and go back to Palings. Stop at the house and find out if Romney Greeve is at work in or near the summer-house, painting that picture of his. If he is, and there's no one watching him, then put your car in neutral and let it run quietly backwards downhill along the drive till it gets near the summer-house. Then go to the phone, where I'll call you. And if he *is* painting, I'll arrange to phone from a call-box in the town and ask for him. Your man will fetch him, and as soon as he goes to the house, you nab the picture and have it in the back of your car, and drive off along the London Road. Soon as I've finished phoning, I'll set off the same way and we'll meet a mile past the house. Whoever gets there first waits for the other."

Polegate thought for a minute. "Tell you what, sir. They say you might as well be hanged for a sheep as a lamb. You ring up and say he's wanted at the inquest. Then he'll be right out of the way, and he won't have no reason to lay the blame on me." He still looked a bit anxious. "And if anything happens, you'll square it with the Chief?"

"If anything happens," Travers told him, "I'll start a detective agency myself and take you on the staff."

Polegate grinned. "And when you go past the gate with that big car of yours, sir, don't go sticking your head out. There's a man of ours on duty there."

So Polegate set off. Ten minutes and Travers was ringing him up. Then he drove to a new call-box and got Palings again. Describing himself as the clerk of the court, he asked that a Mr. Romney Greeve should come to the place of inquest forthwith, by the Coroner's instructions.

In just under another ten minutes, Travers was a mile beyond Palings, on the London Road, but Polegate was already waiting. When the road was clear the picture was transferred, and Travers covered it with a rug.

"Easy as pie, sir," Polegate said. "All four of 'em were out there, but the other three had their backs turned, and I was in and out in a jiff. I told the man on the gate that he hadn't seen a thing of me this morning." And he winked.

Travers grinned. "The fun'll start when our friend turns up at the inquest. By the way, is there such a person as the clerk of the court?"

Polegate had never heard of one.

"All the better," said Travers. "Nothing like putting things in to make other things more difficult." He held out his hand, and afterwards wondered why. "Keep a shut mouth and a brazen countenance. Tell Major Tempest you saw me, and how I was called away suddenly to town, and I'll be back some time this evening. Let Palmer know too. And if things turn out as I think they will, you're on a ten-pound note."

In an hour Travers was on the fringe of the outer suburbs. Then came the traffic, and it was an hour later before he drew up the car outside the shop of Julius Lebene, the picture restorers, in James Street, and caught Frank Lebene in the act of going out to lunch.

Travers lugged the picture into the office. "A ticklish job for you," he said. "It's got to be done quickly and most expertly. I even suggest you put two of your best men on it, working from opposite corners. As you see, it's a landscape of sorts—a garden scene with vista, shall we say?—and quite a charming piece of work. I want it removed. Most of it, if not all, has been done since the morning of Wednesday last. Got that?"

Lebene nodded.

"Immediately underneath it," Travers went on, "your men will come across a heavy coating of cadmium or yellow ochre. The artist, if he were asked, would say it was the foundation for his picture, because he wanted—with perfectly good technique—to give it a luminosity. I want all that foundation removed, too, and it was put on only last Tuesday night."

Lebene grimaced. "And what then?"

"Then," said Travers, "we shall see what we shall see."

Lebene nodded again. "I get you. You suspect the foundation was laid on yet another picture, and you want us to expose it." He shook his head. "I doubt if we'll manage it. The paint's all too fresh. But what about the final picture? How long ago was that painted?"

"Bad news for you," Travers told him. "I suspect it wasn't painted more than a few days ago, so it's fresh, too."

Lebene blew out a whistle. "Well, it's your funeral. I don't suppose my men will mind having a shot at it. There's a special kind of stuff of our own that we use when we have to be particularly careful—an emulsified spirit. Turpentine'd be hopeless."

At three o'clock that afternoon, Ludovic Travers sat in an upstairs room watching Lebene's two men at work. He had been there for an hour and a half, and the climax was at hand. As he looked, the picture was nothing but a thin film of yellow, and the men were waiting for it to dry off.

"Any ideas yet?" Travers asked.

"Only what we told you, sir," the foreman said. "There *is* another painting underneath, and we've seen some flesh tints."

Ten minutes, and with eye-glasses affixed, the two were at work again; dabbing dexterously and blotting, dabbing and blotting, and slowly the yellow seemed to go. More than once a spot of paint was added to replace something that had been removed, and then Travers craning over, saw the faint background of the thing for which he had hardly dared hope.

Another ten minutes and the foreman was straightening his back.

"Well, sir, we've made a fine mess of it, but you can see what it is, and the guv'nor reckoned that was all you wanted."

Travers grabbed it in a flash and took it to the window. There on the canvas, smudged and faint and yellowish though it still was, was what would put into Polegate's pocket a ten-pound note.

"A portrait, isn't it, sir?"

"Yes," said Travers, as if it were a Rembrandt. "A self-portrait."

"Do I happen to know the artist, sir?"

"I'm afraid you don't," Travers told him. "This happens to be his own portrait by a gentleman who specializes in miracles!"

CHAPTER XI
TRAVERS EXPLAINS

AT HALF-PAST SIX that evening, Travers was drawing into the police-station yard with the idea of depositing the picture in safe custody before putting in an appearance at Palings. But Tempest, he learned, was in his office, and—without the picture—he sailed gaily in.

Carry was there, and the Major was looking worried, with the reason not hard to seek. For as soon as Travers entered he was told of the day's amazing happenings; at least, Tempest began with a hint at such and then was cut off.

"I know," Travers said. "Romney Greeve has had his picture stolen, and most mysteriously he turned up at the inquest."

Tempest's eyes bulged, then he smiled. "You've seen Polegate."

Travers shook his head. "Lord, no! I stole his picture myself, and I lured him away to the inquest to leave the coast clear."

The soothing processes began. The Major's indignation became remonstrance, and remonstrance petered out in injured dignity, till curiosity got the upper hand as Travers related the afternoon's revelations in Lebene's studio. Carry came in again, bearing the picture, and Polegate was with him.

"Why, it's Romney Greeve!" said Tempest. "It's the very living image of him."

"That's right," said Travers. "And if you'll let me, I'll try to explain not only what he had in his mind, but also those queer vagaries in Mrs. Service's eyesight. You haven't heard about that? Well, I'll tell you."

At last the lecture was ready to begin. Travers had the picture standing on the desk and held a steel measuring tape in his hand.

"First, I call your attention to the fact, which you can check for yourselves, that the side door which looks out from the summer-house towards the drawing-room windows, measures exactly an inch short of three feet, and is five feet two inches high. There's no actual door, and never was. There are twin doors in the front which apparently are kept folded back in the summer, but the side entrance is a kind of convenience and decoration. If you remember, it is flanked by two comic stucco pillars, for instance.

"Now we take this picture. It measures across, as you notice, precisely three feet two inches. In other words it is wider than the doorway, or entrance if you like, and the reason is that it was designed to fit behind the entrance, with an inch and a half against the interior brick-work, which made its real frame and held it and supported it.

"Now you may ask why the picture isn't five feet two and more inches in height, so as to fit the entrance in the same way lengthways. I think we shall see that a minute or two later. First of all, we'll begin to construct a theory.

"Romney Greeve was a camouflage expert in the war, and he knew, therefore, the deceptive values of paint and colour and confused line. If the time was dusk, the eye was more likely still to be led astray, and that was the basis of his method of making himself be in two places at the same time."

"I've got it!" broke in Tempest. "I see now what he did."

Travers shook his head somewhat ruefully. "That's what I thought. The trouble is, the more we know what he did, the less we see any sense or reason behind it. That's what's been worrying me all the way down from town. When I started away I knew that before the night was out you'd have Romney Greeve under lock and key. Now I know you won't."

Tempest shook his head doggedly.

"Let me go on with what I was saying," Travers told him. "It was that Romney Greeve hit upon that idea. I'm dead sure that if inquiries are made at his home, we shall find Romney Greeve was away that night when the nocturnal intruder was seen by the gardener in the summer-house at Palings. I know that it never could possibly have occurred to Sergeant Polegate to connect that event with the finger-prints of the four cousins, but I'm going to ask you to let him make a further very close examination in his office of the measuring tape that was picked up, and try to find some trace of a print to compare with Romney Greeve's."

Polegate departed unblushingly. Travers carried on.

"I say, then, that he came down by motor-coach, hopped off where it passes the entrance to Palings, and slipped into the grounds with a torch to measure that doorway accurately. He was seen, and bolted, but he had his measurements. Then he set to work to paint a self-portrait, in the attitude of writing. He made an excellent job of it, hardened it off as well as he could, rolled it up and had the sections of wood ready to clap together at a moment's notice for a frame. Picture, frame, easel and a certain folding-stool—later cut off the painting—were sent down to Palings in advance, in charge of Service.

"All I can do now is to recall supporting evidence, such as the special demand for a bedroom that overlooked the summer-house; the announcement that he was painting a certain scene in the garden—and he a still-life painter—and that utter rubbish he was talking about writing an article for the *Dilettante*. In fact, he prepared a thoroughly good excuse for being in the summer-house at all, and for writing.

"That brings us to the night before the murder, when he undoubtedly smuggled round the rolled-up picture, fixed the frame of it together, and when it was dusk, tried the effect of the illusion. I'll wager he asked some of the others if they saw him—and undoubtedly they did. But we'll leave all that because it contains a fair amount of conjecture. We'll get on to what the evidence proves unanswerable facts.

"We'll ignore how Romney Greeve was intending to kill his uncle because there'll be enough bother about that later. It might have been to shoot him from the summer-house using the contraption at the tree, or to be at the tree himself and shoot him from there while he was plainly in sight in the summer-house. But what we *know* is this. As dusk fell, he checked the time and knew he had a few minutes before the gong would go. He could see people in the drawing-room, and the only one he couldn't be sure of was Mantlin. But he flashed up in the side entrance that picture of himself writing, and squinted round the main entrance to see if Mantlin was near enough to be a danger.

"The time went on and zero hour was very close. Was Romney in the summer-house still, holding a string to pull a trigger? Was he in the shrubbery, ready to fire from there? I don't know, but I do know this. He heard Mantlin or caught sight of him. If Mantlin went in the summer-house and insisted on seeing the progress of the painting, the game was up. So he whipped away the picture and called to Mantlin to know what the time was. Mantlin, then at the far side of the lawn by the other twin doors, saw him sitting there writing and told him. He also made as if to turn to go that way, and immediately Romney told him not to come in as he was busy."

Polegate came back, and never batted an eyelid while he announced with hushed voice his discovery.

"You're right, sir. I found two prints and managed to bring them up."

"Splendid!" said Travers. "And now where'd we got to? Oh, yes; to where Romney told Mantlin to keep out, as he was busy. And he was busy. He was in a minor panic, so he whipped the picture away. He turned it back to front, and, working like blazes, smothered it with yellow paint, which he could justly claim was a foundation for the landscape. Then he stood it aside and heard the gong actually going. In the meanwhile, Mrs. Service had been gazing out from the bedroom window at the mysterious appearances of Romney Greeve—now sitting writing, disappearing into thin air, appearing again, and so on.

"In spite of his panic, did he fire the shot? Again I don't know, but I do know this. He wanted badly to get that picture up in his own room again, so he sneaked out. He was caught, but he was allowed to take the picture away. In his bedroom he cut down the picture and frame to its present size and the following morning, bold as brass, began painting—though he had always announced that it was an *evening* picture with certain *evening* effects he was so keen on."

"Why did he cut it down, sir?" Carry asked.

"For two reasons," Travers told him. "Firstly so that it should be no longer the size of the entrance, or even the shape, and he took good care to camouflage that by painting his landscape the breadth-way and not the length. The other reason was that to paint a landscape of the size of five feet odd by three feet odd would have been absurd. It wouldn't have been a picture but a monstrosity. Even the size he reduced it to was pretty huge, as you see. And, by the way, I'm positive if you question the sergeant who saw the picture taken away, he'll state that it was much larger than this, though I doubt if he'd be able to judge whether or not it was the exact size of the entrance."

"Well, that's good work," said Tempest. "It's damn good work. But where are we?"

"If you'll pardon me, sir," said Carry, "you were saying you were worried about certain things on your way down to-night. May I ask what they were?"

"By all means." His fingers fumbled at his glasses. "In the first place, we do all admit, don't we, that Romney wouldn't have gone the length of shooting his uncle unless his plans were watertight and complete. Therefore, if he did shoot him, there was no need for him to have left such a loose end as made him run the enormous risk of creeping out of a window—in defiance of police orders—and getting hold of that picture. Therefore this seems to me to be incontrovertible fact. *Romney Greeve did not kill his uncle.* I say he was having yet another rehearsal, and was going to do the job the following night, *when that contraption was completed.* In the state in which we saw it, that contraption was incomplete. Not one of us could suggest any possible way in which we could have efficiently used it. But the great point is this. Romney Greeve was startled to death when he came into the room and found someone else had killed his uncle. He got out of it as soon as he could, and all he had time for was to get rid of his gun, which he threw in the pond. Later on he went back for the picture."

"That seems logical enough to me," Tempest said. "But about the gun. Which gun was it he threw in the pond? The rifle or the little revolver?"

"Undoubtedly the rifle," Travers said. "If you examine that summer-house, you'll see there's a ledge under the roof, just beneath the slates, where you could hide anything. But I say it was the rifle he threw away, because the revolver wouldn't have needed an elaborate contraption. The rifle would, if the firer was to control it from elsewhere. Which brings us to the thing that disturbed me most. If Romney Greeve intended to kill his uncle with the rifle, he certainly never did so, for we know he was killed by a very heavy revolver bullet."

"Yes," said Tempest, and rubbed his chin. Then he looked up. "But why shouldn't he have had both rifle and the gun that did the trick? Why shouldn't the rifle have been a blind?"

Travers shook his head. "Now you're getting too involved for me." His face suddenly cleared. "But there's one thing I have thought of. Let me put it to you. I say that Romney asked for that one particular bedroom for one vital reason. From that window he couldn't be overlooked."

"But he was overlooked!" said Tempest. "Didn't Mrs. Service see the summer-house plainly that evening, when she thought her eyes were playing her tricks?"

Travers smiled. "That end doesn't matter. It was the morning Romney Greeve was worrying about. If you wish, I'll make it my business to run across Mrs. Service some time to-morrow, and see if she can bear me out that he was up very early that Tuesday morning. Perhaps his shoes were wet with the dew and one of the staff noticed it. But I do put it to you that he got up at dawn, knowing that then he could fix up that contraption without being overlooked." Then his face positively beamed. "I believe I can prove it! What about the books?"

"The books?"

"Yes. Those two volumes of the 'Decline and Fall'? The two volumes that were in their places on the Monday when Service shut up the house for the night, and weren't there the next morning? Why shouldn't this have happened? I'll go further and say it must have happened. Romney Greeve was up as soon as it was even half light, and came out of the house through the drawing-room, opening the french doors. In the shrubbery he found the kind of place he had in mind, or he may have found it that other night when he came down specially to measure the summer-house entrance. He made the hole in the laurels and sighted over the top of the chair he'd already placed where his uncle's head should be. Then he took a shot with the rifle so as to know where to make the gun secure to his contraption. It was a sporting gun, mind you. All it'd make is a crack. You know that, Major, and I know it, for my brother-in-law has got one almost like it. Anybody upstairs who happened to be awake would hear a crack—and no more. No reverberations, mind you—only a crack; and that person would wait for another sound, and when there wasn't one he'd know he'd been mistaken. And that sighting bullet went into the books, as we know."

Tempest was shaking his head. "An amazingly risky thing to do."

"Is Romney Greeve a sportsman who understands rifles?" Travers challenged him. "Is he a practical man? Look at his face on that picture, and what do you see? An artist. A man eminently unpractical in most of the things that are simple to you and me. He was feeling his way over that murder. He'd forgotten what'd happen to the bullet, or maybe he felt the trigger and it went off before he was aware. But whatever made him fire, he had to get rid of those books. The bullet he got out easily enough, or maybe it dropped out where it had just penetrated the second book; so he threw it away, and tied a stone round the books and threw them into the pond. Then he began to make his contraption, and stopped when he thought the household would be on the move."

"Where'd he get the rifle?" asked Polegate.

"Anywhere," Travers told him. "It was a sporting gun. He could walk into a shop and buy it."

"And suppose anybody on the staff came down and caught him with those drawing-room doors open?" asked Carry.

Travers smiled. "Well, suppose anyone did? Hasn't a guest the right to get up early if he likes? Hasn't he the right to go through the drawing-room and throw doors open or leave them open? How could he lay himself open to suspicion in doing that? Also he could always have claimed that he had the same light for his picture at dawn as he had at sunset—the same quality light, that is. He'd got up to paint."

Tempest was forced to laugh. "Well, that demolishes you all right, Carry."

"I don't mind that, sir," Carry told him. "The only sort of argument that's any good in our game is the one that can stand argument."

"Stout fellow," said Travers. "And before I return a vote of thanks, may I point out that in any murder a man's not open to a charge till it's committed. He can make any amount of preparation—as Romney Greeve did—and run no risk till the actual murder's done; always provided he can explain away any actions that might possibly lay him open to a charge of *attempted* murder. And just one other thing. I do call your attention to the excellence of the site from Romney's point of view. As I know well enough, it's easy to be in and out of that summer-house and no one a penny the wiser. All you have to do is slip out of window opening on the far side and into the shrubbery at the thin end."

For another hour the arguments went on, till the issue was boiled down to one main question. Should or should not Romney Greeve be asked to make a statement? Travers was for delay and Tempest for action. Yet even Travers saw that the value of Romney Greeve lay not only in his possible elimination from the list of suspects, but also in what, under pressure and inadvertently, he might let fall. So a compromise was reached. The following afternoon, when the other three were at the funeral, Romney should remain behind and be put on the grill. In the meanwhile someone might have a new brainwave, and there would be the line of attack to be decided on.

Travers stretched his long legs. "And how've you spent your weary day?" he asked Tempest facetiously.

"One damn thing after another," Tempest said. "We've got the body up to the house, by the way, and it's in the morning-room in case you should go sleep-walking to-night. Thought it would avoid publicity if the funeral started from the house. Two-thirty at the cemetery, it is. Service is going, to represent the staff. Mrs. S. doesn't want to."

"Which reminds me," said Travers. "In view of that pussy-footing of his this morning, and other things we've had in mind, don't you think it would be a sound idea to get his regimental history?"

"You're too late," Tempest told him. "I've already got it in hand. And the four cousins' too. I did them the same time as I did Tom Bypass's. I got the details from Mantlin." Then he smiled dryly. "So as not to be invidious, I'm getting Mantlin's as well."

"Bendline'll be over to-morrow," Travers reminded him. "Why not ask him, in the strictest of confidences, to explain why he made that grimace when you mentioned Mantlin's name?"

Tempest nodded. "Perhaps we might." Then the same dry smile. "But he didn't commit the murder. He's not a miracle-worker."

"You never know," said Travers genially.

So Travers, somewhat tired and decidedly hungry, drove back to Palings. Palmer was still up and was all concern. The four cousins had gone early to bed, but Travers's meal was brought as usual to the comparative privacy of the drawing-room. Service lent a hand in bringing it in.

"Something I ought to report to you, sir," Palmer said, as soon as the two were alone.

"Then stay here and wait at table," Travers told him. "And don't even let yourself hear yourself speak."

Palmer's story was this. During the morning he happened to be in the butler's parlour with the two Services, when the man in charge of the telephone popped his head in and asked for news of Romney Greeve. Service said he was at the summer-house, whereupon the man said he'd fetch him, and would Service in the meanwhile keep an ear cocked in case anyone called. But no sooner had the man gone than Service hopped up. Palmer went too, with Travers's bedroom in mind, but when he reached the landing he heard a voice, and looking back cautiously round the stairs, he saw Service surreptitiously using the phone. As his back was turned, Palmer made no bones about coming nearer.

"He was crouched over the phone, sir, if I may put it that way, and he was talking to someone called Ethel."

"Ethel!" Travers nearly shot off his seat.

"Ethel, sir. I distinctly heard him say, 'You're to stay where you are, Ethel,' and 'No one's ever likely to know, Ethel.'"

"And then?"

"He had the phone back, sir, and was standing looking perfectly normal when the man came back, sir—so to speak."

"And he didn't see you? Service, I mean."

Palmer shook his head. "He had his back to me all the time, sir."

Travers finished his meal at the double, called up Tempest and found him still in his office, then got the Rolls out from the coach-house again and drove to the town.

Tempest was waiting for him like a man who expects something sensational and too dangerous to trust to the phone, but when Travers told him the news, he too almost leapt from his seat.

"Ethel? You're sure he said 'Ethel'?"

"Palmer was dead sure," Travers told him.

Tempest nodded. "That's the best thing we've got hold of yet." Then he picked up a paper and dramatically flourished it. "This just came in about our friend Service, too. Headquarters records of his regiment say that no man of his name served in any of their battalions during the war!"

CHAPTER XII
WHITE ROSES

TRAVERS AWOKE that Friday morning with the overnight thoughts of Service in his mind. That information which had promised so well had given extremely limited results, for the call that Service had made on the automatic dial had simply registered itself as a local one, and Telephones could give no receiving number. But the possible search for Ethel Greeve had narrowed down. At the moment of the butler's call, she had been somewhere in the town. And if Palmer had heard aright. Service had appealed to her to stay where she was. So what Tempest had determined was to send Service to the town on the Friday morning and have him discreetly followed. The excuse would be the fetching and selecting of a funeral wreath, which would be deposited anonymously on behalf of the police.

There had been an argument too, about the information imparted by Mantlin. In Service's favour was one thing only: that it was extremely difficult to imagine him firing a shot from a heavy gun with sufficient steadiness of hand and dexterity to hit a possibly moving target. Somehow Service and revolvers didn't match, as Travers put it. As well imagine an archbishop climbing a greasy pole.

But against the butler were the facts that Mantlin's evidence had hitherto been unsuspect; and that Service was nearest to the gong and where its noise was loudest. And the occasion was from his point of view very apt for murder. If Service had killed Greeve at any other time but that birthday period, he himself would have been the main suspect, however shrewd his planning. As it was, the house was filled with suspects, with—as he well knew—the best of motives for the killing.

It was barely half-past seven when Travers made his way out by the front door. The weather was holding good, and as he sniffed the air it came to him that he would walk through to the far confines of the garden to see that view which Charles Mantlin had so admired. But as he came round the summer-house to the lawn, he caught sight of Hugh Bypass on a seat beyond the rhododendrons. Travers gave him a good morning. Hugh made room for him on the seat.

"Well, I suppose we shall soon be seeing the last of you?" Travers remarked with a nice mixture of geniality and regret.

"You think we'll be allowed to go?" Hugh asked anxiously.

"I imagine so," Travers told him. "Mind you, I'm not the authorities. I'm merely a hanger-on."

Then Travers remembered something else about Service— that slight deafness he had assumed when he had been asked the name of his regiment. The brief delay had given him time to think of a regiment other than that to which he had belonged; so yet again he had something to conceal.

"Service will find it a bit of a wrench, leaving here after all this time?" Travers remarked. "About thirteen years, isn't it?"

Hugh thought back, and agreed.

"Where'd he come from?" Travers asked. "I mean, it looks to me as if he was in some good houses in his time. Your uncle was lucky to get him."

Hugh screwed up his eyes in thought. A few seconds' desperate cogitation and all he could recall was that the cousins— himself included—had come down one year for their visit and found Service installed. Before that, he said, the staff had all been women.

"Pity he's deaf," said Travers casually.

"Deaf?" said Hugh. "What made you think that? He has remarkably good hearing."

And then he said something that made Travers somewhat blush, thinking as he had been that one so guileless as Hugh Bypass would never gather the point of the delicate questioning.

"I do hope, Mr. Travers, that the police are not connecting Service in any way with what's happened here. I have a very high opinion of him—and his wife too." He gave a quick, appraising look. "I wonder if I might tell you something, strictly between ourselves? It's nothing to do with this terrible affair."

So he told Travers about that visit of his to his uncle, and how the butler, on behalf of himself and his wife, had offered their poor help.

"They're two honest, genuine people, Mr. Travers. Only once a year we come down here, but we've got to know them and they us. We ask after them, and they remember our children and inquire how they're doing." He shook his head determinedly. "You don't tell me that people like that had anything to do with murder."

Travers had a score of arguments to off-set Hugh Bypass's personal opinions, but it was farthest from his interests to take the line of demolition. So he mildly agreed, and then Martin Greeve was seen coming across the lawn from the house. He gave Travers a most courteous good morning, but his news was for Hugh.

"I've just seen Tom," he said. "He's feeling none too well this morning, and I think it'd be madness for him to go to the funeral."

Travers left them talking and went back to the house. The sight of the plain-clothes man at the telephone brought something to his mind. Towards the end of the morning, he had learned from Palmer, it was Mrs. Service's custom to inspect the bedrooms. As soon, therefore, as the plain-clothes man, from his point of vantage near the stairs, saw her go up, would he let Mr. Travers know?

And as Travers spoke to him, his eyes lifted to the huge, convex mirror that hung on the wall above the telephone, and he profited by his nearness to give it a closer look.

"I'll wager that's worth a bit of money, sir?" the man said.

Travers shook his head. "That's what I thought when I first caught sight of it. But it isn't old—I can see that now. A very good reproduction, though."

"Just shows you how you can be taken in, sir."

"You're right," said Travers facetiously. "Honest men like you and me don't stand a dog's chance these days." Then, though the real point of the quip had not yet come, he suddenly broke off. His eye, regarding the mirror no longer as a possible thing of value, saw it as a mirror in the corner of which appeared all at once the figure of Service descending the stairs. So Travers moved unobtrusively away, and it was not till later that he knew how much he had missed.

Tempest was along soon after breakfast, to fix up the butler's trip to town and arrange for the shadowing. One piece of news he brought with him. The white-handled revolver had been got out of pawn. It was French, as Tom Bypass had stated, but of different make and bore from the one recovered from the pond. Moreover, both revolvers had been shown to the landlady, who, after some deliberation, had picked on the pawned one as the one she had seen in Mr. Bypass's drawer. In other words, so admirable a witness would she make for the defence, that that line of attack was definitely closed.

But though the telephone that morning was left on two or three occasions artistically deserted, there was no repetition of the butler's surreptitious attempt to use it. Maybe, as Travers said, in vain was the net spread in the sight of the bird, but there was an encouraging sign when Service was about to set off for town. There were one or two things he would like to see to while he was there, he said, concerning the catering arrangements for the house.

"Whatever you think necessary," Tempest told him; and elatedly to Travers when he had gone, "We've got him! He's planning to get into communication with her, for a fiver."

Travers hoped he might be right. Then Tempest left to await results at the other end, and inside five minutes Travers was being warned that Mrs. Service had gone upstairs. So he made his way up to his room and was lucky enough to find the housekeeper on the top landing, where the window overlooked the garden. She gave him a little bow. It was courteous, and deferential even, but there was in it something vaguely unfriendly. Travers laid himself out to be his most seductive best.

"I'm afraid I've got an apology to make, Mrs. Service," he said. "I've been meaning to tell you how sorry I am for all the bother I'm making for you in the house."

"You're no bother, sir," she told him gently.

"Well, I'm glad you take it that way," he said. "And I hope Palmer's no bother either."

She smiled then. "Mr. Palmer's very nice in the house, sir. It does us good to have a little company."

"Perhaps it does." He hunted for more words. "It's a lovely old-fashioned garden you have here."

Her eyes followed his own through the window. "I like old-fashioned things, sir."

"And old-fashioned ways?"

"Yes," she said, "and old-fashioned ways. I think there's nothing like them, sir."

"I don't know that you're not right," he told her gravely. "I know I like the times when I was a boy—not that I don't like these too."

She smiled quietly again. "You're only a boy now, sir—if you don't mind me saying so."

He laughed. "I think Palmer might tell you different." Then his face straightened. "Still, perhaps I am, in some ways. But you, Mrs. Service; you're going to feel it, leaving here after all these years?"

"Yes, sir, I am."

"You've lost a good master."

She nodded. "Yes, sir; he was a good master to me. No one could have wished for a better."

"It must have been a great shock to you?"

She hesitated queerly. "Yes, sir, it was—and yet it wasn't. You see, sir, I knew."

Travers almost bolted out of his five wits. "You knew!"

"Yes, sir—through the tea-leaves."

He stared blankly for a moment, then was conquering the overwhelming desire to laugh.

"The tea-leaves?"

"Yes, sir. There was a death in the cup, and I knew it was his."

Travers nodded gravely. "You can tell fortunes by tea-leaves?"

She thought for a moment. "Yes, sir, I think I can. More than once I've had proof of it."

Travers nodded again. "It's a gift, I expect. I had a nurse, I remember, who always believed in *Old Moore's Almanac*."

"It's a funny thing, sir, but so do I. I've proved it true a dozen times, sir."

"Have you really?" He let the smile fade from his face. "I wish I could find something in the teacup. Something that would tell us what we want to know."

She was suddenly biting her lip. "You mean . . . who did it, sir?"

"Yes," said Travers. "That's something that has to be done. The law's a bigger thing than you and me."

She made a step forward, hesitated, then her eyes rose pleadingly to his. There was a quick glance back along the deserted corridor.

"May I say something to you, sir?"

"By all means," Travers told her gravely.

"You don't think anyone in this house would do such a thing? You don't think any of his nephews would have killed Mr. Greeve?"

Travers frowned, at a loss for words.

"I'm sure none of them had anything to do with it, sir. Even the little I know of them tells me that."

Travers patted her arm. "Of course they didn't. And it's nice to hear you standing up for them like that."

He was wondering what else he might say to bring the conversation round to Romney Greeve, but all at once she was bestirring herself.

"I beg your pardon, sir, for keeping you here like this. I'll be going now. There's a lot to do."

And before Travers could devise words to keep her there, she had moved off along the corridor. And as he still smiled to himself at her old-fashioned dignity and the old-fashioned persistence of her quaint beliefs, a door opened along the corridor and Tom Bypass came out. Travers waited for him.

"Sorry to hear you weren't feeling any too well. How are you now? Any better?"

"Just a bit," Tom told him. "It's up and down with people like me."

"A sea voyage would put you on your feet," said Travers.

He shook his head. "I doubt it. But I'm trying it though, as soon as you people let me get away." He smiled ironically. "And that won't be yet."

"Why not?"

"Well, you seem to have an idea that I'm not the plain and honest fellow I really am."

Travers shook his head reprovingly. "Statements like that, my dear fellow, can only spring from a guilty conscience. The law is never prejudiced." He smiled. "All the same, I have a pretty shrewd notion—strictly between ourselves—that you know who did it."

"You flatter me." His lip drooped. "But why?"

"Irony," said Travers, "has always a basis of superiority. You have suddenly decided to cultivate a certain cynicism—and it doesn't fit you. Therefore you are being superior because you know as well as anybody that you can never be—well, found guilty of murder."

The other's eyes momentarily narrowed, then he smiled. "You're a good fellow, I believe, T.T.—sorry. You didn't know that we'd nicknamed you T.T.?"

"Lord, yes!" Travers told him. "Even a boob like myself soon found that out. But you were saying—?"

"Was I?" He frowned. "Oh, yes. Guilty of murder we were mentioning. Perhaps you were right. After all, you can't prove a man guilty of what he hasn't done."

"Now you're disappointing me," Travers told him. "You're not being ironical in the least. All the same, people have been hanged for what they've never done." His fingers went to his glasses. "And you *could* have committed that murder easily enough."

Tom Bypass stared. His eyes narrowed again.

"How?"

Travers smiled. "That, if you look at it properly, is a hopelessly illogical question. If you committed the murder, you know the answer; if you didn't—well, it remains mere conjecture."

"We're both blethering," Bypass told him. "You going down? It's a pity to be indoors a day like this."

They walked together through the drawing-room and Travers turned back at the door. Tom Bypass gave him a look that was definitely and amusedly ironical.

"Still don't feel like telling me how I did it?"

Travers shook his head.

"Or when you first found it out?"

"I'll tell you that," said Travers. "I first had a shrewd idea of how you could have done it when you were in bed."

He looked puzzled. "Last night?"

Travers shook his head. "No, this morning." He was turning away with a smile and a nod, then turned back again for a last thought. "And the funny thing is, it was only five minutes ago that I realized it."

Tempest came back in none too good a humour, and Service was with him. The butler was carrying two bunches of flowers—a larger one of pink roses and a smaller one of white.

"I happened to be coming through the gate as Service got off the bus," the Major said, "so I gave him a short lift. What do you think of the flowers?"

"Not those, sir," Service said, as Travers fingered the white roses. "Those are just a small tribute from Mrs. Service and myself, sir." He seemed rather nervous about it all. "I hope you gentlemen don't think we're taking a liberty."

"I think it's amazingly kind of you," Travers told him, and promptly admired both sets of roses, and particularly the white—apparently Mrs. Service's selection.

Tempest motioned Travers into the drawing-room as soon as the butler had gone.

"Amazing thing, but he didn't do anything suspicious down in town. We had two men sitting on his tail, and all he did was to go to the florists, and a confectioner's and a grocer's."

"No phones he could have got at in the shops?"

"If there were he couldn't have used them," Tempest said. "A man was at his elbow all the time. What do you think? Shall we give him some more rope, or have him on the grill?"

Travers favoured delay; and maybe Romney Greeve would let something fall that afternoon. Then Tempest's face suddenly brightened.

"A confidential chit came through about Tom Bypass just as I was leaving." He peeped out to where Tom himself sat in a deck-chair in the sun. "He was one of the best shots with a revolver his regiment ever knew. But for his health he'd have been in that team of six that were sent to the States for some competition or other soon after the war."

There seemed a certain satisfaction in the way Travers was nodding.

"You've found out something?" Tempest challenged him.

Travers shook his head. "After the fiasco of that picture yesterday, I'll own up to nothing till it's reinforced."

"But you have found out something?"

"I don't know." He shook his head again, then he smiled. "What I'm going to do between now and this afternoon is to sit down and try and find out whether you committed that murder yourself."

Tempest looked at him open-mouthed.

"Yes," Travers went on. "And if I find a score of good reasons, from personal idiosyncrasies and suspicious things you may have let fall, then I'll know I've lost my sense of proportion altogether, and I'll throw my hand in." He blinked for a bit as he polished his glasses. "Every man-jack who was in this house that night has been thrusting clues on us. Everyone has a motive—and yet only one fired the shot."

"Mantlin's done nothing suspicious," Tempest said. "Neither has Hugh Bypass."

Travers shook his head. "Mantlin stood in the same place two nights running, and each night asked a question."

"But everybody was in the same place on the Monday night as he was on the Tuesday," Tempest reminded him.

"I know that. That's what's driving me insane. And there was Hugh Bypass. Didn't he bolt upstairs at the first mention of the police?"

Tempest shook his head. "A mild, inoffensive little man like that? You're barking up the wrong tree."

"Exactly," Travers told him. "But what if I told you I'd got something else against him? Something concerning himself and his brother? Something that's been right under our noses all the time, and"—he smiled—"something that may turn out to be perfectly innocuous."

"Well, what is it?"

"I won't tell you," Travers told him bluntly; "at least not yet. But when we've finished with Romney Greeve, we'll do an experiment if you like. After that there may be some cards to lay on the table."

"It's up to you," Tempest told him. "But who's the experiment on?"

"On Hugh Bypass," said Travers. "And just because he happens to be a mild, inoffensive little man."

Just before lunch was due, Travers came to the hall; that is to say he was opening the door from the drawing-room when he caught sight of Mrs. Service coming from the morning-room. She was giving a last dab to her eyes, and with no wish to intrude on her tears, he drew back. But when she had gone it came to him that he himself had not seen the last of Hubert Greeve.

As he closed the door of the morning-room behind him, he felt at once the sweet oppression of the flowers. There they lay about the coffin: a mass of lilies from Hugh Greeve; wreaths from the staff, indoor and out; a wreath of deep red roses from Romney Greeve; white carnations from Tom Bypass, and a wreath of smaller lilies from Martin Greeve. Travers kept back his own ironies in the presence of that coffined death, and wondered if the four cousins were so sure of some inheritance that they had been so unsparing of tributes.

That anonymous bunch of pink roses had been spread to a fan, and lay flat on the coffin itself. At the coffin head lay the tribute of the Services. Travers read the words on the white envelope that was tied about the stems with narrow black ribbon:

With Respectful Sympathy,
from J. and A. Service.

And it was as he stooped to see if those white roses had smell, that he noticed something peculiar. When he had seen them in the hall and had touched them, he had pricked his finger on a thorn. Now, as he looked more closely, he saw that from their stems every thorn had been neatly removed. But even as he became aware of it, he was shaking his head like a man who rouses himself from sleep or delusions. There it was again! The very thing he had laughed about to Tempest! Clues everywhere, or the delusions of somebody obsessed who thought he saw them.

For there was a perfectly good reason why one so kindly and thoughtful and old-fashioned as Alice Service should have removed those thorns. She too may have pricked her finger when she formed them into the spray and tied the ribbon about them, so it had been in her mind that whoever else handled them at the graveside should run no risk. And in any case, Travers determined that were the reason right or absurd, it should bother him little. Whatever else his eye met or his ear overheard, he would ignore. Clues, clues—and no rhyme or reason. To blazes with clues; long live logic. And yet it had been very queer, that business of Hugh Bypass!

CHAPTER XIII
ALL ABOUT MONEY

THE SCENT of flowers still hung heavily in the morning-room while the grilling of Romney Greeve went on. Polegate was at the funeral, but Carry was there, and a stenographer sat in the far corner; and from the first moment he entered the room, the suspect must have known that something ominous was in the air. Then Tempest gave his official warnings and invitations, and with his notes in hand began the series of suggestions.

At first Romney Greeve aped a kind of mental deafness, as if his ears refused to credit the astounding things with which the law was charging him. Once only did he interrupt.

"I put it to you," Tempest had said, "that in order to create an atmosphere after the murder, to throw the police off the scent in fact, and make them suspect some outside man, you invented a fictitious person called the husband of your Aunt Ethel, and then in his name wrote a threatening letter. You didn't know—"

Romney protested strongly, and somehow the protestations carried conviction.

"I'll swear on anything you like that until I met my brother and my cousins on the way down here last Monday, I hadn't the vaguest suspicion that my Aunt Ethel was still alive. I hadn't thought about her for years. I tell you it's preposterous. I never wrote any such letter."

Tempest proceeded, fact following fact with such unanswerable logic that Romney shuffled more than once in his seat. And then suddenly a subtle change came over him. He stirred indeed in his chair, but like a man who settled comfortably to it with an easy mind. The mental deafness went and he seemed to be taking a fatherly interest in the astounding things of which Tempest was accusing him. Once or twice he smiled, and so obvious was his ease and so curious the change in him, that Travers began to feel a disquiet, and when he caught Carry's eye, even the inspector gave a raising of the eyebrows.

The long accusation finished, and Tempest laid aside the notes.

"Now, Mr. Greeve," he said, "I take it you're prepared to sign a statement to the effect of what we've put to you? You seem to have had no complaints."

"No," he said. "I haven't any complaints. But I take it I'm allowed to make my own statement?"

"By all means," Tempest told him. "Make the statement and then put your name to it when it's read over to you."

He bowed courteously. A little smile, beneath which there was still some remnant of uneasiness, hung about his lips.

"I don't know that I disagree with anything you've said, except that thing you've called a contraption. That never was meant to be serious. It was merely something to mislead everybody." He smiled more openly. "Still, I'm beginning at the wrong place. You've got the whole thing wrong. I never had the least intention of killing my uncle, or anyone else—not in earnest!"

Cold eyes confronted him. The smile grew less warm and confidential.

"I won't even admit that I've done anything foolish. How was I to know anyone was going to kill my uncle?" He leaned forward, spreading his hands. "Let me ask you to do one thing—to be absolutely unbiased and try to imagine my uncle never was killed. Suppose you have me here and now to ask me about—well, certain suspicious happenings that have come to your notice, that might even look like attempted murder. If you'll do that, you'll see what a mistake you've made."

"Carry on," Tempest told him grimly.

"Well, you see, the whole idea in my mind was the writing of a detective novel. I was hard up. I don't conceal the fact, and there's no disgrace in it. So I thought I'd have a shot at it, especially as I know a man who could have placed it for me. And I'll own up I had my uncle in mind. I sort of sat down and thought, and he was the only man I could think of who would fit the case of the man to be murdered." He leaned forward again. "You see, it was personal experience I wanted. You do agree, don't you, that the only way a raw amateur like me could write a detective story would be to write about people and places he knew?"

"Carry on," said Tempest curtly.

"Well, whether you believe it or not, that's what was in my mind. I said I'd pretend it was my uncle who was being murdered, and it should naturally take place down here. I admit I came down here that night and measured up the door, and it was my measuring tape that was left behind. I painted the portrait and I did everything you say. The little rifle I'd had for some years, and I was pretty sure it'd serve my purpose. All I intended to do in my book was to shoot from the summer-house, while everybody knew—from the picture, of course—that I was writing that article I'd been talking about. Then I had the idea of making that contraption in the tree, so that the police—the police in my book, of course—should be misled.

"I didn't shoot deliberately at those books. As I was making the fake contraption, I suddenly wondered if I couldn't improve my book by reversing everything and really shooting from the shrubbery after all. That was why I sighted the gun, and then it went off before I knew." He blew out a little breath. "I tell you I was scared stiff when that happened."

"Carry on," said Tempest, and nodded.

"There's nothing else to say," he said, "except that what you found out was right. Only, I do ask you to think of what I felt when I came into the room that night and found someone had really murdered him." He shook his head as if still bewildered by the mere recollection. "That was why I went out with the others and threw the rifle into the pond—and why I had to get out later and make sure I'd disguised the portrait."

"And that's all?"

"Yes," he said. "I think that's all."

"I see," said Tempest. "And all those things you did were what authors call, I believe, the acquisition of local colour."

"Exactly! You see, if I did everything myself, it'd be easy as anything to write it down afterwards in book form."

"And instead of letting your imagination have the slightest rein, you went to extraordinary lengths to get what I might call this verisimilitude."

Romney spread his hands again. "That's something I should have mentioned. I had the idea that it might help the book if I were in a position to counter any criticism by saying that the whole thing had been actually done—so to speak."

Tempest nodded. "And you were very hard-up at the time. And in spite of it, you spent a considerable sum of money in coming down from Essex to here, merely in order to get the measurements of a doorway, when a confidential letter to Service would have served the same purpose."

He gave a shrug of the shoulders. "I'm sorry. If you won't believe me, you won't. But I will say this for myself. Money has never really worried me as it should have done." He smiled ruefully. "If I have a pound in my pocket, Lord knows what I'm likely to spend it on. Also, you see, I couldn't have come down here openly and taken the measurements—not in view of the fact that I was due down in a week's time. Let alone that my uncle wouldn't have welcomed me."

Nobody had any questions to ask, and Tempest said his own final words.

"I make no comment whatever on what you've told us, Mr. Greeve. All I ask you is whether you have anything further to add in support of your statement before it's read over to you."

He frowned, then smiled. "Well, there is just one thing. Very fortunate I remembered it. If you like you can prove for yourselves the truth of what I say. All you've got to do is send a man at once with a note from me to my wife, and she'll give him all of that detective story I've written up to the present." Again he smiled ruefully. "I'm afraid it isn't much; just an account of imaginary circumstances, and how the man came down and measured the doorway. Oh, yes, and how he got the rifle and painted the self-portrait."

Sensation in court was a dull description for what happened in various minds when he so casually announced all that. Then Travers leaned over to him.

"You were writing your story from what angle then?"

He thought for a moment, then his face cleared. "Oh, I see. Of course. Why, from the angle of the murderer. I was letting the reader into the whole mechanism, so to speak, and showing how the police afterwards put clue to clue and found things out."

"You'll write that note for your wife?" Tempest asked.

"Why, certainly," he said. "Or, if you like, you can get a phone message through. There's a neighbour of ours . . ."

* * * * *

The door closed on him, and Tempest let out a whistle.

"Talk about spiking our guns! What'd you think of it? Ever hear anything so plausible?"

"A pack of lies from beginning to end!" said Carry contemptuously. "All that about writing a book and letting us see how much he'd written! He'd got all that worked out beforehand, sir. He thought that'd give him an alibi."

"Devilish ingenious though," said Travers.

"You don't believe it?"

"I don't know at the moment just what I do believe," Travers told him frankly. "I can't for the life of me imagine a man going to the lengths he did to get verisimilitude. What I think perhaps is, that he suspected what we knew as soon as he came in the room here. He pretended to be nonplussed at first, hence the village-idiot attitude. Then he assumed that look of sympathy with us—poor blind fools that we were."

"Well, you heard me warn him," Tempest told the room. "If he lets out a word I'll hold him on some pretext or other."

"All the same," said Travers, "there's just one little thing that's emerged. Assume, as we're reasonably entitled to do, that the detective novel business was all part of the scheme, and he really intended to kill his uncle by firing from the summer-house. That rifle would have been quite adequate, you remember, even from there. Suppose all that, and we're up against two things. The fact remains that he *didn't* kill his uncle. The other fact is that even if he'd had that gun trained on his uncle that night and was ready to fire the shot, he couldn't have done it."

"And why not?"

"Because of Mantlin. Mantlin was masking his view all the time. If you like, we'll go along and prove it."

There was no sign of Romney Greeve or Tom Bypass, and the proving was done. Carry sat in the chair for Hubert Greeve, Travers stood at the end of the screen for Mantlin, and Tempest himself took sighting tests from the summer-house.

Tempest came back shaking his head. "As you say, he couldn't have done it even if he'd wanted to. But about that threatening letter. Did you believe him when he swore he didn't write it?"

"I think I did," said Travers. "It was about the only convincing thing he did say."

"Well, we know old Greeve didn't write it—if the experts are right. The question is then, who did write it? And was it genuine after all?"

"I think I've got an idea, sir," Carry said. "I've been thinking a lot about that letter, and when he said what he did this afternoon, I sort of put two and two together. Now he didn't know a word about this aunt of his, so he said, sir, and we think he was telling the truth. But who did know about her? Who was on the spot and heard all about it first?"

"Mantlin, of course."

"And who was he particularly friendly with, sir?"

"Tom Bypass."

"That's it," said Carry. "Tom Bypass wrote the letter, after Mantlin had given him the tip about the likely changing of the will. What's more, sir, I think I can prove it another way. How if that man that was supposed to be seen in the garden on the Monday night was a fake like some other things? And who was the only one supposed to see him? Tom Bypass!"

Tempest nodded. "I think you're right. How it's going to help is a different thing. Still, I'll get a phone message through to Chelmsford, and we'll see what's in this famous detective story that was supposed to take the wind out of our sails."

Carry and Travers took a stroll round the garden.

"The Chief's getting a bit worried, sir," Carry said. "Did you see the *Beacon* this morning? A pretty broad hint that it's time he called in the Yard. Between you and me, if nothing happens in a very few hours, I reckon he'll do it." He grunted. "Though what they can do that we haven't I don't know. They'd never have rumbled all that picture business, sir, like you did."

Travers shook his head. Carry went speculating on.

"And the funny thing is, sir, I never knew a case in my life where clues and things so stuck out everywhere. Now take that letter, sir, that Romney Greeve reckoned he didn't write. What about those lies Service told over it—how he'd never seen it, and yet it was proved he'd picked it up and held it while he read it?

And something else I've been thinking of, sir. About that Martin Greeve and the cards he dropped two nights running. Now I've got an idea that might fit in, if we can only make use of it. Why shouldn't that have been all part of a scheme with the two Bypasses?"

Travers pricked his ears and listened. At the finish he was nodding away with his mind made up.

"Here's the funeral party back, but you and I'll have a word about it later. And we'll fix up an experiment that'll make the Chief's eyes pop out of his head."

Service showed Bendline into the drawing-room after tea, and Tempest immediately took him out to the summer-house.

"Everybody very pleased over the will?" he asked.

"Well"—the lawyer made a face—"they were and they weren't. You know what I mean. On balance I think they were satisfied when they came to think it over. Ten thousand isn't thirty thousand, but it's better than a bad joke."

"Any surprise at Mantlin not being there?"

"I explained tactfully," Bendline said, and left it at that.

Tempest hemmed and hawed for a minute and then came to the point.

"Now a very ticklish question which Mr. Travers here and myself consider vital to us in this inquiry. We guarantee your name will never be divulged as the author of the information, if you can see your way clear to give it. It's about Mantlin. When we mentioned his name to you here the other day, we both had the idea that you'd run across him before."

Bendline smiled. "Well, there's no secrecy about that."

"I know," said Tempest. "I'll go further and say that we had the impression that you had run across Mantlin in some way that reflected none too well on Mantlin himself. That's what we'd like you to tell us."

Bendline thought for a moment, then shook his head.

"I'm sorry but I can't go into that."

Travers smiled. "You see how easy it is, Mr. Bendline. You've got to say nothing at all, really. No committing of yourself or anything. Already you've told us that you did have business connected with him that wasn't in every way to his credit."

"As you wish," countered the lawyer. "I take it then that I've given Major Tempest the information he wants."

"Damn you, Travers," said Tempest, with mock-seriousness; "now you've gone and put your foot in it."

Travers looked so apologetic that old Bendline had to laugh. Some general good-humour must have been engendered, for he was all at once changing his mind.

"It's highly unprofessional, mind you, but I'll state a case, and leave you to make what you can of it. We'll call two lawyers A and B, and a client C. C gives A certain monies to invest in a certain stock. Being a most inquisitive woman, and a busybody, she can't take A's word for it that everything is fixed up, but she wants to see everything for herself. A puts her off and puts her off and at last she consults B. A tries the same tactics with him, but finally agrees to hand everything over. In the meanwhile, by a strange coincidence B has discovered that A has had to raise money. That's all there is to it—except that the shares were purchased *after* the date originally quoted."

"And after the affair was placed in B's hands?"

"Sorry," said Bendline, "but I can't say any more."

"And that's a pity," added Travers, "for I was just going to ask if it was after lawyer A had raised the wind."

They saw the lawyer to his car, then went into the house in search of the four. They were still in the dining-room, talking animatedly.

"I hear I have to congratulate all you gentlemen," Tempest said, and for a moment tried hard to drop the policeman. "I'm sure I do congratulate you, though you haven't perhaps got all you were entitled to."

Travers beamed round too and remarked that it was all very gratifying. Hugh returned thanks and for a minute or two the room hummed with good-feeling and almost hilarity. Tempest applied the damper.

"I'd like to see you some time this evening," he said to Hugh, "about you people getting away. I hope it may be first thing on Monday, but I doubt if it will be before."

Faces looked blank. Hugh remarked mildly that they'd all been counting on getting away in the morning. Travers whispered something in Tempest's ear.

"I'm sorry," the Major said, "but I'm afraid that's out of the question. But perhaps you'll see me this evening. Not till just before dinner, though, as I may have more information then."

"Why was I to say that bit about not till just before dinner?" he asked Travers, when they'd left the room again.

"Sh!" said Travers mysteriously. "Carry and I have worked out a little surprise for you. We're all going to be in the drawing-room just before dinner. Carry and Polegate will be writing or something in a corner somewhere, and you'll leave me to do the talking to Hugh Bypass. You see, you'll be busy. You're going to be writing at another table; far too occupied to attend to anything, if you follow me. At a signal which you and I will arrange later, you'll go over to Carry's table and speak to him with your back turned to Bypass and me."

"And what's behind it all?"

"That," said Travers, "is what's going to constitute the surprise."

Tempest left for a hurried visit to his office. Travers strolled out to the garden and there ran across Polegate, who emerged unexpectedly from the shrubbery.

"Hallo!" said Travers. "What are you looking for?"

Polegate grinned sheepishly. "I've been poking about in that leaf-mould, sir. Thought someone might have buried that bullet after he picked it up."

"Well, I wish you joy of the job," Travers told him. "But how did you get on at the funeral?"

A crowd of sensation-mongers, Polegate said, but they'd been suitably dealt with.

"By the way," Travers suddenly said, "you didn't happen to see a bunch or spray of white roses at the grave-side?"

Polegate looked at him. "Funny you should have asked that, sir. The two Services sent them, didn't they, sir?"

"That's right. Why?"

"Well, I was right on Service's tail, though he didn't know it; supposed to be watching out in case he communicated with this mysterious Aunt Ethel—which he didn't, as far as I could see. Then when the coffin was lowered, I saw he had those roses in his hand, and as soon as they threw the first earth in, blowed if he didn't throw the roses in! A waste, I call it, of perfectly good flowers."

"Yes," said Travers thoughtfully. "I suppose it was. And somehow I'd like another look at them. I don't know just why, but I would."

"You never will now, sir," Polegate told him. "They're under six feet of soil."

"So I believe," said Travers imperturbably, and remembering something else, began feeling for his pocket-book and a certain ten-pound note.

CHAPTER XIV
TEMPEST RESIGNS

THE STAGE was set. At a table by the bookcase Carry and Polegate were writing. At a table near the gong Tempest had writing materials too, while Travers sat at the table where the two Bypasses had sat on the night of the murder; he in Tom Bypass's chair and with Hugh's placed ready. Travers looked round to verify the placings, then gave Polegate a sign. The sergeant went out in search of Hugh Bypass. Tempest, with a grimace, sat down at his table and began to write.

Hugh Bypass came in. Polegate showed him to the vacant chair and then left to resume his work with Carry.

"Sit down, Mr. Bypass," said Travers genially. "Cigarette?"

"Not just before dinner, thanks," Hugh said.

"Then I won't either," said Travers. He lowered his voice so as not to disturb the work of the room. "Major Tempest asked me to see you about this departure of yours. Things are not going any too well with our inquiries, and we're on the point of calling in Scotland Yard."

Hugh made an involuntary raising of the eyebrows.

"That means, of course, that whatever officials the Yard sends down will want to interview all you people again and hear your evidence at first hand. In other words, there's little point in putting you to the expense of letting you all go away some time to-morrow when you may have to be fetched down again as early as to-morrow night."

Hugh pulled a long face and admitted the argument had reason.

"That's all right then," Travers said. "But Major Tempest hasn't any objections to your going down to the town, provided certain guarantees are given." He had been rising from the chair but suddenly sat down again. "Oh, and while you're here, there's just one little thing you could do for us. It may seem foolish to you, but I do assure you that there's heaps of sense in it."

He leaned forward and gave a little clearing of his throat. Tempest must have taken it for a signal for he got to his feet, and while he made his way across the room, Travers was putting his question.

"When was the very last time you heard either of your parents mention your Aunt Ethel?"

Somewhere about ten seconds later, Travers gave another little cough. Tempest left Carry's table and came back to his own.

"I really can't think," Hugh Bypass was saying. "I've got a vague idea, if you know what I mean, but I can't get to grips with it."

Tempest's voice cut excitedly in on the quiet conversation.

"I say, who's been at this table?"

Travers peered round at him. "Who's been what?"

"Been at this table. Someone's been smudging all this writing."

Travers looked puzzled, then he grinned. He took Hugh Bypass somehow into the amusement and grinned at him too.

"My dear fellow, who on earth should have done that?"

"Heaven knows," said Tempest, "unless it was you."

"I?" His face puckered up in bewilderment. "But I haven't been near your work!"

His eye caught Hugh's again. Hugh spoke up.

"Mr. Travers was talking to me the whole time. I'm afraid—"

"That's all right," said Tempest, suddenly placated. "Maybe I did it with my own coat sleeve as I got up."

Travers got to his feet with a species of wink at Hugh. The two went to the far door with their own whispered conversation, and Travers bade him a cordial good night. Tempest regarded his return with much nodding of the head.

"I think I'm wise to what you were up to."

"I guessed you were when you sheered off so suddenly," Travers told him. "And what about the application? Wise to that, too?"

Tempest rubbed his chin and said he wasn't so sure.

"Right," said Travers. "Then we'll rearrange the room again as it was at the time of the murder, and see how it all fits in."

Tempest took the place of Mantlin at the end of the screen, with nothing to do but watch. Travers was Hugh Bypass, Carry was Tom, and Polegate undertook Martin Greeve. To give more of the atmosphere of dusk, only the light at the far end of the room was on.

"Everything depends, of course, on that trick of Hugh Bypass," Travers began. "It first came home to me when I was with him before breakfast this morning, though I didn't get the application of it till later. When he thinks at all seriously, he screws up his eyes and leans back, or he tucks his head in his hands. As Polegate can bear me witness, I was able to get up, tiptoe across the carpet, smudge the writing and sit down again—and he wasn't aware of a thing. What's more, he seems unaware of his own idiosyncrasy. He swore blind he had me under his eye all the while."

"Quite a natural proceeding, sir," said Carry.

"I think so," agreed Travers. "If you're sitting close to a person and talking, it implies that you have the person under your eye. A man might sneeze, and in the fraction of a second when his eyes were closed, the man he was talking to might whip poison in a third man's glass—and have a magnificent alibi. As far as we're concerned, the thing is that the trick must have been perfectly familiar to his brother. Proceed from that to the special association existing between Tom Bypass and Martin Greeve—the attempted suicide of Martin, and Tom's visit, you remember?—and you have those two forming an alliance to commit murder. Hugh Bypass may have been in it himself, and if so it was a triple alliance.

"Still, we'll assume for the moment that all Hugh did was to be the unknowing medium, as it were. Now for Martin's part in the design. There Carry has an idea that seems to me absolutely supported by everything else. Martin's dropping of a card on two nights running couldn't have been mere accident, occurring as it did at the same special second of time. The theory is, then, that by dropping a card, he could influence the movements of his uncle's head, and when he stooped for the card, by a touch on his uncle's leg, he could influence the movement still more.

"Most important, isn't it? Remember how we tried to get information of where the old man's head was facing, and all the evidence we got was confused? Mantlin said one thing, Service another, and Tom Bypass vaguely corroborated Mantlin. If we'd known for a certainty, we'd have known where the bullet originated. The theory now is that Martin Greeve could influence the apparent origin.

"Let's go slightly back to something—the man Tom Bypass was supposed to see on the Monday night. Through which doors? The ones on the right there, not those by that screen. Suppose, then, this man were claimed as the murderer of old Greeve, then the bullet must have come through the open doors on the right there. But if Tom Bypass were shooting him through the centre of the skull, then it would be necessary to make Greeve turn his head towards the right-hand doors in order to convey the impression that the shot came from there."

"And afterwards, of course, Tom Bypass would swear his head had been turned quite a different way," said Tempest.

"Exactly! If Greeve's head were proved to be turned to the right—his own right—then the bullet might have come from the shrubbery. If he turned his head to his own left, then it came through the other doors, from a gun fired by Tom Bypass's bogus man. *But remember this one thing.* It wasn't necessary for the murder to be committed that one night. There was still another night. Not till the head of old Greeve was in the right place could that murder be committed." He looked at the three with a desperate intentness. "We must have that in mind. A lot depends on it, and I repeat it. It was essential for Tom Bypass's scheme that his uncle should look towards Mantlin, and look right round. Then the bullet would have caught him in his left temple. Turn old Greeve right round the other way—a position to which Tom himself would have sworn—and that head is in a position for the bullet to have been fired by the non-existent man whom Tom Bypass saw through those other doors, out in the garden."

"Aunt Ethel's husband," said Polegate.

"That's it. The man who was supposed to write the threatening letter. Which brings us to the other motive of Martin Greeve in dropping the card. If his own head was bent down, he would have been out of the way of his cousin's shot!"

Tempest nodded. "And what gun was he supposed to shoot with?"

Travers made a wry face. "There we come to hypothesis. Still, we'll be logical. Tom Bypass was a crack shot. He left the service in ill health, therefore he hadn't done any shooting for years. He had, however, a small, white-handled revolver which lay about in his drawers, and somewhere he had ammunition for it. A week or so before he came down here, things arrived at a climax and he resolved to kill his uncle. But that revolver, having been seen by his landlady, would be a damning piece of evidence. So he bought another sufficiently like it—"

"Rather difficult at short notice, don't you think?" objected Tempest.

"I doubt it. He may even have seen one before, and that's what may have induced him to use his own revolver. But the undeniable fact is that he pawned a certain revolver, and took good care to bring the pawn-ticket down here with him. I say he bought a second revolver sufficiently like the one he knew he was an expert with; he put that second revolver in the drawer for his landlady to see—to refresh her memory, if you like—and then pawned it.

"His own revolver was essential, because firstly, he could rely on being able to use it; secondly, he had to have a small revolver, and thirdly, he daren't have run the risk of acquiring a new, traceable gun to do the actual killing with. And as to how he used it, I suggest he had it up his sleeve with elastic attached. When the time came for firing it, he would manœuvre it to his palm; fire, and then it would disappear up his sleeve again.

"On the Monday evening there was a rehearsal. On the Tuesday there was a chance to commit the murder, but the decision would be in his hands. May we suppose that he decided at the one certain split second that everything was as he wished it, and that he did fire?"

"But he didn't!"

"I know he didn't," said Travers calmly. "But let's imagine, then, that it was the Wednesday night when everything was in order. Service comes in to sound the gong, which gives its warning rumble. Down goes Martin's card. Greeve turns his head. The gong is deafening, and Tom Bypass and his gun are the nearest things in the room to it. He fires. Greeve falls. Tom can swear Martin didn't do it. Hugh can swear Tom didn't do it, though the said Hugh was at the moment of the shot engaged in wrestling, eyes tightly shut, with a problem his brother had conveniently put to him.

"But what happened on the Tuesday night, as you'll say, was vastly different. Just what it was we don't know, but Tom Bypass was a most amazed and frightened man when his uncle was killed. Tom Bypass, mind you; cool as a cucumber and suave as they make 'em, was so rattled that his own desire was to get out and dispose of his gun, which he did by throwing it in the pond, which his own common sense—unlike that footling Romney's—must have told him would be the first thing to be searched. Then he got his nerve back. Either because he discovered who'd actually done it, or because he was dead plumb sure no one could prove he'd done it, he could regard the whole appalling business with an ironic complacency." He smiled. "He could even sit in this room the other night, Major, and pull your leg."

"That's been pulled out straight long ago," Tempest said dryly. "But what about it all? Where's it leading us?"

"You'll pardon me a minute, sir," broke in Carry, "but just why couldn't he have used that Colt and thrown away the other gun for a blind?"

"He couldn't have concealed it," Tempest said. "At least, not in the way Mr. Travers suggested."

"It would negative everything we've been building up," added Travers. "Also, why pawn the gun if he was going to use another? If he used that other gun, of a vastly different calibre, how could the little white-handled gun implicate him? Far better leave it at home in the drawer."

"Unless he really wanted the money?"

"A man in Tom Bypass's position hard up for twenty-five shillings?—which was what he got for it." Travers shook his head. "But there's an unanswerable proof. If you'll take the position of Hubert Greeve and let me still be Tom, we'll prove something else at the same time."

Carry sat in the dead man's chair. On his temple was placed a blob of red ink to mark where the bullet had entered, and a black blob on his forehead for the spot where it had emerged.

"Now then," said Travers, fingers coiled round an imaginary gun. "You turn his head this way, Major, till the shot came from me."

"Can't be done," Tempest said. "I'd have to twist his neck."

"What about moving my shoulders, sir?" suggested Carry.

"That's not in the bond," Travers told him. "If he moved his body or shoulders, it must have been noticed. Also, you'll notice according to the marks that he sat very close to the table; so close that for your own ample centre-piece to fit in, you've had to move the chair back a bit. If he'd moved his body, then, he'd have moved the table—or the chair."

"It's final," said Tempest. "Tom Bypass didn't fire that shot—even with the Colt."

Travers suddenly chuckled. "Screw Carry's head round, will you, till I can shoot him from here. Move your shoulders, Carry, if you like. . . . That about it? Then you go back to your screen, Major. . . . Now do you see another reason why even if Greeve shifted body and shoulders, Tom Bypass could never have fired that shot?"

"My God! yes," said Tempest. "He'd have hit me!"

He had appreciated the fact so alarmingly that there was a moment's amusement. He even smiled himself, but it was his face that straightened first.

"Mantlin in the way. Funny, isn't it? That was exactly the end of that conference we had this afternoon. Mantlin was in the way of Romney Greeve." "Yes," said Carry. "And if he hadn't happened to stand where he did, the old man might have been shot twice, let alone the way he *was* shot."

"What a birthday party!" said Tempest. "Think of it. Two of them planning to kill him from inside, and another trying it from outside. It doesn't bear thinking of."

"Three desperate men," said Travers. "Four, maybe, for Hugh may have been in it up to the neck. And Mantlin. If he'd got to the state where he misappropriated funds entrusted to him—that's what Bendline said in so many words—then he was pretty hard pressed."

"And the butler," said Carry.

"Yes, and the butler." He shook his head. "Some people's consciences are going to trouble them shrewdly the rest of their lives."

"Well, I don't know," said Tempest, and heaved a sigh. "It's got me hopelessly beat. The more we find out the less we know. And I don't know about you, but the more I think the more I get fuddled." He shook his head. "We'll leave it for a bit. All get some food and then meet here again at ten. If no one's found any fresh ideas, then we call in the Yard straightaway."

The spectacles of Ludovic Travers had never been so polished as in that last remaining hour. Somewhere inside him he knew himself on the edge of discovery. It was as if a word stayed tiptoe on his tongue and disappeared as the lips shaped to speak it. Then an idea began to form itself, till it was like a dark thunder mass that has gathered slowly from innumerable clouds. It weighed on his mind with a kind of terror, and he knew that if he were right, then the truth was hidden deep in the brains of those who would keep it there.

Ten o'clock came, and the others with it.

"Any ideas?" Tempest asked Carry.

Carry shook his head.

"You, Polegate?"

"No, sir. Nothing new."

"You, Travers?"

"What about yourself?" Travers asked.

"None at all," Tempest said. "Except that I can't get away from Mantlin. I know he couldn't conceivably have done the murder. He was in full view every second, but he made that fortuitous appearance and stopped two people maybe from committing murder—and yet the murder was committed!"

"He seems to you a kind of central point?"

"In a way, yes. But it gets us nowhere. And what about yourself? Anything new?"

"No," said Travers, "except that whatever you do, I'd like to pin my faith to miracles."

Tempest pulled a face. "What sort of miracles? Not the toys and camouflage?"

"I don't know." He shook his head. "I've made mistakes in this case, and I've jumped to false conclusions, but somehow I never was more sure of anything than what I'm going to say now. I believe everything we've discovered was part of some intricate larger plan. It may even be that we were meant to discover just so much—Romney Greeve's contraption, the various things in the pond, the obvious likeness of Monday evenings events to Tuesday's, and so on. I believe that each of a certain number of desperate men decided that it was to their general interest—and indeed their vital safety—for old Greeve to be killed. I believe they planned to a split second, each man to his own specialized job, with the whole dovetailing in with not a hair's breadth of error. Some, like Hugh Bypass, and possibly Service, may have been parts of the mechanism without being aware of it till too late, which might account for Service's remark that it was necessary to lie, and to keep on lying." He smiled. "Fantastic, isn't it?"

"I don't know," said Tempest soberly. "But if you *are* right, the sooner the Yard's called in the better. There's a prestige behind them that'll force the pace and get a suspect on edge."

"I think you're right," Travers told him. "But I don't think the truth will ever come out—if my theory is right. A conspiracy to commit murder means a conspiracy of silence afterwards."

"Or a conspiracy of lies," put in Carry.

"Exactly," said Travers, "and that'd be worse. The organizing brain that planned the scheme would be quite capable of organizing lies and silence." He remembered something. "By the way, didn't you send Service's prints to the Yard?"

"Prints not known," Tempest said. "I took an absurdly wide view and sent all the prints. None of them are known."

"And you're throwing in your hand?"

"Yes," said Tempest. "I'm throwing in my hand. I'm phoning the Yard from my office inside ten minutes."

Travers smiled. "Well, my little holiday has come to an end. Shall I call off Palmer, or will you?"

"You do it," Tempest told him. "And don't forget to come and have a word before you go for good."

Travers saw him off at the door, and just as the car was about to move, remembered something.

"Anything ever come in about the various regiments."

"Yes," said Tempest. "Everything was satisfactory."

"Mantlin all right?"

"I think so," Tempest said. "He was wounded—I remember that—and then he put in his time with a concert-party behind the lines." He smiled. "The really astounding thing is, I believe I must have been at one of their shows myself. I seem to remember the name. You didn't run across them, did you? 'The Moonbeams'?"

Travers frowned in thought. "No, I can't say I did—or else I've forgotten." He frowned again. "I can hardly imagine Mantlin being attached to a war-time troupe, can you? What was his capacity? Not a ventriloquist by any chance?"

Tempest laughed, then stared. "Why'd you ask that?"

"But was he?"

"I haven't the foggiest notion," Tempest told him.

"That's a pity," said Travers, drawing back for the car to move. "You see, he's the one man in a concert-party who's expected to perform miracles."

PART III
TRAVERS STAYS THE COURSE

CHAPTER XV
TRAVERS LAUGHS

THAT SAME NIGHT Travers saw Service and announced his departure the following morning. And after breakfast on that Saturday morning Travers went up to his bedroom, where Palmer was packing, and had a word with him.

"I think we ought to give the Services some little present for their kindness," he said. "Have you any idea as to what might be acceptable?"

Palmer thought for a bit. "I don't know that I have, sir. If I may say so, sir, Service and his wife are now very comfortably off. Something purely ornamental, sir, might I suggest?"

"You might," said Travers. "A box of chocolates for the lady; civilian neckties for Service." He watched for a moment the dexterous folding of a jacket. "You'll be glad to get back, I expect."

"I've been very comfortable here, sir," Palmer said. "I don't know that I've ever been more comfortable, sir. Mrs. Service is a particularly nice woman, sir."

"Yes," said Travers reflectively. "I should think she is. She has tastes that are old-fashioned enough to be original. This generation requires a sign, but it wouldn't hunt for it at the bottom of a teacup."

Palmer gave a sparrow-like, sideways cock of the head.

"Teacup, sir?"

"Yes," said Travers. "Mrs. Service tells fortunes from tea-leaves. And she believes in *Old Moore's Almanac*"

"If you'll pardon me, sir, I think there's a lot of truth in *Old Moore's Almanac*" said Palmer resolutely. "I've proved it, sir." He shook his head. "But I can't say I believe in all the things Mrs. Service believes in." He sniffed gently. "Lucky stones, sir, and the Language of Flowers."

"The Language of Flowers?" Travers was suddenly thoughtful. "Mrs. Service believes in that?"

"Yes, sir. She was reading a book about it the other night. Service was quite annoyed about it, sir. He spoke very sharply, sir, though not in my actual hearing."

"Know where the book is?"

Palmer looked up quickly at the abruptness of the tone. He shook his head.

"I was out of the room, sir, when I happened to hear him. The book itself I haven't seen since, sir."

Travers took a hasty glance at his watch, frowned for a moment, then turned to the door.

"I'm going out. Get the bags downstairs and then wait."

He drove to the outskirts of the town and there slowed, with an eye out for a stationer's shop. The poorer the district, the more likelihood of a find. Two shops were drawn blank, and he tried a bookseller's in the main shopping centre.

"I doubt we haven't got such a thing," he was told. And then a woman assistant cut in.

"Was it anything about the Language of Flowers you wanted? Because you might find it in a dictionary."

In a dictionary it was. Travers invested six shillings on chance, and drove far enough out of town to be unhustled by traffic police. His eye an down the list of flowers with their usual meanings;

Rose . . . Love.
Rose, damask . . . Beauty always fresh.
Rose, yellow . . . Spite or jealousy.
Rose, white . . . I am worthy of you.
Rose, moss . . . I love you.

Travers frowned prodigiously, finding no grain of sense in Mrs. Service's choice of white roses. The six shillings seemed indeed wasted, till his eye caught a page of reading matter that rounded off the flower list.

That language known as the Language of Flowers is universally current, and was not unknown to the ancients. Even natives of remote and almost barbarous tribes have been known to make use of this inarticulate form of speech.

Besides the meanings usually assigned to individual flowers which we have given above, certain modifications and arrangements occur, which also vary with the locality or country.

In Spain, a rose divested of both its thorns and leaves signifies, "Nothing is left of our love." If thorns alone are removed, the meaning is, "All obstacles to our love are now gone." With white roses, themselves the emblems of purity and love, the meanings in the same circumstances are suitably varied. Divested of leaves and thorns, they convey the meaning, "Nothing remains to hope or fear." Divested of thorns only, the meaning in some countries is, "I remain pure." In others it is, "Nothing remains but the memories of our childhood." Yellow roses devoid of thorns mean that a meeting is safe. . . .

Travers frowned to himself as he read that last paragraph again. Still in the background of his mind was the original curiosity that had teased at it and made him wonder why the roses should have been tampered with at all; but nothing had been farther from his thoughts than the strange idea that was now hammering at the door of his mind. Almost mechanically he laid the book on the seat beside him and moved the car slowly off.

By the time he reached the drive his mind was made up. Service should be his own conviction, unless new proof arose. Then as he came into the hall, still putting coincidence to coincidence to make that proof for himself, his eyes rose to that mirror above the telephone where the plain-clothes man still sat. It was the same man who had been there before when he had taken an interest in that mirror. Now he watched with even more curiosity as Travers moved this way and that with an eye always for what the mirror showed.

"Think it's a good one after all, sir?"

"I've known worse," Travers told him non-committally, and moved off to push the bell for Service.

As Travers waved him to a seat in the morning-room, the butler was none too much at ease. The gentleman's manner had been lacking in its wonted geniality and was dimly dry and off-hand.

"The time has come," Travers began, "for you and me to arrive at an understanding, Service. Certain aspects of your conduct need explaining. What you don't seem to realize is that murder has been committed in this house. Yet certain people—yourself included—have concealed facts and distorted others. You understand me?"

The old butler shot a look at him.

"Lies have been told. Have you told any, Service?"

The butler licked his lips. "No, sir."

"And suppose I prove that you have? You realize the consequences? That you can be taken into custody and be brought up on a charge, and have your name in the papers—and Mrs. Service's name?"

He stared, then shook his head quickly. "No, sir. Not her name, sir."

Travers leaned forward. Certain precautions, he said, had brought him to that very room some nights previously. Inadvertently he had made a noise which Service, accompanied by his wife, had come to investigate.

"You suggested reporting it to the police," Travers said. "Mrs. Service dissuaded you because it would have to mean the telling of more lies. You see, Service, according to your wife, you'd told some lies up to that moment. And what did you tell her? That there'd got to be still more lies."

Service shook his head. "You must have made a mistake, sir."

Travers smiled. "You think you'd get away with that in a court of law? You think you could brazen me out?" He leaned forward again. "What *was* your actual regiment in the war?"

Service shot another look at him. The truth and a lie were poised, and compromise won.

"I'd rather not say, sir."

"Now that's very much better," said Travers genially. "Not the truth, Service, but we're getting near it. Which brings us to a certain lady—the sister of your late master. Ethel, her name was. You remember? You read all about it surreptitiously in a certain threatening letter that came to Mr. Greeve."

"No, sir."

"Then how do you explain that the letter bore your finger-prints in such a way that any jury would be convinced that you read it?"

"I don't know, sir."

"But you called this lady up on the phone! The words you used were overheard."

There was a sudden change in the butler's attitude. He pulled himself up with an assumption of dignity that was only too plainly an anticipated pose.

"I must refuse to discuss the matter, sir."

"Splendid!" said Travers. "You were ready for me and you did it rather well. But with regard to this communicating with the lady, you haven't tried to get into touch with her since—nor she with you. We've taken every precaution with correspondence, and unless you've been too clever for us, there hasn't been a thing, coming or going. However, we'll leave that for a moment. Just answer a simple question that's nothing to do with murder. What was your last situation and who was your employer?"

"I was with an American gentleman, sir; Willis by name."

"Here, or in the States?"

"In the States, sir. In New York."

Travers smiled. "Splendid. And don't tell me he's dead?"

"Yes, sir. He is, sir."

"I knew it," said Travers with humorous exasperation. "I said to myself that it'd be just our luck that you'd have been with a gentleman abroad who'd now be dead."

The old man's face, that was meant to be a mask, had on it such depth of misery that Travers was suddenly ashamed. He got to his feet.

"The pity of it, Service. You and your wife plan so carefully—even these pitiful lies—and all you do is proclaim the truth."

"The truth, sir!"

Travers sat down again. He leaned forward till the face of the butler was not two feet from his own.

"Yes, Service. The truth. Look at me and ask yourself the question. I know who you are, Service, and who Mrs. Service is. Isn't that so? Do I know—or don't I?"

The old man's eyes lowered. "I don't know, sir . . . but I think perhaps . . . you do."

Travers shook his head at him as if he were a naughty child.

"Why did you go and do it? Why didn't you come to Major Tempest or myself and tell us the truth in confidence? We'd have kept your secret."

Service licked his lips. "Perhaps I should have done, sir." He looked up with a pathetic kind of appeal. "You do know, sir?"

"Yes, I know."

"And you'll never let out a word to a soul, sir?"

"Not till you give me leave," Travers told him gravely. "And now tell me all about it. How'd you first come to get here?"

It was the war that caused all the trouble, Service said. After their marriage they had come to England and lived on her money till he could find a suitable post, which he did—for both of them; he as butler-valet to a gentleman in town, and she as single-handed housekeeper. The war came and Service joined up. Then his employer joined up, and Mrs. Service stayed on in the flat as caretaker. Then he was killed, and the flat had to be left, with Service supporting his wife with part of his pay to eke out the government allowance. Then after the war a job somehow eluded him. One—as the usual married couple—was found, but proved too taxing for Mrs. Service, whose health broke down. Their savings slowly went, and then when they were at the end of their tether, Mrs. Service had seen her brother's name in the paper and had written to him for help. He offered her a home without her husband, and this she refused. A compromise was reached, and she and Service were only too glad to take their present post.

"We assured him, sir, we should never attempt to take a liberty," Service said, "and we kept our word. He promised to see us provided for if anything happened to him, and I must say, sir, he kept his word handsomely too. If ever anything got out, he threatened that the arrangement would come to an end."

"He treated you none too well," Travers remarked.

The old man shook his head. "He was hard to put up with sometimes, I admit that, sir—but we were both very grateful. And I was an interloper, sir; I knew that. Now my wife, sir—his sister—he was always very considerate to."

"It was he who gave you your present name?"

"Yes," said Service. "It was like him—in a way, sir. It was a sort of reminder we were never allowed to forget."

Travers nodded. His sympathies had always gone out queerly to the old man, and now he felt like shaking him by the hand.

"And why didn't you come to Major Tempest and tell him?"

Service shook his head. "It was the young gentlemen, sir. We didn't want anything to get out to disgrace them, sir."

Travers shook his head. "They'd never have been ashamed of you, Service—nor their aunt. If they had, it was you who should have been ashamed of them." He shook his head again. "And yet you ran risks. That asking after their children, and how you and your wife once offered to lend help when Mr. Greeve refused."

"That was a risk we couldn't help taking, sir," Service told him quietly. Then he looked up. "Was that how you came to find out, sir?"

"No," said Travers; "though it ought to have told me something. But you told me yourself—and Mrs. Service, she told me too."

"She told you, sir?"

"Yes. A bunch of white roses that you threw in the grave. No thorns to them, Service."

The old man had looked startled. Then he shook his head.

"I told her she shouldn't have done all that, sir, but she would have her way. A very sentimental woman, sir—sometimes."

"She's none the worse for that," Travers said. "And as for yourself, once you'd announced that you were going to tell lies— you needn't blush for it now, Service—I had to be on the look out for lies. And you had the idea that Palmer was spying on you. He came to the hall with you and went up the stairs. The telephone was deserted, so with one eye on that convex mirror you pretended to phone, and watched him listen from the top of the stairs. You tried to lead us on a false scent and merely implicated yourself. If you hadn't mentioned the word *Ethel* it wouldn't have been so bad. We were bound to follow up that."

Service was shaking his head, then he smiled quietly. "As you told me yourself, sir, I'm afraid I don't make a very good liar."

Travers clapped him on the back. "Forget all about it. Don't tell even your wife. There's no need for her ever to know."

"Thank you, sir." He got to his feet. "And you won't say anything to Major Tempest, sir?"

"If you wish it, I certainly won't."

His thanks were never spoken, for something queer was happening to Travers's face. It was puckering to a smile. The smile became a chuckle, and then he laughed.

"Damn funny, Service, if you only knew it!"

"Funny, sir?"

"Yes," said Travers, and chuckled again. "The only thing I've actually unearthed and discovered and incontrovertibly proved in a week's sleuthing, I've just promised never to divulge. The world, my dear Service, owes me respect which I shall never receive."

"I hope I shall always respect you, sir."

Travers smiled with a sudden sheepishness and clapped him again on the shoulder.

"I hope we both shall, but not because of what's happened this morning. Now you'd better be getting back or your wife will be wondering things."

For five good minutes Travers sat on in the drawing-room, beneath his eye those grim mementos of the night of the murder. His thoughts by one tremendous effort were concentrated upon one certain second of time; then by deliberate intent they were allowed to expand, and play about the actors in the scene. Something in his point of view he knew was inherently wrong. Something conflicted with logic. The fantastic, he felt, was still there, and yet there must be logic. A conspiracy there might have been, and yet from out the dovetailed detail that had gone to make a murder, one man alone should stand out clear—the man who had fired the final, necessary shot.

His eye rose to the clock. Ten minutes to ten. Maybe in a few minutes some detective-inspector and his sergeant would be coming into that room from the Yard. And as he thought of that, a tap came at the door. But it was Service who entered.

"Might I have a word with you, sir?"

"By all means," Travers told him.

"There's something I'd like to clear my name of, sir, if you'll allow me."

"Please do," said Travers, "if you think it's necessary."

"About that letter, sir, the one you thought I read. I didn't read it, sir, not in the way you thought. It was the master himself who showed it to me, sir, and made me read it. He had an idea at first, sir, that I was concerned—which I wasn't, sir."

Travers smiled. "My dear fellow, as soon as I knew who you were, I knew that. You must stop all this morbidity and dismiss everything from your mind."

"The police have finished here now, sir?"

There had been something hopeful in the question. Travers shook his head.

"I doubt they're only just beginning. The law won't stop till there's no sense in going on."

Service hesitated curiously. He opened his lips, and closed them. He moved his feet to go, but held his place.

"Still something on your mind?"

"Well, no, sir." He shook his head. "There was just something I wondered if I ought to communicate to the police, sir—when they come."

"Well, tell it to me and let me judge for you."

Service's face brightened. "Thank you, sir; I will, sir. It was like this, sir. On the Tuesday night I was standing here, just where these marks are, sir. I had the gong-stick in my hand, like this, and I was looking down towards the master, and when I began to sound the gong, sir, I saw something which I thought at the time very strange."

"Yes?" said Travers, and nodded.

Service hesitated, then made up his mind. "If I might take a liberty, sir, will you stand by the screen where Mr. Mantlin was standing?"

Travers went to the spot at once.

"Just as he stood, sir."

Travers's hands went to his lapels. His right shoulder just touched the screen.

"A little bit back, sir, if you don't mind. A little bit more, sir. That's it, sir. That's exactly where his feet were. Now if you look, sir, without moving your feet, you'll see there's well over a foot between you and the screen, and you have that white garden seat behind you. On your left hand, sir, in the garden. What I really mean, sir, is that when I look at you, there's something white between you and the screen."

"I see. That's how you knew just where his feet were."

"It isn't that, sir," Service said, and his voice lowered. "The curious thing I wanted to say I saw, sir, was this. Mr. Mantlin was perfectly still, sir, just as you are now, yet I distinctly saw something come between him and the screen. It looked like some-thing dark, sir, and I saw it as plain as I see you now. It showed up right against the white, sir."

Travers frowned. "When was the exact moment?"

"When I was sounding the gong at the loudest, sir."

Travers thought hard, then whipped round. "Where did this dark thing come from? Was it inside here or out in the garden?"

Service shook his head. "That's what I've wondered, sir."

Travers thought aloud. "It might have been either. The only certain thing is, it was between the white back of that seat and Mantlin." A sudden thought. "It couldn't have been between Mantlin and you?"

"Oh, no, sir. I mean, it didn't seem like that, sir. It seemed farther away, now I come to recollect."

"What shape was it? How high from the ground?"

Service pondered. "Well, it's hard to say now, sir, but I seem to remember it was like a dark sort of bar suddenly going across. It was about—well, up to your coat pocket, sir. That was about the height."

"A dark sort of bar. A dark something." He shook his head, and then his eyes again fell on the clock.

"Keep this to yourself, Service. Not a word—even to the police. I'm going now, but I'll be back later. Tell Palmer I'm waiting."

He went through to the hall and waited impatiently while the man got Tempest on the line.

"I've just thought of something I've got to do," he said. "It means slipping up to town, but I'll be back all right some time later. . . . That's right. Oh, and when do you expect the Yard people down? . . . You haven't got them yet! . . . Of course it was a wise thing to spend another night in thinking it over. . . . No, don't do that. Wait till I get back. . . . Why? Well, you can't make a fool of the Yard."

He was about to hang up, with Tempest's voice still desperate at the end of the wire. He smiled, and listened again.

"What have you found out? . . . Are you there? What have you found out?"

"Nothing yet," Travers told him, "but I'm off to look for something. . . . No, I don't know what it is or where I'll find it, but it's like a bar, and it's something dark."

CHAPTER XVI
TRAVERS INQUIRES

WHEN LUDOVIC TRAVERS came afterwards to analyse those workings of his brain that had led him to set off on that mad, hurried rush to town, *away* from the scene of the murder, he was appalled that a person so mentally sober as himself could be so easily lured into folly by that species of will-o'-the-wisp known as a hunch.

When Service had mentioned the queer thing he had seen that night, it had come all at once to Travers's mind that the position of every single soul in the drawing-room at the time of the murder had been accounted for—reasonably, if not with absolute certitude. Hugh had been placed where Tom could ask him a question. Tom had sat where he could be in Hugh's sight, where he could watch Martin and best shoot his uncle. Martin had been placed for the game of cribbage, and in that unsuspicious seat he always occupied. Service was at the gong and Romney engaged in his own intricate schemes in the neighbourhood of the summer-house. But the position of one man alone had never been accounted for—and that man was Mantlin. Every man's movements had some semblance of reason; Mantlin's had not always taking into account the fact that his movements had been precisely the same on the Monday night as they had been on the fatal Tuesday.

Mantlin, therefore, must be inquired into. And in the agile, whimsical mind of Ludovic Travers had been that paradoxical, Chestertonian dictum that he who wishes to get behind the scenes must always be behind the times. It was the past of Mantlin that must be inquired into, and the only thing available from the past was his army career, and above all, that concert-party work with its suggestion of possibilities in the working of miracles.

And in that context, a trip to town was indicated for a somewhat fortuitous reason. At the mention of "The Moonbeams," the mind of Travers had become for a split second a white sheet of nothingness. Across that sheet had flashed a picture; the recollection of an hour in the Hampstead house of Brighton Craigue, the actor-manager, with Brighton displaying his collection of war-time posters and relics.

All that, then, was the reason for the Rolls on the London Road, Travers meditatively at the wheel, and Palmer rigid and dignified alongside him. And while he drove steadily but far from furiously, Travers elaborated his original thoughts and analysed their impulses. Three main questions suggested themselves.

What and whose was that *dark something* that Service had seen? It had appeared between Mantlin and the white back of the garden seat, and therefore on the face of things the only person concerned was Romney Greeve, since he alone had been out of the room. But the butler had caught no sight of Romney Greeve himself against the white of that seat. True, his body in the garden might have been masked by the body of Mantlin in the drawing-room, but so perfect a coincidence was scarcely credible. As for what the dark something was, why tease the brain by testing the billions of possibilities?

As for Mantlin's position, Travers had ideas. Why should not some interested party have made a bet? Martin Greeve might have said, "Bet you I beat the old man to-night. But don't come in and bother him and put him in a foul temper till the games are over." That might account for Mantlin coming in—and two nights running, if the bets had been on two nights—and inquiring who had won. But, feasible though the theory sounded, it could never be checked. If both Mantlin and Martin Greeve were interested parties, would it be likely that either would acknowledge that a bet had been made for the purpose of establishing some subtle immunity from the crime?

And then again something else concerned with Mantlin's position came to intrigue the mind of Travers. *Just why had Mantlin's route from the garden taken him that roundabout way which avoided the summer-house and brought him to the right hand french doors?* On the face of it it seemed beyond doubt that there had been collusion between him and Romney Greeve. The natural way home was by the summer-house, with a peep in to see how Romney had been getting on, and so in by the doors most in use and nearest the cribbage game. Somewhere in him Travers felt a vital import in that queer route of Mantlin, and yet for the life of him he could find no solution save in some deliberate understanding with Romney Greeve.

Then there had been Travers's own flash of illumination at Tempest's first mention of the word *concert-party*, and the wonder if Mantlin had belonged to it in the capacity of ventriloquist. For Travers himself had seen behind the lines a concert-party with a ventriloquist as the star turn. Yet if Mantlin had any gift in manipulating his voice, how did it help? Even if the words he uttered had appeared to come from the screen, his body had not been elsewhere. The throwing of a voice might deceive every ear in the room, yet the fact remained that every eye in the room had seen him where he undoubtedly stood.

It was exactly noon when the Rolls stopped before Brighton Craigue's door. The actor-manager was at home, though obviously puzzled why Ludovic Travers was seeking him out at so unusual a time. Travers explained circuitously.

"Oh, yes," Craigue said; "I'm practically sure I've got that particular programme. 'The Moonbeams' were pretty well known. Squat there, will you, and I'll bring the whole lot along."

He came back triumphant. "Here we are! Two programmes-one for 1917 and one for 1918. See which one you want."

Travers had a look and took down the essentials.

THE MOONBEAMS
1917

Sidney Shea . . . Bass-baritone.
Tom Lewis . . . Tenor.
Buster Carr . . . Comedian.
Hepburn Drew . . . Entertainer.
Frank Farnim
Lester Scott . . . Female-Impersonators.
Pianist—Arthur Lofty.
Producer—Jack Hay. *General Manager*—Tom Press.

For 1918 there were two alterations. Harold Meene appeared in place of one of the female-impersonators, and George Mekers was the new tenor. But a sudden, tremendous depression had come across Travers's mind at the non-appearance of the name of Charles Mantlin. A consoling thought followed hard on its heels. Maybe the performers had chosen stage names and Mantlin had been one of those names he had just written down. And if only there had been a ventriloquist!

"Got what you want?" Craigue asked.

"So far, yes," Travers told him. "But I have an idea that a lot of these members of concert-parties were pros, in real life. I suppose you don't happen to know if any of them returned to the music-hall or the stage after the war?"

Craigue had a look at the list, and shook his head.

"Hardly in my line," he said. "But why not try the agents? Tebbitt's a good man, and his office is open till one—or should be. Phone from here and ask him or his manager to hold on till you get there."

The trail was hit once more. Palmer was dropped at St. Martin's with the baggage, and warned that it might be after midnight when Travers came finally home. Then Travers circled round to Charing Cross Road again and so into Shaftesbury Avenue. Solly Tebbitt was expecting him.

"Buster Carr?" he said reflectively, and pushed the desk bell. "I have an idea he's Ernie Carr. You know, the double act with John Griffin. Griffin and Carr—you know 'em." And to his secretary. "Bring me Ernie Carr, miss. Or you can't tell me off-hand if he was known as Buster Carr?"

The secretary knew. Ernie Carr, known then as Buster, had done a red-nosed act round the cinemas.

"Where's he now?" fired Solly.

The secretary knew that, too. Griffin and Carr were on at the Palaceum. The programme she brought in showed their act as timed for five past two that same afternoon.

"Ring up the management from here," Solly said. "Or if you like, Mr. Travers, I'll fix it for you. You only want five minutes with him, I take it?"

Inside three minutes it was all fixed up. Travers, ravenous after a morning's fresh air, rushed off in search of a quick lunch.

At a quarter to two, Travers was being shown into a dressing-room occupied by two gentlemen in violent plaid trousers and shirt-sleeves. Buster Carr, a plump, perky-faced gentleman, was making up his face at one mirror, with his partner at another.

"Meet my partner, Jacky Griffin, Mr. Travers," he said. "And now what can I do for you, Mr. Travers? Don't mind if I go on with the job. You won't disturb me."

"First of all," Travers said, "I only want your help if you were the Mr. Carr who belonged to 'The Moonbeams' during the war."

"'The Moonbeams'?" He nudged his partner in the ribs. "Was I in 'The Moonbeams'? I should say I was! I was the one that got them started, and I was with 'em when they packed up." He laughed. "I'd say I was with 'The Moonbeams'!"

"Well, it's someone who was connected with 'The Moonbeams' that I'm anxious to get in touch with," Travers said. "The trouble is I can't find his name on any of your programmes. A Mr. Mantlin. Charles Mantlin."

"Charlie Mantlin?" He laughed hugely. "Do I know Charlie Mantlin! Bit of a toff, old Charlie. Do I know him!"

"But his name isn't on your programmes."

"Well, you see, it wouldn't be. He wasn't anything not regular. He come to us as a bloke what knew all about electricity, and he was sort of foreman to old Tommy Press."

Travers consulted the programmes. "Oh, yes, Mr. Press was your stage-manager."

"That's right," Buster said. "Then once Curly Drew got in a bit of a muddle and Charlie lent him a hand. Anything like that he'd do. You know, sort of made himself useful."

"Curly Drew?" said Travers, and had another look. "That would be Hepburn Drew, the entertainer."

"That's right. That's what he called himself on the stage, see? Curly, we used to call him. Walter his name was." He ran his eye over Travers. "Tall, thin sort of chap he was. Something like yourself." Then he laughed hugely again. "Wish I was making the dough he is!"

"Well, I'm afraid I'm not getting much farther," Travers told him ruefully. "What I'm looking for doesn't seem to be there." Then his face was suddenly more hopeful. "I suppose you didn't have a ventriloquist in your party?"

"Ventriloquist?" He shook his head. "No, we never had no ventriloquist. Was it a ventriloquist you was looking for?"

Travers smiled. "I expect you'll laugh at me, but what I was looking for was a miracle-worker!"

"Miracle-worker!" His face looked comically puzzled for a moment, then he guffawed. "Blimey then, you ought to have seen old Curly. He was a miracle-worker and a half!" He nudged his partner again. "You've seen his act, Jacky? Ain't he what you'd call a miracle-worker? He's the one you ought to have seen, guv'nor."

"But he's down here as an entertainer."

"That's right," said Buster. "All sorts, he was. Bit of sleight-of-hand; card manipulation, see? Anything to make 'em laugh. Regular riot old Curly was. And his finale! Blimey! if you'd seen his finale. Still"—his tone dropped to the casual and conversational—"you can see it any day if you want to."

Jacky Griffin's voice followed as a mildly interested comment.

"Mysterioso. On at the Hippodeon."

"Yes, but how did Charles Mantlin come in?" Travers asked.

"Didn't I tell you," Buster said. "You see, it was like this. There was a lot of things on a table, see? Then Curly used to come in and ask for two of the audience to come up and see everything was all right; only it used to be a fake, see? Charlie used to slip round in uniform and be there handy, and when Curly asked for two to come up on the stage, Charlie used to hop up quick, and he used to be the one that was asked to examine Curly himself, see? The other, he used to examine the table and the things on it, just to see there weren't no hanky-panky—no strings attached or anything, see? Then Curly used to reckon the stage was too crowded, and he'd make the two of 'em go down, and just as they was getting down he'd change his mind and tell Charlie he could stop up. Of course he had a whole lot of patter, different from what I'm a-telling you now. So you see, Charlie used to be a kind of assistant while Curly did his act. And what an act! I tell you, guv'nor . . ."

Twenty minutes later Travers drew the Rolls up before the Hippodeon, had a quick word with the attendant and dashed in.

"What time is Mysterioso's act?" he asked the foyer commissionaire.

"Two-thirty, sir. In exactly ten minutes."

Travers slipped him a shilling, then caught sight of the manager. Though the house was full he arranged for a seat in a box, and after the act Mr. Travers might certainly see Mysterioso in his dressing-room. The commissionaire was informed to that effect. Then, as the applause was heard for the ending of an act, Travers made his way to his seat.

The curtain was down and the house lay in darkness. As the orchestra played the prelude to the act, stagey and falsely Oriental though it was, it had something of the force of a tragic symphony. When it ceased there would come out of the past a something symbolically dark; a something that had killed a man in Nature's artificial dark, and had left a darkness in which, but for chance, a murderer might escape.

The music softened till it was almost inaudible. The curtains rolled back, and ail that was seen was a stage that was nothing but a blackness queerly illuminated. Two Chinamen appeared from the wings, gold robes superbly decorative against the black, and there they stood impassive, arms folded and eyes downward. The back-stage curtain parted and a man appeared.

He was as tall almost as Travers himself, and as thin. His step was somehow lithe and his gestures deliberately foreign, with a peculiar shrugging movement of the shoulders. His clothes were black and had the look of a court costume, with knee-breeches and shoes with buckles. The two Chinamen bowed low, disappeared behind the curtains and reappeared bearing a table. They retired again, and in a moment came back with various appurtenances which they stacked on the black-carpeted floor.

Then it was seen that a pack of cards had appeared as if from nowhere and lay on the table. Mysterioso bowed to the audience, picked up the pack, and with subtle manipulations whisked the cards into innumerable cascades. He flashed them across his body, behind his neck, to within an inch of the ground, till, when every law of gravity had been defied, they seemed at last to nestle like homing birds in his hand.

The applause was subdued, not because the audience was not interested, but checked by the fascination the man himself seemed to exude. Then came tricks of the stock kind, where the apparatus itself worked the miracles: glass balls that balanced on each other, a cage of singing birds that disappeared when a cloth was waved, the head of a Chinaman rising a yard above his body after decapitation with a wand—effects of mirrors and dark backgrounds which Travers himself applauded, so deftly were they done.

Mysterioso clapped his hands. The table was at once bared, and on it were placed a tambourine, a book and a cornet. The Chinamen again bowed low and retired to the stage corners, where they stood once more impassive. Mysterioso, it was suddenly remembered, had gone behind the back-curtain, but now he reappeared. The music became once more almost inaudible but yet curiously intense.

Mysterioso spoke, and his voice was not disappointing. It was that of a foreigner who knows English but speaks it none too well.

"Vill two gentlemen of ze audience pliz come up? Two gentlemen, pliz, to see zat I deciv nobody. Two gentlemen, pliz."

There was a stirring on the right, and a man rose with a kind of sheepish resolution. He, as Travers knew, was the placed man. Then another man rose, and mounted the special steps self-consciously. Mysterioso explained to the audience.

"Von of zese gentlemen vill pliz examine me myself, to see I have nozzing up my sliv; to see zat I am joost like yourselfs. Ze ozzer gentleman vill pliz examine ze table to see zat it is only a table like you have in your homs, and zat zeere is on ze table only an ordinaire tambourin, a book and a trompette. Sank you. Now, sare, vill you pliz make an examination of myself vile ze ozzer gentleman he examine ze table."

The two scrutineers did their job and were ushered to the steps again. Then Mysterioso—always *alias* Curly Drew—did his old trick, for the placed man was called back to be still the surety for the audience that everything was above-board.

Mysterioso approached the table, hands in full view of the audience. He peered at the table.

"Vat do I see? A book. I vould like to read zis book. But I will not fetch him—no. He mus come to me."

Then an amazing thing happened. While he stood with eyes on the audience as if indifferent to the book, it suddenly rose from the table and presented itself before his eyes. With one hand he fingered its pages, then gave a grimace.

"I do not like zis book—no!"

The book stood for a second in thin air, then slowly settled again to the table. Mysterioso's eyes surveyed it, and all at once the tambourine rose of itself and began to shake. He watched it for a moment as it lifted itself in the air, then made a *moue* of contempt.

"You call yourself music, eh? But you are not music. Go back to your table."

Travers rose quietly from his seat and began making his way downstairs. He knew that the cornet would next be conjured from the table, and as he came out to the foyer again, he caught the sound of its notes. Then as the commissionaire led him away to the dressing-room, he heard the tumultuous applause that greeted the act. In two minutes he was following on Mysterioso's heels and giving his explanations.

"You've just watched the act, have you?" Mysterioso said. "What'd you think of it?"

"First-class," Travers said. "As effective a show as I've seen for many a long day.

"It ain't bad." He gave a little nod of approbation. "And now just what can I do for you, Mr. Travers?"

Travers's next move was to his own flat, no other phone being sufficiently sound-proof for what Tempest had to be told.

"Tempest," he said, "I want you to get everybody at the house and in the drawing-room as they were that night. You needn't set the stage till I get there, but they've all got to be in it."

"A reconstruction?"

"That's it. And I'd like to have Dr. Shinniford there."

"But he had nothing to do with the murder!"

"I know he hadn't. Still, you'll know all about it when I see you. And you'd better have Mantlin."

"But, my dear fellow, how on earth could he have done the murder?"

"I know he couldn't. That's just the point. And I want you to have half a dozen men—uniformed or otherwise—lying handy. Half-past seven the balloon will go up."

A pause, and the voice became wheedling. "What is it you've found out?"

"Just what constitutes a *dark something,*" Travers told him. "Two hours' time and I'll spill the whole works. Don't forget. Shinniford, Mantlin, a few men, and the balloon rises at seven-thirty."

And before Tempest could try another extorting word, he hung up.

CHAPTER XVII
TRAVERS MAKES SOME COMMENTS

DUSK WAS ALREADY in the sky by the time Travers and Tempest had thrashed things out, and in a few minutes the stage would again be set. Travers himself had changed his clothes before leaving town, and now wore a black morning-coat, a black waistcoat with a smallish neck opening, and dark trousers, so that with the black necktie he seemed dressed for a company directors' meeting of the chaster sort.

"It's a tremendous bluff," Tempest was saying. "There's only one consolation. If it doesn't work, we can get on very well without it."

"It'll work," said Travers. "Consider the atmosphere and the way you're going to make people's flesh creep. Once they're worked up there'll be no thought of sniggering. Besides, open your eyes wide."

Tempest duly opened them, and before his question could come, Travers flashed his hand to within an inch of his nose.

"There you are. You winced."

"Of course I winced," said Tempest. "You get up to monkey-tricks and give no warning."

"Then take warning," Travers told him. "Stare at me and expect my fist to come."

But even then Tempest made a slight flinching.

"That's why the bluff will come off," Travers said triumphantly. "One man knows what to expect, but he won't be sure either just when or just how—in spite of his senses. Carry and yourself must watch him like a hawk, and if he does flinch—then he's your man."

Tempest had a last objection. "I don't like your taking Service into your confidence. He may be implicated for all we know. Why shouldn't he have been tipped to sound that gong extra hard?"

"I could rig myself up; I know that," Travers told him. "But I'd rather he helped me, Besides, I give you my word he's all right. One day I may be able to tell you why."

The drawing-room seemed more crowded than ever when Tempest came in. There was a quick lull in the talk, and eyes turned his way as he stood surveying the scene. Both sets of doors were open; each piece of furniture was in its place as on the murder night, and only the butler was missing.

"Now, gentlemen," he said, "we'll get to business. I want to impress on you the importance of obeying orders and doing precisely what you're told, and no more. Inspector Carry, you stand just inside those right-hand doors and do as you've been instructed. The gentlemen who were in the room on the night of the murder will please take the seats and positions they occupied then."

"What am I to do?" asked Romney Greeve.

"All in good time," Tempest told him. "That's right, gentlemen. You by the screen, Mr. Mantlin, just as you were. And Mr. Martin Greeve, please have the board and cards arranged just roughly as they were. Have some cards in your hand and drop one when the time comes."

His eye fell on Tom Bypass, and he watched him for a moment; his hands restless and his cheeks a deathly white, and the lips no more than a thin line of pallid colour. Tempest went over to him.

"You're sure you're feeling all right, Mr. Bypass?"

"I'm all right," Tom told him. "Only I wish to God you'd hurry up and get on with it."

"All in good time," Tempest told him imperturbably. He raised his voice. "Now, gentlemen, I want you to realize the desperate seriousness of what's about to happen. At this moment, the man who killed Hubert Greeve is *inside this room*. A murderer is in this very room! He may be saying to himself that the police aren't sure—that they're bluffing, in fact. If so he's going to make a mistake that will cost him his neck.

"What we're going to do is reproduce the actual murder. The very shot will be fired, and as the murderer fired it. Nobody must move therefore, or the consequences will be on his own head. To guard against accidents—and anybody being so foolish as to run a risk after this serious warning—we have Dr. Shinniford here. You might be so good as to sit over there by the bookcase, doctor.

"About the bullet that will be fired. It will go near enough to prove the case the police have to present, but if instructions are implicitly obeyed it will do no harm to a soul. Remember, gentlemen; the police accept no responsibility after this last warning. You ready, Mr. Martin Greeve? You think the light is about correct?"

"It's about the same." His voice was none too firm. "We could just see the cards and no more."

"Right!" snapped Tempest. "Sergeant Polegate, you and Mr. Romney Greeve will go to the summerhouse and remain there till sent for. I shall stand just here facing the card-table. Oh! . . ."

His voice trailed blankly away, then he smiled grimly.

"We've forgotten the essential thing. Mr. Hubert Greeve should have been here. I wonder . . ." His eyes went round the room. "Oh, Mr. Mantlin. You were only a spectator on the night of the murder?"

"That's right." His face had a peculiar pallor of its own, and his look was strained.

"Then perhaps you'll help us out," Tempest said quietly. "You're just about his height. Take that chair, will you, and remain perfectly still, with your eyes on the man you were playing cards with. Closer to the table, please. That's right. . . . Quiet now, gentlemen. And take your thoughts back to last Tuesday. It *is* Tuesday. You're all here on Mr. Greeve's birthday and the hour is seven-thirty." His voice hushed. "A murder is about to be committed. Dead silence, gentlemen, please. And not a move!"

As he spoke, the clock on the mantelpiece tinkled the half-hour. Service must have been listening with the far door ajar, for he tapped and at once came in. At those opened french doors by the screen there was a gentle cough, and another man appeared.

It was Ludovic Travers, and yet, curiously enough, it was somehow not. There was an unfamiliarity about him: the dark clothes, perhaps, after the grey, but principally it was the slight Balfourian, meditative stoop of his shoulders, and the way his long, sensitive fingers were wreathed about the lapels of his coat. The last light from the west caught the white of his collar till it seemed like shining ivory, but on the shadowed side by the screen it was no more than a dull lightness.

He stood by the screen impassively surveying the card-table, and Tempest raised his hand. In the unbearable hush of the room a faint rumble made itself heard. Men's teeth were gripping tightly, but the fingers of Travers were as imperturbably unmoving where they wreathed about the lapels. The rumble grew louder—swelled to what seemed a deafening clamour, while men's nerves frayed to snapping point. Then while the few seconds seemed eternity, the climax came, for as ears strained for it and knew it could never come, there was suddenly the roar of a shot!

What happened then was an uproar and confusion that whirled about the room. As the gong began its rumbling, the eyes of Mantlin had shifted to that figure by the screen which was so complacently aping himself. Carry had stepped inside the doors, and Tempest had crouched as if to spring. But at the split, infinitesimal second before that shot roared off, Mantlin had backed with a quick jerking of his chair and then had made his downward leap. And as he moved, there was a moan and a slithering, and Tom Bypass sank to the floor, with his brother springing towards him, and Martin Greeve getting startled to his feet.

"You damn set of fools! You've shot him!"

But in that confusion no one heard. Mantlin left the bait of the opened french doors and was now away. Shinniford he smashed aside in mid room and with his fist he caught Service a thrust in the mouth that dashed him sideways. As Carry and Tempest reached the far door, he was through it and away. Then there was Carry running back madly and calling to his men in the dark of the garden, with Polegate running up, and Shinniford making for Tom Bypass, and Hugh and Martin lifting the fallen man.

A moment or two and the room had a deathly quiet again, with only the noise of pursuit that came through the open doors. A young moon had lifted above the trees, and made new shadows where Ludovic Travers stood.

"What is it, doctor? A fainting fit?"

"Something of the sort," Shinniford said, and frowned. "He'll be round in a moment."

"A damn silly thing to go and do, if you ask me," said Martin. There was a truculence in his tone that never rang true. "And what about that bullet?"

"There was no bullet," Travers told him. "It was blank that was fired. It sounded louder because, however it may have seemed to you, Service wasn't beating that gong at all loud."

"Then what was the sense of it?"

"Guilty consciences," said Travers gently. "You don't suffer from guilt of conscience, Mr. Greeve. You've never known what it is to kill a man. You've never even thought of it, or planned it with somebody else."

Martin shot a look at him, then his eyes lowered. When he raised them again, Travers had gone.

Up in the bedroom, Service laid the spare arm carefully on the bed.

"So that's what it was I saw, sir." He nodded down at it. "Whoever'd have thought it? What things are coming to nowadays, I don't know, sir."

"It's no new thing that," Travers told him. "It was only the way Mantlin used it. How long ago was it, by the way, when he began that trick of always clutching the lapels of his coat?"

"How long ago, sir?" He thought for a bit. "Now you come to mention it, sir, I don't think it was more than two years ago—not as a regular habit, sir."

"A pretty long preparation," said Travers, "and either he funked it, or else the particular circumstances never quite arose." He cocked his ear. "What was that?"

There was a noise in the corridor, and Service took a quick look out.

"It's Mr. Tom, sir. They've taken him into his room." He shook his head. "I'm glad—more glad than I can say, sir—it wasn't one of the gentlemen who did it. You're glad too, sir."

The thoughts went like a lightning flash through Travers's mind. Then he smiled. Far better think now that Romney Greeve *had* been merely carried away by a passion for local colour, and that purely by chance had Martin Greeve twice dropped a card, and that poor devil Tom Bypass asked Hugh a question.

"Perhaps I am, Service."

The old man smiled for a moment, then his thoughts went back.

"You were telling me about this—er—arm, sir."

"Yes," said Travers. "I got it from a magician—a conjurer perhaps you'd call him. A spare one he always has to keep. You see, if everything on the stage is dead black, the back-cloth black and your own clothes black, then this beautifully made hand, with the fingers made to snap tight, looks perfectly normal and above-board grasping one's coat lapels. The false arm, being spread out as it were, conceals your own real one. Then that real hand and arm, dead black, do the work, and they're absolutely invisible against the background. Mantlin, as you saw yourself, drew back a little from the screen, to allow room for the play of that black arm and hand that controlled the gun. While everybody saw his two hands grasping the lapels, he shot through the open carved work of the upright of the screen, and apparently never moved a muscle. Then he was the first one to bolt from the room to chase the man he said he heard outside. Somewhere we may find that arm he used." Then he shook his head. "No; he'd plan better than that. He's destroyed it long ago."

"However he had the nerve to risk coming in the room with it, I don't know," said Service.

"He came in a roundabout way," Travers said. "He was not afraid of the room. It was Romney Greeve, still in the summer-house, perhaps, that he was afraid of."

A sound came through the partly opened window; a sound of distant shouting and confusion from some-where down in the valley below the woods. The two men listened.

"You think they've got him, sir?"

"Sounds like it," said Travers. "I think I'll go down and see."

He stood for a while by the summer-house, listening again for the valley sounds, but now everything was quiet, and he knew somehow that Mantlin had been taken, and they would not be bringing him back. He would be on his way to the town with the handcuffs on him, or maybe he had killed himself and they were taking him to the mortuary.

As he shook his head there was the nearer sound of voices, and Hugh Bypass came from the open doors to the lawn. He regarded the sky contemplatively, then caught sight of Travers and walked across.

"How's your brother now?" Travers asked him.

"Much better," said Hugh, and shook his head. "But the doctor says he's to stay where he is."

"Yes," said Travers lamely.

"We've been talking about things," Hugh said. "Was it really Mantlin who did it?"

"Undoubtedly," Travers told him.

"But how on earth—?"

Travers smiled. "The old story—heaven and earth and strange philosophies. But I'll tell you about it some time." He broke off suddenly and his fingers went to his glasses. "I wonder if you'd tell *me* something, in the very strictest confidence. Last Tuesday night, didn't it rather look as if when Mantlin mentioned the police, you bolted upstairs?"

"Yes," said Hugh. He shook his head, blinked a bit, then gave Travers a shrewd look. Then he sighed. "Well, I'll tell you. I didn't really go because of the mention of the police. I mean, it was only because I happened to think of something when I heard the word. You know how you think of things? I sort of thought about the police and how they'd search everywhere, and then I thought of my room, and I remembered I'd left something there I didn't want anybody to see—well, not particularly."

"And that was?" hinted Travers gently.

Hugh tittered slightly. "You sure you won't laugh at me?"

"Heaven forbid!" said Travers fervently.

"Well then, it was a speech."

"A speech!"

"Yes. You see, it fell to me, as the eldest, to make a speech after dinner that night." He hesitated. "It was always rather difficult. One had to be extremely tactful, you know." He shook his head ruefully. "I'm afraid it was always beyond me—till I fell into temptation."

Travers was staring blankly. "Into temptation?"

"Yes," said Hugh, with another gentle titter. "And after that everybody congratulated me, and said how marvellous a speech I'd made, so I had to go on with it."

"Yes, but go on with what?"

"Well, you see, I put my difficulty to an agency. You know, one of those firms that advertise in the personal columns that they can write speeches for any occasion. I went and saw them and put the problem, and they helped me out. After that I always relied on them—and I must say they did amazingly well." He sighed humorously. "I admit I found it a bit hard to memorize the speeches."

"Yes, but why panic and run upstairs?"

Hugh whispered. "You see, I'd left my speech on the table in my room, and it had the firm's name and particulars on it. Suppose anybody had seen it, after the deceit I'd practised!"

Travers laughed gently. Somehow, at that particular moment, the incongruity of that particular panic acquired a grotesqueness that was ironically hilarious. And a quick thought—or a resolution—was flashing across his mind. Two chapters of "Kensington Gore" had already been written, and he had been puzzling his wits for the title of the third. Now he knew it. It should be what he himself had told Tempest on a late occasion: CLUES—*police, for the misuse of.*

But as he opened his mouth to speak, Martin Greeve came up. He turned back at the sight of Travers.

"Don't go, Mr. Greeve," Travers said quickly. "We were having a perfectly wonderful discussion on clues, and evidence and things." He buttonholed Hugh again. "As I was saying, Mr. Bypass, the particular instance you just mentioned is a case in point. Clues, in fact, are the very devil. We were instancing this case, Mr. Greeve, as an example of how the most innocent actions could be misinterpreted. Mightn't it have been considered strange that you should drop a playing-card two nights running at the same second of time? And even that Mr. Tom Bypass should have been asking his brother a question—"

Martin Greeve had been sidling away.

"Yes," he said, and shot a quick look at Travers. Then he was mumbling that he must go. There was something he had to do. Hugh stared and made a step his way, but Travers's hand felt for his arm and held him back.

"Mr. Greeve is busy. Probably going to pack."

"Yes," said Hugh, shaking his head. "And he's worried about my brother. More like brothers themselves, those two."

Travers frowned into the darkness, then shook his head. Let the dead bury its dead. He turned again to Hugh.

"But we did make an awful hash of this case, between ourselves. If we'd taken Service's word that a certain head was turned straight down the room, then the very line of the bullet would have told us that Mantlin did it, miracle or no miracle. Simple, isn't it?" His mind flashed again to that third chapter of his own book. "And that's how it is with the things we call clues. They're the trees that keep one from seeing the wood. The perfect case to solve is the one that has no clues. In the multitude of counsellors—whatever they say—there's precious little wisdom. Avoid side issues and you get mental clarity. In every case there's one essential clue. The trouble with too many counsellors and too many cooks, as with too many clues, is not so much that they spoil the broth, as that they land you in the soup!"

He paused for a moment's breath. Hugh was an admirable listener, and that chapter was beginning to take shape. But Hugh, who had indeed been listening to the spate of words like a man mesmerized, suddenly broke in:

"Mr. Travers" he was being most apologetic—"I've an idea. It will probably be distasteful to yourself, but I'm convinced you'd make a wonderful thing of it if you cared to do it." A little deprecatory cough. "It's this. Why don't you write a book about—about clues and things?"

Travers's mind was suspended for one blank moment in the unexpected. Then, while he chuckled quietly to himself, the figure of the plain-clothes man appeared in the light of the open doors.

"Is that you, Mr. Travers, sir? You're wanted on the phone. I think they've caught him and they'd like you to be at the station."

Travers's face sobered for a moment, then he linked his arm in Hugh's and drew him towards the house. Service closed the french doors behind them, but Travers was drawing Hugh Bypass to the right, where the screen offered a choice of way. He paused for a moment, and his long fingers felt inside the pierced carving of the massive upright, where there was a roughness or a blistering of the wood as if a flame had seared it. He stooped and whispered:

"The only clue that mattered. The one essential clue, and we never dreamt of looking for it!"

Arm linked in the other's again, he moved off towards the far door. Again he paused for a moment before moving on.

"My dear Bypass, I'm dreadfully sorry. You were saying something. About a book, wasn't it? Yes—a book. An admirable idea, and one that really appeals. All about clues and things. And evidence, and theories, and miracles. We mustn't forget miracles. And in that context, has it ever occurred to you that the old miracles have long ceased to be miraculous . . .?"

Still trying it out on the dog, he prattled his nothings in the ear of the attentive Hugh. The plainclothes man, hard on their heels, strained to listen, and grinned to himself at the elongated figure and the ample gestures of the free hand. As he was to confide that night to his missus—a queer bird, that Mr. Travers!

THE END

CPSIA information can be obtained
at www.ICGtesting.com
Printed in the USA
BVHW04s1440150418
513424BV00016BA/205/P